THE EQUATIONS OF LOVE

LAURENTIAN LIBRARY 19

THE EQUATIONS OF LOVE
Tuesday and Wednesday— Lilly's Story

Ethel Wilson

Macmillan of Canada
Toronto

First published in paperback 1974

ISBN 0-7705-1171-6

Printed in Canada for
The Macmillan Company of Canada Ltd.
70 Bond Street, Toronto, Ontario M5B 1X3

" Now, my young friends," [*said Mr. Chadband*]
" what is this Terewth . . . firstly (in a spirit of
love) what is the common sort of Terewth . . ."

BLEAK HOUSE

TUESDAY AND WEDNESDAY

TO

WALLACE AND R.H.T.

I

THE FRESH light of the rising sun touched, and then travelled—losing as it travelled its first quality of morning —down the Golden Ears, down the mountains northeast of Burrard Inlet, down the Sleeping Beauty, down the Lions, and down the lesser slopes descending westwards to the Pacific Ocean, until the radiant sunrise deteriorated into mere flat day. Milkmen were up and about in Vancouver and some railway workers and street railway workers and some hospital attendants; but the phenomenon of sunrise, being only the prelude to another day, slid away unobserved by anybody.

Because Mortimer Johnson's bedroom faced westwards and was darkened as much as possible, the sun had risen fairly high before Mort woke up. Then, because he had to get up some time or other, he got up. He got up quietly and gently pulled the grey blankets back again over the warm bed because he did not want to disturb his wife Myrtle who still slept. Mort emerged from bed in his underclothes and stood sleepily regarding the curved pile in the bed, which was Myrtle. He stretched and rubbed himself slowly over his stomach and sides and back and shoulders and arms. The feeling of the woollen combinations rubbing on his skin gave him a slow obscure pleasure. Mort's angel, who usually woke at the same time as Mort (but sometimes awoke at night and plagued him to no purpose in dreams), stepped for a moment

3

outside its domicile, also stretched, and then returned to its simple yet interesting spiritual or shall we say psychic quarters. Mort's angel had some time ago found out that the insecurity of the quarters wherein it often rocked as in a rough mountainous sea before settling down again facing in a different direction, was due to a weakness in Mort's potentially strong inner structure, but, as it had discovered that it could do nothing about this weakness, had rather given up.

A man's angel, after a long residence within or around a man, knows its host (or charge) very well indeed; far better than you or I, who, looking, see perhaps only a stocky middle-aged man, strong but now flabby, frowsty at the moment but when his face has been washed and shaved and his hair parted on the side and brushed back (as it will be in an hour's time), and his shirt and suit and socks and boots pulled on, and his hat put on, too, at a debonair angle, are justified in believing that this is Mr. Johnson who is coming to do the garden, and seems a very nice man and you hope you'll get a little satisfaction at last. You are inclined to believe this, because Mort turns upon you his kind brown eyes and tells you that he is a gardener, that he doesn't pretend to be a carpenter or a plumber or a mechanic, but one thing he can truthfully say is that he's a gardener and that he loves gardening above all things in the world, and that he has a green thumb. Mort's angel used to kick him a little when Mort said things like this; but the angel does not kick any more, because it—the angel—realizes that the two things Mort really loves are his wife Myrtle and himself—the first inconstantly and the second with a varying intensity that sometimes includes his fellowman in some vicarious

4

way identified with himself; and that when Mort makes these statements (that he loves being a gardener, or a shepherd, or a plumber, or a horse-breaker, or a plasterer), he really means them, at the moment, and it often gives his interlocutor a great deal of pleasure and a sense of security, poor thing.

After Mortimer had looked at his wife as he continued to rub himself, his early morning thought arose, the first thought of each morning. Was Myrtle pleased last night and will she be pleased this morning when she wakes up, or am I in wrong again, because if she acts like she did yesterday, I'll slug her. He then applied the usual solution to this important little puzzle and walked barefooted and picking up dust into the adjoining room which was kitchen and everything else, and struck a match and lighted the gas ring and put on the kettle for a cup of tea. When he had made the tea he put the things on a little tray the way Myrtle had taught him to do fifteen years ago, and then he brought the tray to the bedside and put it on the floor because everything else had something on it, and pulled up the blinds and let the morning in, but no air, and bent over Myrtle and poked her.

"Wake up, Myrt. Wake up, Queen," he said in his pleasant hoarse voice that could sound so easy-going or so angry. "Here's your tea, honey," and he watched for the first raising of Myrtle's heavy lids. One of these days if she doesn't treat him good he certainly will slug her.

Myrtle was no beauty. She had once had a faint disdainful prettiness. Now she stretched herself like a thin cat in the bed. Her hair was both straight and frizzy. Her nose was thin and would some day be very thin.

5

Her eyes, which she would soon disclose, were of pale indeterminate colour. She was a complete mistress (or victim) of the volte-face, of the turn-about, and this dubious possession was one of the reasons for her control and enslavement of Mort. The other was her eyelids. When she slowly raises her heavy eyelids as she soon will, but not until she feels inclined to, you will see their power. Myrtle's eyelids, and her small amused smile, which is not a turning-up but a turning-down of her lips, induce a sudden loss of self-confidence in the individual towards whom the look or non-look, the smile or non-smile, is directed. She can make you, or Mort, feel insecure and negligible, just by the extra quarter-inch of her dropped eyelids and by that amused small turned-down smile. It is not fair. If you should in your beauty, your new hat, and your recent tennis championship appear before Myrtle, she can by her special look and without saying a word, intimate to you and your friends that, for some reason obscure to them and to you but well known to her and to the rest of the world, she thinks very poorly of you. If your uncle, the great explorer from the Gobi Desert, accompanied by a Lama just flown over specially with affidavits from the Desert—if your uncle should arrive with distinctions thick upon him, Myrtle's eyelids and her secret smile will set him down where your uncle belongs. If, more important still, you should have finished and hung out your sparkling wash for your husband and ten children before bottling two crates of peaches and running up before lunch that nice dress which you are wearing, Myrtle's eyelids faintly flickering and dropping will discount this and leave you uneasy about something, you know not what. If your son,

6

brilliant young University graduate and soldier that he is, should, so young, be elected to Parliament, Myrtle's eyelids will say that she knows all about graft and politics, and you can't tell *her*. No wonder Myrtle controls and also aggravates her husband Mort Johnson. She is much more aggravating and less lovely than Mona Lisa of whom she has never heard, but from whom she is probably descended. There is only one person on whom the eyelids have no effect, and that is her aunt Mrs. Emblem. Aunty Emblem is able to make Myrtle feel foolish and inadequate any time she wants to. In fact, on Aunty Emblem, the eyelids work quite in reverse.

Well, Myrtle opened her eyes and slowly pulled herself up in bed a bit, and Mort gave her her tea, and then he went and made some breakfast and dressed and shaved and said goodbye and not to hurry and get up for anyone; and he put on his hat at the debonair angle that always gave him such an air, and started down the stairs clumping a good deal, and went out into the street feeling quite pleased with himself because Myrtle was in a good temper and because he had a new job that promised to be easy. He looked very nice as he walked, rolling almost sailor fashion, along Powell Street, and then to the street car. His face was square and pleasant, a bit soft round the jaws perhaps, his smile ready and easy when it came, his brown head and moustache with never a grey hair made him look ten years younger than his age, and his brown eyes that could be laughing, sullen and opaque, or furious—all very nice to look at.

When Mort had gone, Myrtle sat up and really looked about her. What she saw was their bedroom and because she was so accustomed to these two rooms (with sink) at the top of the house off Powell Street, she did not see that the room was dingy and needed cleaning; that it was not carpeted except by one small bed-side mat (which was the cause of daily and nightly outrage and something near madness to the two old men living below); that the bureau was littered with brush, pins, comb, Eno's, face cream, hair, hairnets, powder, beads and old dust; that the blankets and flannelette sheets were unfresh; that there was no attempt at cheer or colour in the room; that, in short, everything was uniformly dingy and need not be so. She had, of course, her eyelids for a source of pride; but the queer thing was that Myrtle did not realize her eyelids qua eyelids—they were but the outward and physical sign of an inward and spiritual conceit, and were her instrument; the fact that she was not clean was irrelevant to her scorn of other people, however clean they might be.

Myrtle's angel had long since become a nervous and ineffectual creature because Myrtle's various entities and impersonations were enough to keep any angel thin. Of all people, Myrtle loved herself in whatever guise she saw herself. If her parents had been alive, she might have loved them, too. If she had had children she might have loved them too since they would have been her children. She had Mort, and (and this comforted the angel a good deal) she really loved him in her own way. She reserved the licence to dislike him, to hate him even. For very irrational reasons she would end the day disliking Mort, even when she hadn't seen him all day; because, perhaps, the butcher had said that so upstanding a man as Mort deserved the best steak in the shop, or because Aunty Emblem in her luscious fashion had said that *there* was a

man, if you like! Or even because his socks had gone
at the toe, or because he was darn lazy, which he was,
or for no reason at all. Then she knew herself wasted
on this louse. But let her friend Irma Flask who lived
three blocks away ask how many jobs it was Mort had
had since Christmas, and say she pitied Myrtle she certainly did, and whether that was that souse Hansen she
seen him with on Thursday, and what a wonderful
provider her sister Ruby's husband was—then Myrtle
displayed Mort as the perfect husband, hers and none
other, and let them that couldn't keep their own husbands
lay off of hers, whatever she had said about him fifteen
minutes before.

"Well well well," said Myrtle, "this won't buy the
child a frock." And she got up and dressed and pulled
the bedclothes over the bed, and did her face, and put
on her hat, and went downstairs, and took the street car to
Mrs. H. X. Lemoyne's. She "gave" Mrs. H. X. Lemoyne
three part days a week, and Mrs. Lemoyne, who was not
very strong, cossetted Myrtle and apologized to her in a
way that annoyed Mr. H. X. Lemoyne whose money
Myrtle received.

When Myrtle got on the street car in a fairly good
humour, she sat down behind a woman of about her own
age, say forty-five, and this woman wore a nice suit and
hat made of soft brown tweed. The woman sat there in a
composed way and it would appear from her suède gloves
and her alligator shoes and the well-made suit and
becoming hat that she had a comfortable amount of
money and was fairly successful in her undertakings and
was happy and satisfied—for the moment—in her mind.
This set up a faint irritation in Myrtle, and her angel

9

heard Myrtle's inner whisper that this woman should not be taking up working people's places in street cars but should be driving herself. Myrtle and Mort became, for the purpose of argument, "working people," as opposed to people wearing alligator shoes. The woman was actually a school teacher on leave of absence, and she had put her small house to rights, prepared dinner ahead of time, packed her nephews down to the beach with their lunches, put on her best clothes of which she was very proud, and was going to have lunch with her favourite sister-in-law to show her the new alligator shoes. Myrtle could not be expected to know this, and so she said within herself "A society woman! You can't tell *me*! You can't tell *me* anything about society women! I know them. I'll bet her husband's no good. They make me smile, they certny do, society women." Having endowed the woman in the brown suit with several unpleasant qualities, and having herself assumed the character of a woman universally put upon, Myrtle got off the street car virtuous but in a poor temper and walked to Mrs. H. X. Lemoyne's and let herself in.

"Oh, *there* you are, Mrs. Johnson!" cried Mrs. H. X. Lemoyne, who was still in her dressing gown and anxious to please. "What a beautiful day!" She was terrified by Myrtle's eyelids, and could be disciplined any minute that Myrtle chose.

Myrtle did not answer (Oh *Lord*! groaned Mrs. Lemoyne who felt silly at once), but walked to her cupboard, took off her things and put on a coverall which she kept there. She then went to Mrs. H. X. Lemoyne. "Anything special?" she asked, with her mood still upon her.

Mrs. H. X. Lemoyne had worked herself up considerably before Myrtle came, because last night an old school friend from Toronto had rung up, and she had enthusiastically arranged a small luncheon for the old school friend. Three other old school friends. "Just pot luck." All this she now explained to Myrtle, becoming, as she did so, voluble and undignified. She explained that she had sent the children off to school with sandwiches and that her husband was not coming home to lunch. She kept on saying "Just pot luck!" Myrtle had not bargained for lunch parties, even pot luck. She patted the back of her hair and used her eyelids while avoiding looking at Mrs. Lemoyne who felt guilty and yet very angry with her own self for being so weak-minded.

"I'm not feeling so good this morning," said Myrtle. "I don't know how long I'll be able to stay. Mr. Johnson brought me some tea this morning. When he saw how I looked he begged me not to come. He said, 'Gosh, you look awful,' and I said, 'Believe me, it's nothing to the way I feel.' He wanted to stay home with me but I made him go because he's got a big contracting job up in West Vancouver, but he sure didn't want me to come. If I'd a known there was a luncheon party on I'd a stayed home like he asked me. He said 'Now you've no need to work like this.' He doesn't like me going out, and him getting good money. He thinks it reflects."

Mrs. H. X. Lemoyne apologized for all of this and felt that she was not paying Myrtle enough for coming and then said she had the dessert ready and what else would Myrtle like her to do. (How cross Hughie would be if he heard me talking like this! But I can't help it), and Myrtle, now that she had vented her ill-humour and also displayed Mort as a superior type of husband, and had tossed in an artful disparagement of other husbands including Mr. H. X. Lemoyne, now that she had done her bit of drama, became fairly co-operative and "did" the house while Mrs. Lemoyne prepared the lunch. Myrtle forgot that last time Mort had figured in her conversation with Mrs. Lemoyne, he was lazy and you just couldn't ever depend on him, and she, Myrtle, was the sole provider for the two of them, and what her parents (who had brought her up in affluence) would ever have said, she did not know. Mrs. Lemoyne, who was a pleasant woman but temperamentally afraid of people, remembered this and was puzzled, but did not stop to argue as she ran about the kitchen.

II

Mort had arrived earlier in the day at the home of Mr. and Mrs. H. Y. Dunkerley. Mr. Dunkerley was a man of affairs, chiefly lumber affairs, and had left the fall gardening in the hands of his wife who was a pretty little thing but not a gardener; he was expected home from Montreal this day, and Mrs. Dunkerley had busied herself in her inefficient way in getting a gardener (gardeners were scarce) and felt very much pleased that Horace would at least find on his return that she had got this good new gardener who seemed to know exactly what was wanted, and would take the whole matter out of her hands. She was a little apprehensive when for the second morning Mr. Johnson did not turn up, but when she saw him now approaching with his pleasantly rolling gait that inspired so much bonhomie and confidence, she felt happy and grateful. "Oh, *here* you are, Mr. Johnson!" she cried.

Mort was feeling contented and happy as he usually did at the beginning of a new job. He was efficient and experienced; he was a gardener; moreover, Myrtle had been in good humour; he was a good husband, the best of husbands, he had given her morning tea; Mrs. Dunkerley looked a nice little thing and he knew how to manage her (you couldn't tell him anything about women, no Sir!). So Mort strolled into the garden, where Mrs. Dunkerley had stood peering down the hill;

he swept off his hat with natural grace, and turned flattering eyes upon Mrs. Dunkerley who thought I can see at once that he likes me—get them to like you and that's half the battle! Was she not deluded!

"Sawry I'm late, Mrs. Dunkerley," confessed Mort frankly. "Fact is, the wife was sick this morning. I done what I could for her (I'm as good as a woman round a sick bed) and I done up the house and left the house and made her promise she wouldn't stir." This was a lie and Mort's angel gave an uneasy turn hardly noticed by Mort who could believe himself any minute that he wanted to.

Mrs. Dunkerley and Mort became fast friends of a kind, because each of them thought that the other had been impressed beyond the point of esteem. Each exploited his or her personal charm upon the other. After a good deal of walking round together and pointing and nodding and discussing, Mrs. Dunkerley left Mort who began to dig over the perennial bed and to change the line of the border as arranged. The day was hot with the sunshine of Indian summer. Occasionally Mrs. Dunkerley looked out of a window and saw Mort Johnson digging steadily, sometimes removing his hat and mopping his brow. "What a find!" she murmured, as she sped away to unpack the fur box and hang out the furs to take away the camphor smell.

Mrs. Dunkerley became very warm as she bent over the fur box and then flapped the furs about. She thought of Mr. Johnson again. I'll take him a bottle of cold beer! she thought. Her admiration of herself rose as she tripped to the icebox. How thoughtful I am! How kind! And how favourably I shall impress him as a good employer, she thought as she crossed the grass; and indeed she looked very kind and pretty as she crossed the grass with beer for the perspiring Mort who now rested on his long-handled spade.

He straightened himself up and shoved his hat back. He was not tall, but with the large masculine air that so became him he smiled down on her and said in a tone slightly, but not quite, familiar, "Say, Lady, aren't you one little angel of mercy! Ever since I had that last go of malaria" (Oh dear, thought Mrs. Dunkerley, I do hope he's not going to have malaria again and all my trouble wasted. I do want this garden to get done before the weather breaks! Such were her selfish thoughts.) "I haven't been able to stand up so good to digging."

"Take it easy, oh please take it easy, Mr. Johnson!" implored Mrs. Dunkerley unnecessarily, looking almost lovingly at him and still holding up the empty tray like a female Ganymede.

Mort tapped her on the wrist, which he should not have done, and said in the affectionate tone that he kept for women "None of this 'Mr. Johnson,' Mrs. Dunkerley! Mortimer, Mort, just plain Mort, that's me!"

Mrs. Dunkerley smiled winningly and said "Very well, Mort!" when a change of expression on Mort's face made her look behind her. A man, bald, red-faced, tubby, well-dressed, having an air of command and possession, stood at the top of the garden. Mrs. Dunkerley turned at once and "Darling!" she cried (with a slightly silly feeling, for she knew how much sillier her attitude must have looked than it really was), and fled across the grass to her husband who had arrived home by the earlier plane. She embraced him.

15

"Horace," she whispered, "I've got us a marvellous gardener! The *nicest* man! Understands exactly what we want and doesn't mind doing the work himself!"

"Well, why would he?" replied Mr. H. Y. Dunkerley who was known as a hard worker and a hard-headed business man who got good returns for his money. "I see you're spoiling him at once, the way you always do." But he gave her a pat, and as soon as they were in the house and out of Mort's sight, he put both arms round her and kissed her affectionately and asked her how she was, and how about a Tom Collins before lunch. He was very fond of his wife, and forgave her most of her silly little fluttery ways. She loved him too, and nothing pleased her better than to see him at home again sitting on the verandah in a long chair, and to bring drinks for both of them, and to question, and interrupt, and tell him every single thing that she had not already told him in letters, and a good deal that she had. She also called him Darling at intervals, a conjugal term that Mort Johnson would have considered sissy and quite unsuited to Mr. Dunkerley's type.

The only person who was not feeling pleased was Mort. While not dangerous to women, he had a way with him and was vain. He had just been experiencing the pleasant sensation of his male power working nicely and smoothly on a pretty little woman—the wife of a lumber magnate, at that—when the pretty little woman had dropped him flat and had disappeared into the house without even looking back. This nice woman had not even introduced him to her husband—a backward jerking finger had sufficed—and the husband had not seen fit to honour him at all, even with a nod. He was, of course, unreasonable, but there you are. He felt reduced in size. His sense of injury mounted, and as Mrs. Dunkerley continued on the front verandah to ply her husband with two drinks, and then with food, and hang upon his lips, and forgot to tell that dumb Chink to give him some lunch, Mort's world changed. His angel, shuffling uneasily, was aware of this, and helplessly saw the turnover of Mort from successful male, successful gardener, old and trusted employee, unique landscaper, the husband possessed of an ailing but doting wife, to a working man insulted and snubbed by a rich man who no doubt had made his money by graft, and the possessor of a wife who had to toil all day on account of people like Mrs. Dunkerley. He had been fawned upon, snubbed and forgotten by a rich woman for what digging she could get out of him. See what Myrt would say to this, and him slaving away in the heat! At this moment the Chinese cook came out and nonchalantly said "Lunch" and disappeared. Worse insult than any, to be ordered about by a Chink. Mort strode to a sheltered spot to eat his lunch. If this was the kind of place it was he wouldn't stay.

III

WHEN Myrtle had finished her four hours, and had left
the five ex-schoolgirls gabbling together, she departed from
Mrs. H. X. Lemoyne's house and took the street car home,
getting off at the butcher's for a pound and a half of
minced round steak for supper and some left over. She
got round steak instead of the pinkish grayish ready minced
meat because this was Mort's first day on his job which had
already become a big contracting job and as she paid for
the round steak she got fonder of Mort. She got some
frozen peas and she would do french fried potatoes, and
she got some ice cream and if she felt like it she would
make some chocolate sauce. By this time she was very
fond of Mort, and by the time she had climbed the two
uncarpeted flights of stairs to the top of the house, she was
the housewife, the loving wife unselfishly arranging a
pleasant evening for Mortimer. She made herself a cup
of tea and sat down in the rocker and kicked off her shoes.
She looked around her as she drank her tea and thought
she'd tidy up the room which was kitchen and sitting-room
and wash room when she got around to it. She did not
think of it as a room that could be made cosy and pretty.
She just thought that she would tidy up a bit when she got
around to it. Steps were heard on the stairs.

These were not Mort's steps, and Myrtle's face hardened.
She knew those heavy, soft, determined steps; they belonged to her maternal aunt Mrs. Emblem. Myrtle put

on her shoes again. "Yoo-hoo, Myrtle!" called Aunty Emblem. "Yoo-hoo yourself," muttered Myrtle and went to the door.

When Aunty Emblem came puffing luxuriously into the dingy room she was indeed the jewel in the dark ear of the Ethiope.

"Those stairs'll be the death of me yet!" she said, smiling at Myrtle in ample fashion, with her plump white attractive hand spread upon her wide soft bosom. She sank into the rocker and it was a pleasure to look at Aunty Emblem as she sat, still panting a little, the rocker giving, forward and backward, to her large slow movement. What a beautiful golden woman she was! What a beautiful gay soft-eyed girl she had been! That was your thought as you looked admiringly at Mrs. Emblem. She had decided to keep her hair a warm gold, and it suited her. Her rouge ran round the side and just below her eyes on her softly curving cheeks, like it tells you to do in the papers, and this suited her too and enhanced the soft pretty sparkle of her large, grey-blue eyes, still young although they seemed to know the world so well. Her little nose was indeterminate but pleasing, with a hint of the ridiculous in it. But her mouth was perhaps her most pleasant feature. No amount of lipstick could alter the fact that her mouth was well shaped and gay and made for happiness, with a catch and a dimple at one corner. When Mrs. Emblem laughed, as she often did, her eyes crinkled and vanished into dark lashes. The pleasant phenomenon of Mrs. Emblem's soft laugh made you want her to laugh again. She must at one time have been a slip of a girl, for her hands, ankles and feet were small and well shaped. She was a singularly single-minded person. From her pretty head and her features nearly buried in agreeable fat, and the long alluring vee of her black dress, to her neat black pumps she was good to look upon, a warming sight.

Mrs. Emblem lunched every Tuesday with her best friend Maybelle Slazenger who worked and had a small two-roomed flat. Because Mrs. Emblem was fond of Maybelle and enjoyed looking after her a bit—enjoyed, in fact, looking after anyone, for such was her nature— she had that day, as often before, prepared a tasty lunch for both of them at Maybelle's apartment. They had eaten too much and talked too long, and Maybelle had hurried back after lunch to her Beauty Parlour, rather late. Then Mrs. Emblem had washed up and tidied up at her leisure.

Maybelle Slazenger's apartment harboured a good many dolls of two or three sexes, with very long and loose-jointed legs and surprised expressions. These dolls lay about in attitudes all day long on fancy cushions and provided Maybelle with a pseudo-human greeting when she returned home in the evening to her small and empty flat, and this greeting filled some need or other. Maybelle said that her dolls had a lot of Personality and one would be inclined to agree with her. So when Mrs. Emblem had plumped up the cushions again and had rearranged the limbs of the lolling dolls, she turned before going out of the door, gave the room a quick satisfied housewifely glance, crinkled her eyes affectionately at the dolls, and murmured as she had often done before "Say, aren't they cute!" She then thought that she would go and have a look-in on her niece Myrtle Johnson later in the afternoon. A shadow in her mind caused her happy expression for a moment to change.

Why, she thought, can't Myrtle fix her place up nice like Maybelle's. There's no reason. If it's a mess like it was last time I'll just have to speak. I'll *have* to say something. Me being her aunty I can speak and no one else will. Mrs. Emblem became unusually irritated—irritated with Myrtle for being irritating, and irritated with herself for allowing herself to be irritated. Then her face cleared and resumed its customary happy and ingenuous expression—an expression which softened and pleased the hearts of strange people even on street-cars.

Her niece Myrtle who now stood regarding Mrs. Emblem under dropped eyelids saw only Aunty Emblem coming in at the wrong time.

"Well, Myrtle, how's everything?" said Mrs. Emblem, rocking.

"Pretty good," said Myrtle.

"Why don't you air this place?"

"Give me a chance. I just got in."

"How's Mort?"

"Fine."

"Working?"

"Got a big *con*tracting job in West Vancouver."

"You don't say. Well, I hope he keeps it. What you do Saturday?"

"Went to a show." Myrtle knew that Aunty Emblem did not mind much what they did on Saturday, but that she wanted to tell Myrtle about the Bridge Club, which she did.

"Say, I'll never forget the time we had Saturday night. Mr. Thorsteinsen and Mr. Jacob called for me and we picked up Maybelle. Maybelle phoned me and said are you going short or long. Well, I'd always rather go long if you're in a cab and Mr. Thorsteinsen called a cab so I wore my black with fringe and it certainly looked good. You should have heard Mr. Thorsteinsen! Say, that man's a scream! Him and me were partners and did we have all the cards. Once I went two spades and Mr. Thorsteinsen went straight up to seven and I had to play it! I nearly died! And then we danced and Mr. Thorsteinsen dances real good!"

"You going to marry him?" asked Myrtle.

"Well," said Aunty Emblem, dimpling, "I don't say as I will and I don't say as I won't. Maybelle says I'm crazy if I tie myself up again, a woman like me. Is that tea hot?"

"It's stewed."

"I wouldn't mind a cup of tea."

Without a word Myrtle emptied the teapot into the open garbage and put the kettle on again.

Aunty looked round the room. Her knowledgeable aunt's eyes rested on the table with unwashed breakfast dishes, the uncleared sink, the faded curtains and the whole drab appearance of the room. She hesitated and then she had to speak.

"Say, Myrtle honey, why don't you have a good scrub-up and get a pot of paint and paint that table and the chairs and the floor too. And there's some stuff down at Woodward's that'd make you nice bright curtains, it wouldn't take much, the windows are short" she said, rocking and looking about her, and so they were, just attic windows really, "and cover them cushions—I'll help—and the place'd look decent. But I guess if Mort hasn't been doing so good . . . but a pot of paint wouldn't set you back much."

22

Well, wouldn't you think a woman even if she's my Aunty doesn't give her any licence to make remarks like that! Her place all pink-looking like a bad house! If me and Mort wanted to spend a lot of money fixing up a dump like this it's our business! Myrtle drooped her eyelids and looked sideways at her Aunt in a way that would have crushed Mrs. H. X. Lemoyne but didn't bother Aunty Emblem.

"Mort's earning good money and I'm earning good money too. There isn't anything Mort wouldn't do for me. If I wanted this dump done up I've only got to say the word. I'm not going to spend Mort's good money on any old landlord's place."

"Well, I'm glad you know that Mort's a good husband. Last time I was here you weren't talking that way. He certainly is a good husband. He's a real man, Mort is. What I wouldn't have made of a man like Mortimer Johnson if he'd been my husband is nobody's business! What I mean he's got the makings. You don't know you're lucky. And I *do* know. I've had my experience. Two sod cases", (Mrs. Emblem meant, by this, that two of her husbands now lay under the sod—no more, no less.) "and one divorce. Mort and me can always get along fine. I hoped he'd be in."

Mort and Myrtle's Aunty always met on the same plane of camaraderie and male and female mutual admiration that was their own natural ambience. Something in Mort roared to life whenever he saw Mrs. Emblem and she played the safe game of advance and retreat with her nephew-by-marriage, and her soft shoulders and bosom shook when she laughed, and she was, exactly, a comely golden old comedy actress playing her part very well. After these performances Myrtle made Mort feel that he had made himself ridiculous ("You certny did amuse *me!*"). The silly fool let her do this, because against her fine dropped eyelids and her faint dropped smile he had no weapons but fury and stamping about, which Myrtle for some hidden reason enjoyed.

"Maybelle and me are going to a show tonight if Maybelle can get around," said Mrs. Emblem, rocking, "so I'll just stop around here a while but I won't have any supper. I been having gas," and she laid her pretty hand on her diaphragm and patted it gently. "A cup of tea'll do me. What you having for supper?"

Myrtle did not answer because she was unwrapping the hamburg steak and Aunty Emblem could see for herself what they were having for supper.

There was a very gentle tap on the door, which had to be repeated. Mrs. Emblem continued rocking but turned and looked at the door as if it would open itself and Myrtle went to the door and opened it and there stood her cousin Victoria May Tritt. Victoria May had nerved herself up to coming to Myrtle's place and to knocking on the door and now she did not like to come in.

"Come in, Victoria May," said Myrtle with something like heartiness. She could play the role of admired hostess to Victoria May who could not make herself at home in the presence of Mrs. Emblem who made herself at home too much. "Come in."

"Oh no, I couldn't come in," said Victoria May, very frightened when she saw Myrtle's maternal aunt Mrs. Emblem whom she admired but feared extravagantly. So far from putting Victoria May at her ease, Mrs. Emblem by her very golden effulgence and geniality and human success emphasized to Victoria May her own inadequacy, her lack of small talk, her feeling of being the extra one wherever she was, her lack of the gorgeous possession—popularity—which Mrs. Emblem so naturally enjoyed. She was at home in a subdued fashion with Myrtle because Myrt was always rather kind to her. Vicky's timidity, her self-effacement, her very boringness induced a certain tenderness in Myrtle. She never wanted to see Victoria May, but when she did, and had to, she treated the little creature not unkindly. As for Mort, he always tossed her a kind and joking word and let it go at that. In consequence of this, Victoria May who, outside her working hours spent in a little shop where she sold notions and fancy handkerchiefs which few people wanted, lived in a timorous world which she carried round with her, and admired Myrt and Mort as kindly, chivalrous, handsome, elegant and an ideal couple.

"Well, come in, *come* in," said Myrtle a little impatiently. "You'd better stay and have some supper. Aunty Emblem can't eat any, she's got gas" (Myrtle mentioned this so that there should be no turning back for Mrs. Emblem).

"Oh no, I couldn't," said Victoria May quite terrified at such a prospect. "I only called by to enquire."

Mrs. Emblem continued rocking and regarded Myrtle's poor-spirited paternal cousin with a golden lazy smile. Poor thing, she thought, poor thing.

"Well, good night, all," said Victoria May huskily and turned and shot down the stairs, safe and alone in her timorous world.

"It beats me," said Mrs. Emblem, "how a person can grow up, and act like that. That cousin of yours always reminds me of some poor dawg that nobody wants."

"Well, I guess nobody does," said Myrtle frankly and went on preparing supper.

"Smells good," said Aunty Emblem. "Mort late?"

An hour later the meat cakes had become blackened and dried at the edges and the potatoes which Myrtle had not french-fried but boiled because Mrs. Emblem was looking on had a pale corpse-like appearance. Myrtle ate her supper. Half an hour later Myrtle was very mad with Mort who was no longer a good husband, and with Aunty Emblem who never could touch fried stuff anyway.

An hour after that Myrt threw the rest of the supper out. She did not care whether Mort had supper or not.

"There's two things about husbands," said Mrs. Emblem, instructively, shoving up her golden pompadour as she rocked (Myrtle wished to goodness that she'd go home), "you got to learn slow cooking or quick cooking if you're going to have a happy home. None of my husbands, not Tod, nor Homer nor Mr. Emblem could ever say I didn't greet them with a good hot meal and a smiling face whatever time they came in and Homer was a railroad man. No Sir! Always a good hot meal."

Myrtle sat down. She was a prey to her nerves. She could not use her weapons and say to Aunty Emblem "You do certny amuse *me*!" because Aunty would laugh and say comfortably "Don't be silly, Myrtle Hopwood. You act like a child. Mort should certny take a stick to you."

"I'd like to see Mort Johnson take a stick to me!"

"That's what I said," Mrs. Emblem would say, pleasantly. "I'd like to see it too."

"Either," continued Aunty, "you have your steak and

26

you have your pie all ready (pity you don't make pies, Myrtle) and everything set, and when your husband comes in you set your steak on the grill, and believe me that brings a man home on the run. That's the quick way. And the slow way is, have your pie—you must have your pie—and leave a casserole in the oven to do slow, chicken and mushrooms maybe, or cream crab or a good rich cheese casserole," the lovely words dripped from her tongue and the dishes appeared steaming golden and fragrant from the oven, "and they cook themselves while you're out with the girls. I've seen my husbands, all three of them, racing home to a macaroni and cheese and a lemon pie and no fuss—yes, *Sir*—not all three together, separately!" and she laughed luxuriously at her joke and her soft bosom and shoulders shook as she laughed. The room was full of Aunty Emblem's success and Myrtle would soon let loose into it her accumulating venom under which her suffocating angel lay.

IV

MORT took his time over lunch. His desire to please had gone, and had been replaced by a slight desire to displease. He wanted to smoke and he had the makings but no matches. He wouldn't ask the dumb Chink for matches and so he could not smoke. This increased his discontent. At last he had to get up and go dig that bed in all this heat again; but the pleasure of digging had left him. His angel sighed within, folded its slim hands and gave up. He had not been digging long when Mrs. H. Y. Dunkerley came twittering, flying, across the grass.

"Oh, Mr. Johnson, Mort," she began, gazing at him appealingly and receiving a polite opaque look, "my husband was *so* sorry!" (I'll bet he was sawry. I'll bet he was nearly crying.) "He wanted to come out and have a little chat with you about the garden, but he had to rush down to the office. *Such* a lot of things piled up for him!" Mort was not touched by the spectacle of Mr. H. Y. Dunkerley flying through the sky all night, coming home to this fine place of his where people could work themselves to death for all Mr. Dunkerley cared, and driving himself down in a swell limousine to his office, lined with plush I bet you; so he said nothing.

"I was thinking, Mr. Johnson, that I have to go out to tea about four, and I could give you a lift down the hill to where the bus stops. It's *such* a hot day! Unfortunately I'm not going to town, I'm driving to Caulfeild, or I'd take you into town—oh," as Mort slapped this pocket, that pocket, in a meaning way, "what is it? a cigarette? matches?" she asked.

"Just a match. Thank *you*. No. I don't smoke tailor-mades."

Anxious to oblige, Mrs. Dunkerley ran into the house and ran out again, bearing matches. Good relations were re-established, supported by the matches and by Mrs. Dunkerley's running about and by a shadowy feeling of Mort's that perhaps he had been unreasonable and it would be nice to have a lift down the hill.

Early, before four o'clock, Mrs. H. Y. Dunkerley jumped into her big car, and with her tiny hands and feet and with much popping of her bright dark head in and out of the window, she steered the car out of the garage. It is really wonderful what these little women can do. She smiled gaily, and beckoned Mort to get in beside her, which he did, after putting away the long-handled spade, and they started down the hill.

"This is very very kind of. you, Mrs. Dunkerley," said Mort politely, enjoying the cool moving air and the pleasant whizz down the long hill, "because I'm kinda anxious to get home to the wife." Almost unknown to himself, Myrtle was becoming established as ailing, and as lying there, pale and sad, awaiting her husband.

"Oh, of course, Mort," said Mrs. Dunkerley in a suitable voice. "You *must* be anxious to get home! There is nothing—serious, I hope!"

I shall probably, thought Mrs. Dunkerley as she drove, hear about Mrs. Johnson's liver, or her kidneys, but it is very nice of him to be so devoted and take such an interest, and I shall certainly take an interest too.

29

"Not serious," said Mort. "The doctor says . . . m . . . the doctor says that there *might* be a slight touch of cancer, though."

"Oh dear me!" said Mrs. Dunkerley, swerving a little. "A slight . . . well well!" What troubles people have, she thought, and how little we know about each other, and she became quite sententious.

"Well, here we are!" said Mort, brightly and bravely, getting out at the bottom of the hill. Mrs. H. Y. Dunkerley took her cue from him and dwelt no more on Myrtle's disease, but said she would see him tomorrow. Then she remembered to pay him, and with a smile and a gesture, she turned to the right and drove rapidly out of sight in the direction of Caulfeild.

Mort stood and waited for the bus. He began to realize that without intending to, and simply because he had been late that morning, he had wished some kind of an illness on to Myrtle, which was too bad. He felt a warm protective feeling for her rising within him and wanted to do some little thing to make up for the disease which he had wished upon her. And so it happened (the feeling rising more and more strongly after he had crossed the Lions' Gate Bridge into Vancouver) that he got off the bus and instead of going home he went to Eaton's Store. He thought he would get Myrtle a pair of nylons, and as he had in his pocket the money which Mrs. Dunkerley had already paid him, what could be easier. As he walked into Eaton's Store he experienced all the joy of the little boy who is getting a valentine for his mother who will exhibit an exaggerated delight. If she doesn't, she will disappoint her little boy very much indeed. It was as this nice and eager and atoning little boy that

Mort walked into the store, but people did not see that he was a little boy, and one or two women in their hurry felt the pleasant feminine glow that the large masculinity of Mort often evoked from women quite unreasonably. People are very deceiving and you never can tell.

He took his place beside a man who was engaged in buying nylon stockings. This was a tubby red-faced well-dressed man whom Mort did not at first recognize because he did not at first look at him very carefully, but I am sorry to say that it was Mr. H. Y. Dunkerley. After Mr. Dunkerley had boarded the plane at Calgary he had suddenly realized that he had forgotten to bring his wife some little present from New York, and so he had taken out his red notebook, and had made a note in it because he left nothing to chance—a note to buy his wife a dozen nylons directly he got to Vancouver, and here he was, buying her a dozen nylons.

"Half a dozen of these," he said, indicating some so thin as to be almost non-existent, "and half a dozen of these."

"Thank you, Mr. Dunkerley," said the nice girl who seemed to know him, and Mort, who as I said was feeling good and in the self-satisfied frame of mind of a man who is buying nylons, even one pair, for his wife, suddenly recognized Mr. H. Y. Dunkerley. He was feeling jocular, or he would never have said to Mr. H. Y. Dunkerley (as he did) in a deprecating half familiar manner as one stocking-buying male to another, "You won't recognize *me*, Mr. Dunkerley, but I was working up at your place today. Buying some nylons for the little lady, I see! Same here. I know I'm only a working

man," continued Mort with a simple-sounding nobility
which had no basis in fact, "but I am sure that under the
circumstances you will pardon me speaking to you."

Mr. H. Y. Dunkerley turned and looked full at Mort
with great dislike. It was too bad no one had warned
Mort Johnson, but, in the very first words that he had
addressed to Mr. H. Y. Dunkerley he had made him very
mad.

Mr. Horace Dunkerley had been born in the province
of Nova Scotia, near a fine place called Antigonish.
He regarded Antigonish, which he had never revisited,
with the same sentiment, with the same romantic attachment that people seem to think that only Highlanders
have for their homes. Or Jews even. The whole of this
romantic attachment—not so foreign to successful business
men as some people think—was impregnated with the
memory of a hard-working but happy boyhood spent in
helping his father who was a hand-logger and had a yoke
of oxen, and his elder brothers. He had been to school
in Antigonish, but not much. He was a woodsman from
the age of ten, and by the time he was sixteen he was
doing a man's work daily. At the age of twenty-four he
had worked his way to British Columbia. By the time he
was thirty, through continued industry, he had come to
own a small shingle mill. Before he had finished paying
for that shingle mill he had established another. And
because he was that kind of person he was now a lumber
man in a big way. He still worked much too hard and
too long, with his head rather than, as heretofore, with
his arms and legs; and while he had worked continuously,
and prospered, he had established within himself a
violent phobia which caused him nearly to explode when

he heard the simple word "working man" uttered,
unless it was applied to anyone who knew what "work"
was in the sense that he, Horace Dunkerley, knew what
"work" was, and had known all his life. So that at
dinners—which he now attended frequently, or in his
clubs—of which he now had a fair number, or on planes
or trains—which he seemed to frequent, when he heard
the word "working man" applied loosely to people who
worked only eight hours or less a day by choice or by
law, he said what he thought about it, in full. So this
was the Achilles' heel of Mr. H. Y. Dunkerley, and
Mort had stuck a needle right in and did not know it.

Mr. Dunkerley showed restraint owing to the fact
that Eaton's stocking counter did not seem the right
place to demonstrate to a stranger the absurdity of the
word "working man" as applied to people who did not
work as hard as Mr. Dunkerley, and of denying the
name "working man" to people like Mr. Dunkerley.
In his club he would have expressed himself violently,
so when he looked in a hostile way at Mort and grunted
"Oh," he was showing great self-restraint, and was not,
as Mort thought at once, being snobbish and haughty.

This "Oh" had a dampening effect on the little boy
who was Mort. In fact the little boy disappeared as
through a trap door, and a slightly truculent man took
his place.

Mr. H. Y. Dunkerley addressed himself to the nice
girl at the counter.

"Charge them," he said, speaking clearly, "to Mr.
Horace Dunkerley; I have a charge."

"Yes, Mr. Dunkerley," said the nice girl, and charged
the stockings, and wrapped them up.

While she was doing this, Mort's face took on a look of wonder. He scrutinized the well-dressed form and compact face of Mr. Dunkerley, and as he looked, he distinguished in the compact face of Mr. Dunkerley a small chubby and serious boy of about twelve years old.

"Say," said Mort, forgetting how rudely he had been treated, "did you ever live in Antigonish?"

"*Certainly* I lived in Antigonish," responded Mr. Dunkerley coldly.

"Was it your father was a hand-logger and had a yoke of oxen just a piece out of Antigonish?"

"Certainly he did," answered Mr. Dunkerley, wishing to escape this questionnaire but unwilling to disclaim Antigonish and the yoke of oxen.

"Well, whaddaya know!" exclaimed Mort with the happy air of discovery. "Well, whaddaya know! You're not going to tell me you're little Horse Dunkerley!"

"Certainly I am Horace Dunkerley," said Mr. H. Y. Dunkerley who seemed to have found a formula.

"Well . . . Say . . . So you're little Horse Dunkerley!" said Mort. He simply could not get over the fact that this successful business man was little Horse Dunkerley and that little Horse Dunkerley had grown into this successful business man.

"And to think I licked the pants off of your big brother Alfy! I sure licked the tar out of Alfy! Where's Alfy?"

"In Yorkton, Saskatchewan," said Mr. Dunkerley. He still looked coldly on Mort because he did not like him at all and not because he had licked the pants off of Alfy.

This coldness became too much for Mort. It takes two to make harmony and Mr. Dunkerley was doing nothing about it. Mort felt outraged that little Horse Dunkerley to whom life had evidently been kind should act in this snobbish way to Mort just because Mort was a working man—and doggone it! employing *him*, Mort, to dig his old garden! Why he bet he never even went to the last war. Just stayed at home and made money.

"Did you go to the war?" Mort asked with seeming irrelevance.

"Certainly I did," said Mr. Dunkerley, desiring to get away.

"Captain, I suppose," said Mort sarcastically.

"Major," snapped Mr. Dunkerley, and pushed past and on and out of the store.

"Were you wanting some stockings?" asked the nice girl who had been listening with interest while pretending not to. She did not say "Do you want some stockings?" which was what she really meant, but used an oblique and genteel form of address in a past tense.

"Were you wanting some stockings?" she asked again of Mort who seemed to be amazed about something.

If he had answered her with scrupulous correctness he would have said "Yes, I was wanting some stockings but I don't want any now. To hell with stockings. I don't care if I never see another one."

But he just said "No" (Well, what did you come in here for then, thought the nice girl) in a furious tone of voice, and walked with his easy rolling gait out of the door, going in the other direction from that taken by Mr. H. Y. Dunkerley. This brought him out onto Hastings Street facing down towards Main Street.

He walked down and down Hastings Street feeling very mad and reiterating inside himself that it was not fair and

he wouldn't go and dig that old garden not if Horse Dunkerley gave him half the earth. He glowered in front of
him. Many women and girls thought Oh what a man, and
some gave him soft looks but he did not see them.

He walked on until he came to a new beer parlour called
The Old Bodega, and though he was an abstemious man
and spent very little money in beer parlours, unless he met
an old friend—he and Myrt went once in a way—he went
into the beer parlour which was cool and pleasant and
smelled, naturally, of beer, and sat down at a small table
and ordered a beer, which he drank, sipping moodily.

When a tall thin man without a hat came in and walked
across to a table beyond where Mort sat, Mort did not
observe him except with a lacklustre eye which saw nothing
because all his cognition was turned inwards not outwards,
and he was occupied in ruminating on the unfair and
unpleasant day that he had had, and he wished he'd licked
the tar out of Horse Dunkerley as well as his brother
Alfy while he had had the chance, the little bastard. So
it was that the tall thin man, looking idly round, met the
eyes of Mort, looked, brightened, got up, came and stood
over him and said "Well, if it isn't the old buzzard himself!" but at first Mort was unaware of him.

Mort then looked up right at the thin man whose face
was double-creased into a long sad pleasant clown-like
smile. Then Mort's eyes came to life. They brightened.
His face came to life. His mouth opened.

"Well, whaddaya know!" he said. "You old So-and-
so!" He stood up, and he and his old friend, whose name
was Pork, slapped each other on the back and said "Well
well well, you old son of a gun!" It was plain from this that
they were old friends, and the fact was that Pork and Mort

36

had been buddies in the same Battalion, and had been at Passchendaele together and had been in lots of spots together, both tough and funny, and had seen each other only at intervals of years and years. Each was thoroughly pleased to see the other, and so Pork went back to his table and picked up his glass of beer and came over and sat down across from Mort, and how comfortable it was, Pork and Mort sitting across from each other and ordering another beer and taking their time saying things to each other and none of this nonsense of not understanding each other—nothing *between*, as you might say. Mortimer forgot about the things that had so agitated and annoyed him as he walked down Hastings Street into the beer parlour; or if he didn't quite forget at first, these disturbing thoughts turned themselves round and round like dogs settling down and then they settled to sleep. Mort was not bothered by them now, as he sat at the table with his old companion Pork, who was no angel but a good old scout. And Mort's own particular angel sat up and dusted itself off and breathed the inner air of harmony.

"Didn't someone tell me you was married?" asked Pork, and Mortimer said he was, to the finest little woman God ever made; everybody liked her and she was the refined type.

"Nothing like a Good Woman," said Pork, and they both agreed, and ordered another beer and that was the last beer they had. Three, no more.

"Workn?" asked Pork.

Mort nodded. "Doing a big *con*tracting job over in West Vancouver."

"*Con*tracting eh?" asked Pork, implying What kind of contracting.

"Millionaire's place. Landscaping," said Mort, pursing his lips and looking into his beer with the air of a man concerned with slopes, haulage and drainage. He had forgotten that he had stopped working at the millionaire's place.

Pork pursed his lips too, raised his eyebrows, put on a certain look, and nodded, impressed.

"What you doing?" asked Mort, rousing himself from the haulage and drainage.

"I work at Love's. Classy morticians," said Pork.

"Morticians?" asked Mort.

"Undertakers to you," said Pork.

"Oh, sure. Undertakers to me. I don't go for them fancy names," said Mort.

"Well well," said Pork, looking at his silver watch, "I'll have to be gettinalong. I'm on duty nights."

"I'll come along," said Mort. "I never seen an undertaker's place. Behind the scenes as you might say. I'll come along with you."

So the two friends got up, and took their time and walked together along Hastings Street and took the street car and changed twice and got off at a very chic building which was large and spreading and of white stucco with window boxes, and a grass plot all around; the kind of building that caused tourists driving in from Bellingham to say "Oh let's stop here, Momma. This looks like a nice kind of place!" You cannot blame these tourists because it does indeed look like a nice kind of place to stay, but it is not, it is not, it finally and inescapably is not. It is a mortician's place, it is a funeral parlour, it is a funeral home, it is the undertaker's, and people who approach meditatively and a bit early for the funeral wonder How on earth did we manage in the old days! Back east when Grampa died it doesn't seem to me we had anything swell like this. We just had the funeral right in the house and old Miss Foster came in to help.

The hot sun was setting, and Mort felt very much at peace as he followed his friend Pork into the side door of the funeral home. A young man in black with a gentle demeanour approached Pork and gave him some instructions, pointing here and there, taking Pork into an inner office and showing him something, and then taking him into another room and showing him something else, and Pork received his nightly instructions, and nodded and said "Yes, Mr. Pontifex, I certainly will. No, Mr. Pontifex, I certainly won't. Well I don't think she can have left that neckpiece in the chapel because I'd have found it last night when I was cleaning, but I'll have another look and if I see it I'll give her a ring, and if I hear anything from the Pinkham family I'll let you know."

All this time Mort effaced himself from the conversation and stood with a great deal of interest in a very handsome kind of parlour lavishly upholstered and hung and carpeted in an anonymous tasteless fashion. There was nothing to induce reverence in this room, but Mort felt a kind of reverence stealing over him like a scent.

The sun, at that time of the year, goes down suddenly, and then it is night before you know it. Pork began turning lights on in various places and this of itself changed the autumn afternoon into night in a funeral home. The young man in black with the gentle demeanour came through the reception parlour with his things on. He nodded kindly to Mort who wondered Does he think I'm one of the relatives, and went out into the street, closing the outside door after him with a soft click. Pork seemed to be somewhere else.

Mort thought Well, I might as well sit down, so he tried a rocking chair as he was partial to rocking chairs. Not a twinge of thought reminded him—at least hardly a twinge —that he should have been home to supper long ago. The gentle influence of the beer, and Pork, and the funeral home, had the assuaging effect on him—and on his angel —of a warm beach on a starred summer night, or of a soft bed on Sunday morning. You do not want to leave it; it is good enough for you.

After a time the door of the reception parlour opened and Pork came in. He was wearing a janitor's overalls and he had a small fur neck-piece in his hand. He said, "Just wait till I put this in the office." When he returned he said, "D'you want to see something?"

Mort nodded. He was pleasantly apprehensive. He had—years ago—seen death many times and in many forms, but this was different. "Is it a stiff?" he asked.

Pork seemed a little shocked. "It wouldn't be my place to show you that . . ." he said, and Mort said, "Of course not." They went along a lighted hall and then they went up a finely carpeted flight of stairs. There was a door. Pork opened the door wide, went inside, clicked lights on, stepped back, and said, "Well, what do you think of *that* . . .!"

Mort went in.

"Well, whaddaya know!" he said.

The coffins stood row behind row in a large oval space; nothing in the room but coffins. Majestic and inescapable they stood, waiting all together. Mort felt stunned by the sudden silent sight of all these coffins. In this room the fact of mortality was delivered straight with a hammer blow, and there was no evasion. There seemed to Mort to be hundreds of coffins. There were only forty-two. Every taste, except those concerned with doom, shape and cost, every aesthetic taste, was catered for. Mort snatched off his hat, which he had put on again, with a vague feeling of reverence for the dead.

"Well well well, whaddaya know," he said again to the coffins in general; and Pork watched his friend, and was gratified with Mort's response.

Mort's eyes began to differentiate between the coffins. Some were open, some were closed, some were half open, some were certainly for the ladies. All seemed to be lined with lavish crinkles of satin arranged by a master. This was nice.

"I guess there'd be quite a bit of money tied up in them coffins," he enquired, turning to Pork, "they'd be worth quite a bit?"

"Caskets," corrected Pork.

"Well, they're coffins to me. But they sure are pretty!" He advanced towards the coffins, tiptoeing uneasily, vigorous but subdued among their horizontal shapes.

A bell whirred somewhere. Pork turned and left, saying "I'll be back." Mort heard him going down the stairs. He began to move from coffin to coffin. He stood and pondered each one. They became less dreadful. He began to enjoy himself. He began to choose his pick.

I guess by the looks these would all be for society people, he thought as he surveyed them. There didn't seem to be a plain working man's coffin in the lot. He was divided between a forbidding box covered with elephant grey and lined with off-white, and a fine job covered with purple brocaded velours and lined with heliotrope satin. Either of these coffins was suited to a certain aspect of Mort's temperament, but he preferred the richness of the purple. There'd be some satisfaction in being buried in something like that. If he wasn't afraid of Pork coming back he'd get in, just for the feel, but he knew Pork wouldn't like it. He now thought of Myrtle. He would choose one for her. After some difficulty and much sticking out of his lower lip and pinching his chin, he chose a coffin prettily lined with shining blue, and stood over it, looking down. He became sentimental, and then he became unhappy. He became luxuriously unhappy, and mysteriously elevated. He looked down into the soft blue satin and—plain as day —he saw Myrt lying there. This, then, was really the end of everything. This was what we come to; and then—no more; this—and no other. He saw Myrt's thin occasion-ally pretty face with its well-known look, the eyelids closed; and the circumstances of Myrt's death and funeral rose and encompassed him. Easy tears filled his eyes and he dried them with the back of his hand. He thought I haven't always been so good to Myrt as I ought to been, though God knows she'd drive you mad the way she acts sometimes but I bet I'll be sawry sometime for the things I done. Mort was softening up considerably so his angel took advantage of this to start the thought that he'd better not stay here thinking up funerals when nobody was even dead, and he'd better get home to supper because Myrt would be mad. Mort took one more look at Myrtle in her coffin, but she had faded, so he tiptoed noisily to the door, and went out with a farewell look at all the beautiful coffins (I'd sure like to pick one for little Horse Dun-kerley with splinters in), closed the door quietly and met Pork on the landing.

"I certainly enjoyed that," said Mort in his pleasant hoarse voice, "I never seen such a sight before! That sure was a very interesting sight . . . I must be getting along home or there'll be hell popping. Now looka here, Pork, you come around and see the wife and me one of these days. Mind you do. Come any time, any time . . ." and Mort waved his big hands this way and that, welcoming Pork in.

"I sure will, I sure will," said Pork heartily. "Would ya like a few flowers for the wife? There some fine gladioluses come too late today and I can't do nothing but throw 'em out."

"*Would* I!" said Mort gratefully and thought to himself Say if that isn't a break! Myrt'll be crazy about the flowers; she'll forget all about me coming in late.

Pork led the way to back premises where there were mops and brooms and pails and a heap of flowers, some fresh, some faded. "If you look among these," said Pork, bending down, "you'll find plenty fresh. The cards is off. They're all in sprays and wreaths and it's no good sending 'em to hospitals . . . You break off the good ones and take 'em along home. I'll only have to throw 'em out anyway," and the two men went down on their hunkers and fumbled clumsily amongst the flowers—chiefly, as Pork had said, gladioluses—and by selection and rejection and careful breaking-off, Mort got a *bo*kay of real nice flowers, although some of the stems were short. He was pleased.

"Well, it certainly has been fine seeing you again, Pork, you sure must come around . . ." and in his mind Mort began seeing his old friend nearly every day. "Thanks for the *bo*kay," he said, turning it about admiringly, "my wife's crazy about flowers. She sure will be pleased. Well,

I'll be seeing you," and Pork let Mort out into the dark street and said goodbye again several times, and Pork went back into the funeral home and shut the door, and Mort went down the street and got on a street car and paid his ticket and sat down and looked at his pretty flowers.

The street car rollicked along, and the queer thing was that the nearer he got to home the more the mist of good feeling and good fellowship and personal virtue cleared away, and left Mort facing his near and inevitable arrival home to the two rooms and to Myrtle who would be at one of her stages—either not pleased, mad, or very mad. However, he had the flowers. He looked at the flowers and saw to his surprise that they had begun to have a used appearance.

V

Mort got off the street car and walked the two blocks or more to his house. Because an uneasiness within him grew, he assumed a general swagger and so tried to equip himself to meet Myrtle, if indeed she was at home. She might have got mad and gone down to Irma's place. However, he tried to prepare himself. So Mort, going apprehensively home, gave the appearance of a fine truculent man walking along fearing nobody and carrying a bunch of flowers.

He did not know that, as he ascended the stairs, two women, not one, sat waiting for him in silence. They waited in silence because they heard him ascending the stairs.

Mort fumbled the handle and walked into the room, flowers first. Oh radiant vision, temporary rainbow, there sat his friend Mrs. Emblem in the rocking chair! Backwards and forwards, backwards and forwards she rocked, smiling at him in her effulgent indulgent way. Well, whaddaya know! Mort swept off his hat and exclaimed joyfully "Why, look who's here!" and then he did a fatal thing. So great was his pleasure and relief at seeing Mrs. Emblem in the rocking chair that he just naturally very nearly gave the flowers to Aunty Emblem. He held out the *bo*kay (which was nothing much to look at, now) to Mrs. Emblem, and then, sinkingly aware of Myrtle sitting silent, he swung the *bo*kay at a right angle over to Myrtle.

45

"Here's a few flowers for you, honey," he said in his husky voice, "thought you'd like a few flowers, Queen." But the harm was done. An innocent husband coming in late and smelling of something does not first of all hand flowers to your aunt and then as a second thought execute a right turn and pass them on to you. Mort did not know it, but he might as well have given Myrtle a handful of prickly pear. He advanced towards her, and, following up the flowers, put his arm round her, and gave her a good kiss. *There*, he thought.

Myrtle's thin nostrils moved. "You've been drinking," she said. Mort was really hurt by this. "I never . . ." he began.

"Drinking!" said Mrs. Emblem, her soft eyes vanishing in an affectionate smile, "if you think Mort's been drinking, you should a seen Homer!" She rocked, recalling Homer. "When Homer'd been really drinking I'd have some nice sandwiches and a cuppa coffee or a jug of tomato juice and I'd say to him Now, Homer, you lay right down on that couch and I'll cover you up and here's a bite if you want it and he wouldn't touch it and he'd go right off and in the morning he'd never know what happened him except that he'd not be feeling so good. Mort's not been drinking, Myrtle! You come right over and give your old Aunty a kiss, Morty," and Mort did. "Why, Myrtle, that's not drink! That's only one," sniff, "or two," sniff, "or maybe three bottles a beer! Well, I must be getting along home. It doesn't look like Maybelle's coming now. You bring Myrtle around to see me one of these days, Morty." And Mrs. Emblem eased herself out of the chair, and Mort helped her into her coat, while Mrs. Emblem said goodnight genially to

Myrtle. Mort took her downstairs and all the way down the stairs he said "I'll take you to the street car. I'll take you home." And Mrs. Emblem said "Oh no you won't." But when they got to the bottom step Mrs. Emblem turned to Morty and put her hands on his shoulders and said "Now, Morty, don't you be a fool. You go right on upstairs to Myrtle. She's waiting to bawl you out for being late and don't you pay too much attention. Don't go crawling around—you don't have to. Act like a man of spirit but you don't need to lose your temper. Myrtle's got to get it out of her system if you know what I mean. Go on now; go on up."

Mort thanked Mrs. Emblem for her kind words saying "Say, Mrs. Emblem, that's real kind of you, but I'd sooner it was you than me going up them stairs. And me taking her all them nice flowers too!"

"Yes, and a crazy way you gave them to her, passing them to me first! Make any woman sore! Go on now. Beat it, Mort." And Mrs. Emblem went down the street with her easy bouncing tread, and didn't even turn and give Mort a chance to linger; and Mort turned and slowly went on upstairs, trying to plan to act like a man of spirit but not lose his temper.

VI

MRS. EMBLEM got onto the street car feeling depressed. She paid her fare and then sat down taking a whole seat so as to be comfortable, and thought I don't know what makes Myrtle act the way she does. Sometimes I think I'll never go around again. I think she gets it from her pa. Hazel (that was Mrs. Emblem's sister, Myrtle's mother) hadn't got a mean bone in her body. At least not much. But Myrtle always acted kinda mean even when she was a kid. Mort's soft and easy and he's scared to death of her and she knows it. It's too late to take a stick to her now, but reelly *and* truly, if Mort had taken a stick to Myrtle years ago she wouldn't act so silly now. And, Mrs. Emblem continued, feeling irritated, it isn't as if she'd anything to be uppity about. Look at her! Look at that dump! I feel ashamed of my own niece every time I go into it! Well, people have to settle their own hash, and Mrs. Emblem rocked along on the street car and got off at Burrard Street and walked to her rooming house and let herself in, and on up to her room, and turned on the light. The room sprang softly and warmly to life, and Mrs. Emblem locked her door, and breathed a deep sigh of comfort. Well she might. A pleasant glow of sentiment was shed by a light rosily shaded and suffused. Mrs. Emblem advanced into the room and turned on two lamps also rosily and cosily shaded. These lights so pinkly suffused revealed the neatness and cleanness of Mrs.

Emblem's room. It was a room with a small ell. The ell
was divided from the main part of the room by long rose-
coloured curtains which at once suggested a delicious
though precarious privacy, an unravished something.
How pleasant it was for Mrs. Emblem to go to bed behind
those curtains, with her very fancy dressing table, made
of a packing case and frilled by her own hands, beside
her, a pinkly shaded light over her head, a rosy quilt upon
the bed, the rose curtains open or drawn, the dying sounds
of night passing up and down Burrard Street in the dark,
some chocolates near at hand, a pink or blue dressing
jacket loosely upon her white shoulders, her curls for
tomorrow tied prettily within a pink or blue silken scarf
finished with a knot or a bow, and the newspaper in her
hands, opened at the Personal Column. She is undeniably
a home-maker. No one has seen Mrs. Emblem lying
luxuriously there; but I see her now, and she looks so
nice, she makes me feel good.

At any moment, just by drawing the curtains and thus
concealing the bed, the main portion of the room can
become a living room. It is furnished with repulsively
ornate chairs and a couch upholstered in a material
which might be rose-coloured plush, but is not, and on
this furniture are large pink cushions of a shiny satin
which look as though they should not be leaned upon,
but should be held upon the knees. A screen placed with
seeming casualness across a corner hides various things.
The two windows look out, between their flowered
curtains, on Burrard Street. Burrard Street has three
things to commend it, and no more. Its name belongs to
the early history of the north Pacific Coast, but Mrs.
Emblem does not know this. It is wide. As you travel

north on Burrard Street on a fine day you see at its northern end a disclosure of Inlet (also Burrard) and mountains fantastically beautiful; and as you travel south you come to a bridge across False Creek, wide, simple, yet romantically and with dignity conceived. But where you look out of Mrs. Emblem's windows there is none of this; Burrard Street is only a street up and down which there goes too much vehicular traffic. There are no books in Mrs. Emblem's sitting room because she does not read books. Books are untidy, and there is no need of them. There is a shiny wooden chest or bench in which there are all-story, fashion or movie magazines put away. It is easy to be funny about the furniture-store romantic appearance of Mrs. Emblem's room, and for Myrtle to say that it is pink like a bad house. But it is not a bad house; it is a good house although it is only one room, and it is as much part of the essential Mrs. Emblem as her crinkly smile or her pink dressing gown.

Maybelle Slazenger who is part owner of the LaRose Beauty Parlour is Mrs. Emblem's closest friend; but she has many other friends, both men and women, and they spend pleasant evenings in Mrs. Emblem's room. When gentlemen come, they bring a bottle, one only. She does not admit Mr. Thorsteinsen or Mr. Jacobs separately, but she does admit them together, and they with other chosen members of the Bridge Club enjoy coming, very much indeed.

Mrs. Emblem's three husbands have each contributed a little, financially, to her present state. She is a good manager, born to be a wife and a mistress; and to each of her three husbands she has been honest wife and true mistress. From time to time she works because she likes the extra money, and because although she is Mrs. Emblem and therefore a happy woman, she sometimes feels a certain vacuity which is not filled by cleaning and polishing her room, shopping (which usually means walking through the shops with one of her friends), going to a show, and playing whist or bridge with Mr. Thorsteinsen, Mr. Jacobs, and Maybelle. She is hardly aware of the poignant communications of sky, of birds, of ocean, forest, and mountain, although she thinks Vancouver is a nice place. She does not see around or beyond the tangible male or female human form and its appearance and peculiar requirements. I think, in order to be perfectly happy, she still needs to look after someone. You cannot help liking Mrs. Emblem. She is so nice; she is perhaps too fat, now, to be beautiful; but she is—to Mr. Thorsteinsen, to Maybelle, to Mortimer Johnson and to me—alluring, and so she had been to the two sod cases and the divorce.

She and Maybelle can talk indefinitely, over a cup of coffee at Mrs. Emblem's place, or over a cup of tea at Scott's (where they will have their fortunes read) about themselves, their pasts and their futures, and what they counsel each other to do. Mrs. Emblem is not lonely—exactly. But she has enjoyed long and varied male companionship; that is what she is formed for, and that is what she—less ardently now—sometimes craves. And yet something holds her back. Perhaps she is growing indolent; perhaps she does not wish at her age to submit herself to a new elderly marriage whose intimacy youth no longer sanctions and makes charming; perhaps she has discovered the joys of privacy and does not wish to lose them, for at least she now owns herself.

She discusses endlessly with Maybelle the advantages and disadvantages of a further marriage, the feelings that she has about Mr. Thorsteinsen, and the opportunity she has for becoming an investigator—or what her niece Myrtle calls a snoop—in one of the large department stores. She would not be a good snoop; she is too memorable, and her golden quality draws, usually, geniality and attention from those who serve her. She knows that she can always get a job at a certain downtown millinery store where she worked steady for two years but they would want for her all day, and she does not like that. Then Maybelle and she discuss Maybelle's problems, which are similar and are also capable of being extended indefinitely over the tea-leaves. In theory she goes to church. But she does not go to church. Her son is married and lives in Lethbridge and she promises to go and visit there some day. The only relative that she has in Vancouver is her niece Myrtle Hopwood who married that nice no-good fellow Mort Johnson, and she likes Myrtle as little as anyone she knows. But she keeps in touch with her, because Myrtle is of her family, child of her own sister. She has watched Myrtle throughout her curious unsatisfactory years without being able "to do anything about it". She is more kind to Myrtle than Myrtle knows, and is ready to befriend her.

After Mrs. Emblem came in from Myrtle's on Tuesday night she took her time and, moving ponderously, gracefully, and slowly, she went to bed, drawing her curtains apart and allowing some fresh air, and noise, to come in from Burrard Street. She did not take off her make-up the way it says to do in the paper, because there might be a fire, or a burglar, or she might die, or might be ill or have to have the doctor, and she would not like to be discovered without her make-up. She just reduces it and freshens it a little. But in the morning she can, and will, take it all off, and, later, put it all on again.

Mrs. Emblem made some cocoa, and this she sipped at leisure as she looked idly at the least important page, that is to say the front page, of the newspaper, which necessitates no turning. You cannot turn the pages of a newspaper in bed and drink cocoa at the same time with complete comfort and safety. But she has some cookies and she will nibble these when she gets to the real page-turning part. The front page has sometimes a good murder which develops on see page two. Apart from that it is very uninteresting, as it deals in long words or in meaningless initials such as OPA, UNO, TUC, FBI (everyone's gone mad), and with countries who do not seem to be able to get on together and have no particular bearing on her life (or so she really seems to think), and with elderly men who have no news value for Mrs. Emblem. The same applies to the editorial page but that is worse. It is a dead loss, except occasionally for the correspondence. The same applies also to the sports pages and to those pages devoted sometimes to church and to music and the drama.

First of all (have a cookie) she turns to the Society page. She does not regard the Society page with the feeling, which must surely be suspicion by the way it works in her, of Myrtle. She likes the people who figure there for her entertainment. She wishes she knew far far more about them and the interesting congenial lives which they lead. She likes them to get married. How they rush about (little she knows) to meetings, to luncheons, to teas, to cocktail parties, to dinners, to more meetings, to Harrison Hot Springs, and to California. More power to them. She has no snobbish admiration for these people who so industriously and sometimes vainly spend themselves, and are so prodigal of their smiles, and rush about so much; but they give her vicarious pleasure and are part of the same show which includes the movie advertisements and the funnies. Mrs. Emblem has one or two favourites among those people who rush about; she likes to see their pictures. She says to Maybelle "I didn't think that picture of Mrs. H. Y. Dunkerley did her justice, did you?" She really is a darling.

She then turns to the funnies. She has her favourites there also, which seem to touch obscurely on something in her own long experience or in her imagination. Sometimes her eyes crinkle and vanish in a smile (have a cookie). Little Orphan Annie, the eternal little girl who never grows up, is profoundly identified with herself. Annie is the normal person, always right in motive and performance and endearingly young, the little monster. Who would not be Annie? Things are not made too difficult for those who read about Annie. Look at the new character who makes his abrupt appearance in the picture. The lines of his jaw, his brow, at once disclose good or evil. You know exactly where you are: would that one's own acquaintance were so marked. The line of his jaw invites your apprehension or your confidence; but beneath it all, you do not worry. Annie will be all right. Mrs. Emblem passes on down the page, slowly perusing all the funnies, including those funnies which exhibit life in its more debasing forms and are anything but funny. And then she turns to the Personal

Column and this is the newspaper's climax (have a cookie).

Sometimes the Personal Column disappoints. There may only be the working man who wishes to meet a respectable woman of between 30 and 40, no objection to one child, object matrimony. Mrs. Emblem dwells but idly on this working man; he does not tempt her, even in thought; his youth forbids. Her interest kindles at the sight of the Scandinavian gentleman well fixed, desires to meet widow fond of dancing and shows, object companionship and matrimony no triflers. She puts the Scandinavian gentleman through his paces and thinks there is no doubt something wrong with him. What Scandinavian gentleman well fixed could not find plenty of companions for shows and matrimony without advertising for them? He must have bad habits. She considers the retired business man who would like to meet up with a single widow, and here she laughs. What does he mean by a single widow? Well, I am not a single widow so that won't do. She is not too sure about the Canadian Catholic non-smoker, or about the English gentleman age sixty-five with means, Protestant, desires to meet sincere widow, although they sound the safest. She lives through each of these mysterious romances each night, weighs them and sometimes makes her selection. They are real life. But she would never dare. She will no more write to the English gentleman than Mort will slug Myrtle although he often declares that he will; these things happen in the mind alone; only the body acts; and Mrs. Emblem will never write to the English gentleman.

Maybelle once had a friend who did answer an advertisement and what that woman went through was terrible.

Mrs. Emblem rustles the paper a bit longer, but she is getting sleepy, so she folds it up neatly, turns out the light, and settles to sleep at once like a beautiful old baby.

Myrtle's cousin Victoria May Tritt has been asleep for some time in her room down on Homer Street. She too read the Personals including the cockroach remedies. She did not read her paper in comfort (and in any case it was not her paper but an old one borrowed) because her light does not hang above her bed. Her light, which has no shade, hangs small and naked in the middle of her room, and therefore she cannot read in bed. Vicky Tritt sits under it straight up on a wooden bedroom chair; she peers at it through her glasses; if she is cold she will put the comforter around her knees. Vicky Tritt does not know what it feels like to be a woman. Mrs. Emblem knows nothing else.

VII

Mort looked at Mrs. Emblem going down to Powell Street towards the car stop and then, because it was no good continuing to stand there, he turned and went slowly back up the stairs.

Myrtle had been prepared to flick him with a scornful look, to sulk a little, to put him in the wrong for being late for supper, and when she had reduced him to a proper sense of his own inadequacy, consider herself satisfied. But when she had beheld Mort returning home sober but gay, apparently unashamed though late for supper, smelling nevertheless of beer, presenting flowers first to Aunty Emblem and then, as an afterthought, to her—she had flared up into active anger.

Mort went back into the room, and there she sat, her eyelids contemptuous. The ineffectual flowers lay on the table and on the floor.

Myrtle's nostrils expanded sharply to points.

"You been drinking," she said coldly.

"Now, Queen . . ." Mort began, hurt, expostulating.

"Don't call me Queen. I smelled you the minute you came in the room. Right away when Irma Flask told me she seen you with Eddie Hansen I might a known what would happen. I might a known you'd get tight . . ."

"I'm not tight!" bellowed Mort resentfully, nor was he. "And what's more I never even seen Eddie Hansen. If Eddie Hansen's in town this is the first I heard of it.

57

Who's Irma Flask to go telling lies about Eddie Hansen.
I never seen Eddie Hansen since he was down at New
Year's!"

"Yes, and you certny made a fool of yourself at New
Year's . . ."

"Quit that! Quit that now! Can't you forget it!"
But Myrtle had put herself in the wrong by assuming
that Mort had been out with Eddie Hansen, and Mort
in his turn was injured. "Eddie Hansen's a good scout
and I wouldn't trade Eddie Hansen for all the Irma
Flasks that ever went down the pike." The conversation
now turned on the relative merits of Irma Flask and Eddie
Hansen. This led to a good deal of recrimination and old
history, but it got Myrtle nowhere, so she side-stepped.

"And me fixing you a good dinner wasting and
ruining food and sitting here waiting, and all the time
you off spending good money drinking."

"I have NOT BEEN DRINKING," shouted Mort very
loudly. He began stomping about, and lifted up a chair
and whanged it down again on to the floor. Up and
down the room he stomped.

"Oh oh oh," moaned old Mr. Raskob on the floor
below, "I wouldn't mind a leetle row just once in a way
but every day every day this banging and banging, it's
too bad I say it's too bad. If they'd only put down some
carpets, if they'd only!"

"Them put down carpets!" exclaimed old Mr. Gluck
glaring up at the ceiling. "They wouldn't put down no
carpets not if you gave them a pair from the Hudson Bay
with frills on free gratis for nothing! They wouldn't put
them down for spite!" It was true that Myrtle and
Mortimer had no carpets and were indifferent to noise.

Mort continued stomping and roaring up and down over their heads. Old Mr. Raskob subsided in a chair and put his hands to his ears. "Every day every day!" he said. "It's driving me crazy. Don't they never have no bedroom slippers?" Mortimer went on stomping and dragging things about.

Mr. Gluck took the broom and banged upon the ceiling, glaring upwards.

Myrtle and Mortimer, upstairs, became united by a glance. Mort changed the direction of his temper.

"Who do they think they are?" he said, as Mr. Gluck banged with fury.

"Yes, who *do* they think they are anyway?" said Myrtle.

"Who do you think you are, hey?" shouted Mort, bending down to the floor. "Who's paying this rental anyway?" he roared to the two old men below. "Tell me that! Tell me who's paying this rental! We got a right to live as well as you!"

"We are very considerate, I'm sure," said Myrtle who never thought of the two old men below except at such a time as this. She looked superior.

Mort gave the chair a final bang and then he sat down on it back to front, leaning over the chair-back. When Mortimer sat down on the chair the worst of the noise ceased. The two old men remained silent and nervous below. (Pity us, pity us, the civilized ones, who live on shelves, one below the other, one above the other. Pity Mr. Gluck and Mr. Raskob, living in that old house, under Myrtle and Mortimer Johnson. Pity those who live in crowded areas, one below another, one against the other. We live on shelves one below the other because we are so civilized.) Now that Myrtle had caused Mort to stomp about, and Mortimer had vented his rage, and Mr. Gluck by knocking on the ceiling had united Myrtle and Mort against Mr. Gluck and Mr. Raskob, Myrtle and Mort's irritation was a good deal purged, and they began to feel better.

But Myrtle saw again the flowers. "Where'd you get them flowers?" she enquired suspiciously. "Looks like you'd been doing something queer, spending money on flowers. And that was a pretty funny way to give me flowers, I'll say! I want to know . . ."

"Now, Queen . . ." began Mort.

"*Don't* call me Queen . . ."

"Now, hon," said Mort, placatingly, "I didn't spend no money on flowers! I got them" (he checked himself. Suddenly there seemed an impropriety, unnoticed before, in bringing Myrtle flowers from the undertakers. He would have liked to tell Myrtle about all those coffins, but just now she wouldn't understand.) "from a friend of mine. Got a big place out Kingsway. Nothing would do but I must go see his place. And nothing must do but I must take some flowers to the wife. He was pulling up his gladioluses for the winter . . ." the picture lay clear before Mort's eyes—Pork in his beautiful garden, tidying up against the winter; Pork offering Mort gladioluses for the wife in his beautiful garden. Myrtle listened to this, her eyelids averted. It sounded all right. Then she remembered Aunty Emblem and her anger rose again.

"Mew," said a kitten, and ran out from under the sink and rubbed itself, arching and purring, against Myrtle's ankles.

Myrtle looked down surprised. "Where'd that come from?" she said, checked in her temper.

"Musta come in with me," said Mort. "Give it here. I'll put it out." He still looked upset.

"It's cute," said Myrtle forgetting how angry she was and bending down to the kitten. "Say, *isn't* it cute!" The kitten, as pretty and graceful as could be, rubbed and rubbed against Myrtle, and uttered its little mews. They watched it.

"That cat's crazy about you," said Mort ingratiatingly.

"Sure is," said Myrtle, and she picked up the kitten. "If it's a tom I'd like to keep it. We got mice. I don't want no cat families round here but I'd like a tom. Some people say you can tell by their noses if they're a tom," and Myrtle held up the kitten and looked at its innocent face and its inscrutable pink nose.

"They crazy. How could anyone tell a cat's sect by its nose! I can tell dogs but I can't tell cats and I'll bet you you can't tell a tom by its nose."

"And a party told me," continued Myrtle, up-ending the kitten who clawed the air this way and that, "that if it's a she, they's a place shaped like a violet under its tail. . . ."

"That's a hell of a place to look for a violet, under a cat's tail," said Mort. But he bent forward, his hands on his knees, and scrutinized the kitten. "That don't look to me like no violet, but I wouldn't know."

"Then it's a tom . . . that's certny no violet . . . Morty, you just take that box the onions are in and dump them out and go down and run across to Baxter's garden and get some dirt."

"That's a hell-of-a-note," said Mort, grumbling a bit

61

but getting the box just the same, "me going across to Baxter's the middle of the night to get a box a dirt for any old cat."

"You go right along, Morty," said Myrtle as she set down a saucer. "Isn't that a cute kitten! Look, it's lapping!"

"What do I get the dirt with?" asked the gardener and landscaper.

"Use your hands . . . take a spoon . . . I don't care . . ." said Myrtle, and Mort clumped down the stairs and out into the dark, with the box and a cooking spoon.

When Morty came back having put down the spoon and left it in Baxter's garden he set the box on the floor. "Mroo, mroo," said the kitten, and with croons of delight ran to the box, scrambled up the side, scratched in the dirt, and sat down. The kitten's face took on a look of blissful angelic abstraction. The kitten wore the same distant ineffable look as does a young child occupied in the same business.

"Well, whaddaya know!" said Mort smiling down at the kitten.

"Say, he's trained! Isn't he the cutest thing!" said Myrtle, smiling down, too. The kitten was irresistible in its bland innocence.

And now, because the dispositions of their minds were turned towards each other, so were the dispositions of their bodies.

Myrtle went to bed. Mort cut himself a couple of sandwiches and then he went to bed too. The dispositions of their bodies were towards each other and the bed springs—which sagged, and the mattress—which was thin and resembled a hammock, impelled them one to another so that, when they slept, they slept as one, together, and Mort's arm clipped Myrtle as it did most nights when Myrtle was not out of temper. Thus they slept as one the whole night through, and their angels, tired, slept profoundly within them. Some angels undergo continual strain. It is too bad.

The kitten, who was not a tom, felt her way about in the dark which was, to her, transparent, and learned the room. Feral, wise, with her inscrutable little hunter's nose and whiskers she felt and explored and recorded each chair leg, each table leg, each corner. She prowled and prowled on silent paws, and sometimes she stopped to wash. When she was satisfied, she accepted and adopted the room. Then she slept fitfully. She slept anywhere, lightly yet deeply, waking and moving often. Chiefly she slept on Mort and Myrtle who lay deep in sleep, warm and approved by her. But sometimes she awoke, remembering something pleasant. Then she jumped lightly down and ran to her box. She scrambled up the side of her box and sat down, quivering, still, looking into the transparent dark with bliss.

VIII

Victoria May Tritt had been, for as long as she could
remember, the youngest Tritt girl, nothing more, con-
veniently anonymous. If one should attempt to record
the life of anyone as unnoticed and as unimportant and
as timorous as Victoria May, the words "anonymous"
and "anonymity" are bound to occur inconveniently
often. It was in Smith Falls that Vicky had been the
youngest Tritt girl. In Vancouver, now, to her land-
lady for purposes of rent and to her employer Mrs.
Ravoli for purposes of wages and instructions, she is Miss
Tritt; to other people she is nothing, anonymous. Life
on such terms as these is arid, one thinks, but it suits
Vicky.

After the eldest Tritt girl married and went to live in
Duluth, and after the middle Tritt girl—Bertha—married
and went to live in Vancouver, and after Mr. Tritt died
and was buried in Smith Falls, Mrs. Tritt and the youngest
Tritt girl came West to be near Bertha. And then Bertha's
husband went to Moosejaw, followed by Bertha and the
children, and Mrs. Tritt and the youngest Tritt girl
stayed on in Vancouver. They stayed there for lack of
any motive power to do anything else; and because the
climate of Vancouver was fairly easy to live in; and
nominally—but not actually—because Mrs. Tritt's
brother's daughter, Myrtle Hopwood, came to Vancouver
at about that time, and the theory was that it would be
nice for Myrtle. It turned out to be neither nice nor

nasty for Myrtle who had an anaemic disdainful prettiness and subjugated and then married a pleasant no-good
man called Mortimer Johnson, and thereafter did not
see very much of Mrs. Tritt and the youngest Tritt girl.
Mrs. Tritt and Victoria May really stayed in Vancouver
because, however insipid, or unimportant, or anonymous
you are, your humanity imposes upon you certain condi-
tions which insist that you spend twenty-four hours a
day somewhere, and that you spend, somehow, twenty-
four hours a day; and so, as they were already in Vancouver, they stayed there.

Victoria May had her small job in the little notions
shop on Commercial Drive. She neither enjoyed nor disliked her job, but because she was neat, silent and con-
genitally honest, she was useful to Mrs. Ravoli her employer.
Mrs. Ravoli ended by taking Victoria May for granted,
as just another notion in the store, and Victoria May
would have been distressed had things been otherwise.
If Mrs. Ravoli had died, Victoria May's plight would
indeed have been desperate, as her timidity would have
prevented her from finding a new place without making
efforts which would have been painful to her. Fortunately
Mrs. Ravoli did not die.

Mrs. Tritt, however, did die. The youngest Tritt girl
was helped through the bewilderment of the funeral by
her cousin Myrtle Johnson and by Myrtle's maternal
aunt Mrs. Emblem whose embracing kindness drove
Victoria May away in flight from Mrs. Emblem and thus
repelled Mrs. Emblem. When the funeral was over,
Victoria May retreated from her benefactors in case they
might want to show her some more alarming unnecessary
kindnesses, only emerging sometimes to see her cousin

65

Myrtle who after all was a cousin, and did not bother very much about her one way or another, which was as Victoria May liked it.

Mortimer Johnson, Myrtle's husband, alarmed Vicky in a pleasant masculine fashion. She thought him handsome, noble, and kind, like a movie star, which he was and he wasn't. He was a jokey kind of man. When Morty arrived home and found Vicky sitting nervously in a chair as if she were about to get up, or standing by a table as if she were just about to leave, he always greeted her warmly in his hoarsely pleasant voice and asked her what was her hurry. The enveloping masculinity of Mort excited Vicky in a pleasing unfamiliar way, but caused her to desire to leave as quickly as possible, which she did; and as she escaped down the stairs she always felt an uneasy glow from Mort's presence and from the kind words that he had tossed to her. She had never seen Myrtle demonstrate her thoroughly bad temper with Mort, and so it was she thought humbly that Myrtle and Mort were an ideal couple. These little incursions into life last her for some time. She wants no more. She could not have less. She receives no mail. She writes no letters. At Christmas time she selects two cards and sends them to her married sisters. She receives, latterly, two cards.

By the time, now, that Vicky Tritt is thirty-nine, she is little Miss Tritt who has drawn her cloak of anonymity so closely about her that the dreaming eye does not observe her. She is anonymous, as a fly is anonymous. To the alert and glancing eye she is like so many others that she is indistinguishable, but is recognisable when seen repeatedly in the same place, as, behind the counter where she sells the notions; or customarily leaning against the rail down by the docks watching—as you do—the seagulls; or sitting, withdrawn, in a pew at St. James Church; but you will not know her again when you see her in another place; the place has to be united with the person before Miss Tritt exists as Miss Tritt. This satisfies her. She has not thought all this out, but she has so ordered (if that definite word may be used) her timorous life that she is able to avoid all notice on the part of potential acquaintances, or, worse than that, of friends. She is sufficient unto herself, in a parched way, and yet she is sometimes lonely with a vast loneliness that for a dreadful moment appals. She goes her way by day and by night and all is well enough; and then suddenly she is aware of a loneliness which is insupportable. What makes her suddenly aware and alone? It is not the crowd in the street, for the anonymity of the continually passing crowd suits her; it is, perhaps, the greeting with delight of woman with woman, of man with woman—not of man with man, which stirs nothing; it is the ascending again of the stairs and going into her bedroom and feeling in the dark for the light which hangs small and naked in the middle of the room; it is the emptiness of time and occupation, the desert that lies between now and sleep; it is the inexplicable fusion of something within her and something without. Yet she does not desire company; like the fakir who has for so long held his arm unused that it is now atrophied, so Miss Tritt's power of friendship is vanished, gone. The fakir forgets his useless arm; Miss Tritt forgets, on the whole, that she is lonely.

But this special loneliness, which at unexpected times overwhelms her because it seems as though it will never end—and it will not—is as it were a revelation of something vast which lies concealed behind a curtain. It is insupportable, like the sorrow of humanity, and one dare not look, for, like the sorrow of humanity, it is there. This much she knows from the frightening glimpse which she for a moment sees. She averts her gaze and must at once busy herself with small tangible objects. She will walk. She will devise activities to keep her hands and body occupied. So she hastens to avoid the revelation of her insupportable loneliness by means of small physical activities which at last—through the similar years— become a routine. This routine at length rules her life, though not unpleasantly. From this routine, arid as it may seem to those whose lives, fortunately for them, can hardly contain their fullness, there grow, at least, small pleasures, and, at last, a continuing blessing.

Seven days are in a week and Vicky has to fill them. Take away the day's work and there remain only the evenings, occasional Saturday afternoons, and Sundays to be filled. Mercifully, she eats and sleeps. She prepares her evening meal in her room—no, not a meal, it is just something to eat. Then, if the season is summer and the day still light, she will walk down to the waterfront—it is not far—and watch the seagulls. They, too, are as anonymous as the crowd of people on Hastings Street and make no demands upon her. How pleasant it is to lean against the rail, down by the C.P.R. dock and watch the seagulls wheeling, alighting, taking off again, and filling the air with their cries. And as if that were not enough, behold the waters of Burrard Inlet, different in colour tonight, and the ships—little and big— coming and going, and across the water the houses and buildings near the water line of the North Shore, all lit up by the evening sun, and the twin spires of the old Indian church by the water, and behind all this the mountains; and behold the sky! Against the peaceful backdrop of mountain, sea, and blue clouded or gloomy sky, there is something moving, always moving. The eye follows the seagull, the floating log, oil on the water, the busy launch, the two squat ferries that ply between the two shores of Burrard Inlet, the big docking ship. One is entertained as in a dream.

Vicky is never alone, leaning on the rail above the water. There is a drifting population that leans against the rail, mostly men, but she does not observe them and they do not observe her. Some are people from the prairie who are actively interested in this scene that lies before them. They comment upon the smell of the salt and the diurnal miracle of the tides which never fails to surprise them. But most of the people come down here because, vaguely, they like it; or because they have nothing whatever to do; or because they are on their way to somewhere else and it won't hurt to stop for a minute.

One man comes fairly regularly. He is not vague. He comes because he has an affinity with the scene, and particularly with the seagulls. He thinks he knows and recognizes some of these calculating active birds which have little to recommend them except their strength, their fine coarse beauty, and their wheeling flight, and that is enough. It is improbable that he knows and recognizes them. He has enormous curiosity about the seagulls. He would like to be one, he would indeed. He checks by the Post Office clock—because he has no watch—the time of the first flight westwards in the evening. Then he watches the regular evening flight westwards of the seagulls. How they pour forth from all the waterfront through the draw of air above Stanley Park. The seagulls cease their wheeling and crying; their behaviour has changed; and now in their evening flight they go, steady, purposeful, silent, flying in ones, twos, threes, and companies, to where they will spend the night. And where is that? Is it at the mouth of the Fraser River? Is it on the western rim of Sea Island? Or Anvil Island? And why do they go, nightly, and return at daybreak? Could they not spend the night here? No, they leave together and fly steadily westwards together, not one turning back.

The man who watches the seagulls with perception is called old Wolfenden, but that is not his name and it never was. He is old and he is obviously poor. He has a scrubby beard. In the summer time he lives in a hollow tree in Stanley Park and will continue to do so until the police discover that he is doing this. Then they will turn him out, but not unkindly. He expects that day.

In the meantime he enjoys outwitting the police because they are young and handsome in their leggings, because they have elegant horses, and motorcycles, and fine prowler cars equipped with devices for finding out law-breakers (he approves of all this, the law should be kept), and he is only an old man with a false name and a dirty copy of *King Lear* in his pocket, and for half the year he outwits these handsome men. The rest of the year, or at least when the weather turns bad, old Wolfenden has a bed in a rooming house in the East End that used to be kept by a Japanese, but is now kept by a Swede; he gets bronchitis and is sent into the hospital. Although old Wolfenden is as alone as Vicky Tritt who often leans on the rail beside him without observing him, he is not lonely. He can, and does, look back along a sorry procession of years which he does not regret. If he regards these years philosophically, and he does, he sees them as a descent from the pride of five months spent on the staff of the *Manchester Guardian* thirty years ago to his present condition. His troubles have been the wrong women and the wrong drinks and himself; he knows this and he spends no time in regretting it. As recently as last year he was paid for a bit of work by a Vancouver newspaper, but as a journalist he has long been unreliable, washed up. "Old Wolfenden? Where is he now? Is he dead?" No, he is not dead. He is living in Stanley Park in a hollow tree, with a copy of Montaigne and some old journals that the man in the newstand near the C.P.R. station gives him sometimes, and some blankets and some scraps. He is leaning on a rail, looking at seagulls and at the other people who lean against the rail. He sees them with the old habit of a writer's eye. He speaks brusquely to an insipid-looking character, a woman, who often comes here. She is, indeed, as regular as he, and seems to watch the seagulls. Why does she come. He says (because he wishes to know) "Why do you come here?" Vicky Tritt is surprised and alarmed. It is one kind of fear if a woman speaks to her. It is another kind of fear if a man speaks to her. She will not commit herself, but says ridiculously enough, "Oh, I just happened . . ."

Liar, thinks old Wolfenden contemptuously, people are fools.

Vicky need not move away, as she soon does, because

71

old Wolfenden has dismissed her; she is too stupid; and now he is watching the *Princess* glide round the corner of Stanley Park, sailing sweetly into Burrard Inlet, entering the harbour.

On Friday evening Victoria May buys one magazine. It is a movie magazine and it does her for the weekend. She buys it according to the face on the cover. She enjoys the life of the movie stars, in which passion or some counterfeit of passion seems to take up a great deal of time. She is pleased when she reads of one of her favourites—whom she knows better than she knows anyone in Vancouver—settling down in her third, fourth or fifth marriage to the true innocent joys of cosy domesticity, found at last. What a hope. On Friday night she looks at the pictures, but she does not allow herself to read the magazine until Sunday morning, in bed. That is part of the routine, and provides a pleasant residual feeling of something enjoyable ahead. Saturday night is her big night, for then she has her dinner at a ca*fay*, and goes to a show. Mrs. Ravoli goes to the shows and so does Mrs. Pavey on the lower floor of the rooming house, and during the week Vicky hears by chance which are the best shows. She likes to go to a show in one of the big movie houses on Granville Street where all the neon lights are. The neon lights are swell and are a show in themselves; but if she has had to buy some aspirin and stockings that week she goes to one of the cheaper houses.

On Sunday morning she rests in bed and reads her movie magazine. On Sunday afternoon she walks down to Stanley Park. On Sunday evening she goes to St. James Church on East Cordova Street, and on Wednesday night she goes there, too. She goes on Wednesday

night partly because she happened to go once and liked
it, and because of the goodness which emanates from
Father Cooper and Father Whitehead and touches her
and leaves her serene, and partly because it is something
to do. On spare nights, she picks up a newspaper from
a discarded pile that lies in the basement of the rooming
house and takes it upstairs with her. This is not pilfering,
because the paper has been discarded. It does not matter
that the paper is old because she is not interested in the
news, but she does enjoy the advertisements. As she is
not going to buy anything mentioned in the advertisements, it does not matter that the paper is out of date.
She sits, often wearing her coat, and with her knees
wrapped in the comforter, and reads about the important
residence overlooking magnificent view, all floors in
quarter cut oak, den with fireplace, two master bedrooms
on the second floor, three bathrooms, owner leaving city.
Two master bedrooms; what can that signify! No wonder
this house is important. She reads Mr. Jollivet's jibing
advertisements and pities the object of them, who is
called Mr. Mackenzie. She projects herself—or some
braver person—into the skin of a girl—or widow—
seeking companionship or matrimony, and vicariously
meets, marries and discards three or four men in turn in
the course of the evening, but without desire or envy.
She takes—and leaves—several positions. She loses
herself in the funnies. She goes to bed. Her routine is
successful, and prevents her from too often being aware
of the desert of loneliness in which she dwells, under-
neath her small shelter of routine. And sometimes, but
rarely, she drops in to see Myrtle, almost hoping that
Myrtle will be out and that Mort will not be in.

One Tuesday evening—it was the evening that old Wolfenden had spoken to her and had driven her away from the railing above the C.P.R. dock—she turned eastwards, towards home, and then she went on as she decided to go and see Myrtle. The sudden dark was descending. The dark would give her an excuse for leaving almost before she arrived. She climbed the stairs and knocked timidly on Myrtle's door. There was no answer. She waited. She would knock once more, and if Myrtle did not come to the door, Vicky would turn and go down the stair, well satisfied. She heard movement and a voice within. She would like to have gone away, but having said to herself that she would knock again, she knocked. Myrtle came to the door. She was not looking pleased, which made Victoria May wish that she had never come. However, when, in the uncertain light of the doorway, Myrtle saw that it was only her timorous cousin standing there, she seemed to brighten and said with something like heartiness "Come in, Victoria May."

Victoria May crossed the threshold and, looking into the room, saw the luscious Mrs. Emblem rocking to and fro. (Oh dear me, I *do* wish I hadn't come!) Mrs. Emblem smiled at Victoria May in her usual pleasant easy manner but thought of the times after Mrs. Tritt's funeral when she had tried to draw Victoria May into her genial orbit, when she had tried to be nice to her, and warm and cheer up this poor spinstery wintery thing. But no, Vicky had shrunk from her, and Mrs. Emblem was sagacious enough to know that Vicky would shrink again from any advances. So that was why Mrs. Emblem said nothing. Vicky stood, stiff, slight and awkward; Mrs. Emblem rocked

74

and regarded her with her lazy golden smile but did not speak; Myrtle stood there waiting; the frying beef smelled good.

"Come in," repeated Myrtle.

"Oh no, I couldn't come *in*," said Victoria May; it seemed important, but impossible to explain, that she should not go in.

"Well, come in, *come* in," said Myrtle a little impatiently. "You'd better stay and have some supper. Aunty Emblem can't eat any, she's got gas."

How many thousand times the same fear had descended on Vicky that now had descended upon her—the old familiar fear that the girls were going to pick sides for games, and no one would pick her, and at the end she would be left over and one of the captains would say to the other captain "And *you*'ll have to take Victoria May Tritt," and she would have to be taken; the fear that came as she looked from girl to girl; the malaise that came at the end of school and at the end of Sunday school, when all the other girls ran off home together or walked together, heads bent together, in twos or threes, all talking at once and then saying to each other "You come over to my place," "No, you come over to my place"; the fear that made her cross the road to avoid speaking to someone she knew; the same fear that came when her mother used to dress her in her good dress and make her go out to a party to which all three Tritt girls had been invited ("Oh *Motherr*, do we *haff* to ask the youngest Tritt girl, she's a lemon!"); that familiar fear of people and their ways which possessed her.

"Oh no, I couldn't," said Victoria May quite terrified now by this prospect of spending an evening with Mrs.

Emblem and with Myrtle who tonight seemed a little
impatient, "I only called by to inquire." There, that was
sufficiently well said. Something came into her throat
as it often did when she was especially nervous, and she
said huskily, "Well, goodnight, all," and turned and shot
down the stairs, safe from them and alone in her timorous
world.

"It beats me," said Mrs. Emblem, "how a person can
grow up, and act like that. That cousin of yours always
reminds me of some poor dawg that nobody wants."

"Well, I guess nobody does," said Myrtle frankly and
went on preparing supper.

Down the darkening street went Victoria May feeling
greatly relieved, and yet she was familiarly unhappy, too,
because she was not as other people are, freely talking,
laughing, even quarrelling together. She could not do those
things any more than swim, and she could not swim. She
walked home quickly, her head poking forward as in haste,
along Powell Street, along Cordova Street, up Homer
Street, as though she had an appointment; but she had
no appointment. (How could she have an appointment?)
When she reached the house she went down to the basement. There was the customary pile of old newspapers
beside the furnace. She took one; she took two; she went
upstairs to her room. She felt around in the darkness and
found the electric light bulb hanging small and naked in
the middle of the room. She turned on the light, locked
the door, took an apple out of a bag, pulled a chair under
the light, sat down and began to read, peering a little.
She read "The Census taker asked a Scotchman named
Mackenzie how many children he had. 4 was the reply,
and that's all I'm going 2 have. Why? Well, I read in the

Almanac, said Mack, that every 5th child born is a China-man." She read to the end of Mr. Jollivet's jibing advertisement, and then on to Information Wanted. "Will Mildred Jabowski née Fink, or anyone knowing her whereabouts, contact Box 803, Confidential." Oh who is Mildred Jabowski and where can she be. Does some fortune await her. Or some threat. Oh Mildred Jabow-ski, is it safe for you to reply?

She bit into her apple, and read on. Here in her room she was at home and secure. She was safe among the people she knew so well, the true companions of her mind, who did not know her, who did not even turn their faces towards her, who demanded nothing of her—not re-cognition, not even a word.

IX

THE morning miracle had again deteriorated into a day which was merely a dull Wednesday which promised to be wet. Early risers, who had gone to bed in Indian summer, now informed themselves that it looked as though the weather had broken. The light which crept late into Myrtle's and Mortimer's bedroom had no quality of morning. Mortimer stirred, woke up, got up, rubbed himself, and sleepily regarded Myrtle. Mort was not wide awake and could not yet remember in what humour Myrtle had gone to sleep, so he put his guard up at once. If she lets one peep out of her, he promised, I certainly will slug her. He had, of course, no intention ever of slugging Myrtle. But whenever he made himself this promise—that he would certainly slug Myrtle if she let a peep out of her—he enjoyed it; it armed him for the day and strengthened his self-esteem which was so vulnerable. Mort then pulled up the blind quietly and let in what passed for daylight. When the weather is fine in Vancouver, fairly impartial residents will tell you that it is finer there than anywhere else in the world. That may or may not be true; but it is at least true that the surroundings of Vancouver, on those days, are more glorious and scintillant than those of any other northern city. Other people will observe that gloomy days are more frequent and more gloomy in Vancouver than anywhere else except in the United Kingdom. I do not know for

sure about that, but this was the kind of day that Mort
now let into the bedroom. Yesterday the mountains
sprawled nearby in frank glorious abandon; today they
were nowhere to be seen. Neither was the ocean.

As Mortimer turned from the window and saw again
the bed, Myrtle had a dream. Her dream seemed to
Myrtle to last for a reasonable time. One cannot prove
these things, but it is probable that the dream lasted
for what is called a split second, or less. This was her
dream.

Myrtle dreamed that she and Mort were as usual in the
kitchen and that a knock came at the door. Mort went
to the door and opened it, and Myrtle saw round his
shoulder the figure of Mrs. H. X. Lemoyne, in a neat
blue suit. Mrs. H. X. Lemoyne had on her face her
usual anxious expression and held out a book of receipts
and a very stubby pencil. She said to Mort, speaking in a
worried manner, "Collecting for the Province."

Mort acted very proud and said loudly to Mrs. H. X.
Lemoyne, "No peddlers or agents allowed in this building!" Mrs. H. X. Lemoyne looked anxiously at Mort,
and then she turned and ran down the stairs, changing, as
she did so, to a medium-sized long-haired whitish dog with
a tail that curled over its back. She stopped on the
landing, and turned to bark at Mort; and the dog's head
was that of Mrs. Emblem in her feather hat. Myrtle was
not surprised at this. Mrs. Emblem barked at Mort. He
did not weaken, but said again, firmly, "No peddlers or
agents allowed in this building," and Myrtle was pleased
with Mort. She was so pleased that a smile broke through
her dream and on to her face, so that Mort saw Myrtle
smiling in her sleep. Her lips parted and she said with

deep affection "Good old Morty, good old Morty," and that was the end of her dream.

Mort was very much surprised to hear Myrtle say this; so much so that he murmured as he looked at his sleeping wife "Well, for gossakes!" He then went barefoot into the kitchen to put on the kettle. The kitten, who had been trying to get a bit of sleep on the potatoes under the sink, ran out to meet him.

Owing to Myrtle's chance (or ordained) dream, the day, although dull, began very well for Mortimer and Myrtle. She awoke pleased, for some reason which she had now forgotten, and Mortimer was in great good humour owing to what Myrtle had said in her sleep, and made tea in the large pot, and set two cups, and pulled on his trousers over his underwear, and sat down on the edge of the bed and drank tea with Myrtle. He began to tell her all about the H. Y. Dunkerleys and why he was not going back there, and Myrtle encouraged him in not going back to subject himself to working for little Horse Dunkerley and his snooty wife who was a society woman and therefore was no good.

Mort was always inclined to believe Myrtle when she told him—as she had told him at intervals, for years—that society people could not fool her. Very simply, he had long since established a situation in which society people —and butchers and vegetable Chinamen, but particularly society people—were always trying to fool Myrtle; but they could not succeed. Myrtle's fine eyelids and her inverted smile stripped them of all their silly pretences at once, and so these society people were foiled in their plans to fool Myrtle.

The kitten who was not a society person had fooled

Myrtle into thinking that she—the kitten—was a tom, and she gave Myrtle and Mort a great deal of pleasure that morning by her ridiculous and pretty antics. Then Myrtle said she must get up or she would be late again at Mrs. H. X. Lemoyne's, and Mort said that he thought he would go and see old Cameron out at Burnaby because sometimes there was a job going at the nurseries. But as old Cameron might have gone into New Westminster, Mort might have to stick around a bit, so Myrtle was not to wait supper or anything for him, although he would probably be back. When Myrtle had gone, Mort slipped downstairs and got a yesterday's newspaper from the ground floor tenant who was a sort of a friend of theirs, and took it upstairs and had a very pleasant morning with the kitten and the newspaper, and then he went out; and that was the last time he ever went out of the house.

X

ALTHOUGH the day was dull and promised rain which came later, Myrtle's inner climate was equable as she went on her way to Mrs. H. X. Lemoyne's. This inner climate—which her angel enjoyed, although without confidence—had, of course, been created and was conditioned by as flimsy a thing as Myrtle's dream wherein Mort had rebuffed Mrs. Lemoyne and had shown himself indifferent and impervious to Mrs. Emblem and had thereby caused his wife immediate and continuing satisfaction. Although the dream had completely vanished from Myrtle, she still had this pleasant feeling—from somewhere—of solidarity with Mort against people in general and—vaguely—a rare feeling of triumph over Aunty Emblem, which was nice.

Mrs. Lemoyne was delighted to see Myrtle arrive in a mood so pleasant and uncontemptuous, and therefore she weakened at once—as she was bound to do, being that kind of woman—and showed Myrtle her new overnight handbag. The fact was that it was Mrs. Lemoyne's birthday, and she had just been regaled by one of those unique and modest self-contained domestic scenes peculiar to affectionate families, in which there is a culmination of happy intrigue on the part of all but one of the family on behalf of that one member of the family. For several days past, Mr. Lemoyne and the three children had plotted, and teased, and then had at last disappeared

on a secret expedition which Mrs. Lemoyne had affected
not to notice, and then they had returned together with
a small blue overnight handbag which with ostentatious
secrecy they had connived into a cupboard which Mrs.
Lemoyne was begged and ordered not to look into.
When on this birthday morning Mrs. Lemoyne undid the
handbag, watched by her children, she enjoyed achieving
the right measure of surprise, and declared that the one
thing in the world she had always craved was a blue
overnight handbag. Everyone was very happy, although,
when the parcels were all unwrapped, the children
experienced a faint feeling of anti-climax, not being yet
old enough to know that pleasures fade. Mrs. Lemoyne
had acted her parts well, and with the private joy of a
wife and mother who sees her husband and their children
united in some small happy successful plot for love of her.
She was, you may see, a simple woman, affectionate,
anxious, not always very wise, often very silly, loved and
bullied by her family, and easily put into a dither by
people like Myrtle. So after this happy breakfast time
when she had received her small queer gifts and the nice
handbag, as soon as her family went off to business and
to school, she put the handbag, wrappings and all, back
into the cupboard because she could not bear the disparagement of Mrs. Johnson's glance to fall upon it; she
loved her handbag so much.

But when Mrs. Johnson arrived, pleasant and agreeably
affected by the dream in which Mrs. Lemoyne herself
had—unknown to either of them—played a part, Mrs.
Lemoyne could not resist taking out the blue handbag
and with shining face showing Myrtle what a beautiful
present her husband and children had given her for her

birthday. Myrtle was very nice about the handbag and neither disparaged nor despised it, merely saying that her aunt Mrs. Emblem had one like that—only her aunt's handbag was bigger and had fittings in it. This did not really take from Mrs. Lemoyne's pleasure in her present, although she thought What a fool I am, why can't I keep things like this to myself. The day passed very well.

Since Myrtle knew that her husband had gone to Burnaby about a job, and that you never could tell where old Cameron might be, she did not go straight home, but went down to Irma Flask's place and thought she might stay there and have supper with Irma because Mort might not even be home to supper, and anyway he could cut himself a sandwich. Myrtle knocked at Irma Flask's door and said Yoo-hoo, Irma, but since Irma had gone to North Vancouver she was not at home. Old Mrs. Uren, Irma's mother, invited Myrtle to come in and sit, but, as Myrtle did not enjoy sitting with old Mrs. Uren, she said that she had to hurry home anyway, and then she walked home. Rain was falling fitfully. She had forgotten the kitten who greeted her with innocent delight and said she was hungry. The kitten occupied Myrtle for some time. She then had some tea and had a good lay-down and went off to sleep. Time thus passed. When she woke up, day was fading. Myrtle began to get fidgety and did a bit of tidying up. She had begun to have that waiting feeling, that waiting feeling, and to become, quite unreasonably, a little irritable; and that was the way Myrtle spent the afternoon. The evening approached.

XI

IF THERE was one person more than another that Mort liked seeing, it was Eddie Hansen. They had worked together at a logging camp up Jervis Inlet when jobs were scarce in Vancouver and Mort could get no work in town; and they had got drunk together more than once when Eddie had come down to Vancouver, and if there was one person more than another that Myrtle couldn't stand the sight of, it was Eddie Hansen.

Eddie Hansen was tall and fair and pleasant-looking and slow moving, with a quizzical look caused by a dropped eyelid, and as he moved among other men he was almost head and shoulders above them. He was a powerfully built logger, a high rigger, and was well known and well liked up and down the coast, and he got good money. When he was on his job which was now at a big logging camp at Knight Inlet, he never drank, but when he came to town as he did two or three times a year, then he drank.

Eddie was technically and legally a widower. Actually he never thought of himself as a widower at all. He was no widower. The word widower carries a dominant overtone of loss. Eddie had nothing to do with loss. He had forgotten what his wife Signe had looked like and he did not care; he never liked Signe anyway and he had forgotten her. He did not care for women except sometimes. Then he forgot them again. But he had a lot of friends up and down the coast and in Vancouver. He liked Mortimer Johnson, and sometimes he dropped Mort a letter which read like a telegram without the word Stop in it.

"DEAR MORT:

Well how are you Mort may bee Ile be down by fridy boat if I doent get tite on the boat Ile go to Olys place and if I do get tite I gess Ile go to the same old place ware I all ways went you no Mort well so long and Ile be seeing you dont you forget it Mort and oblidge

EDDIE H."

Eddie had sent Mort a note of that kind when he came down at the New Year's which Myrtle remembered with so much resentment and which she unwisely cast up at Mort whenever she sniffed one sniff on him. But this time, when Eddie was to land in Vancouver on the very Tuesday that Mort went to work at little Horse Dunkerley's, Eddie sent Mort no letter because he remembered how that wife of Mort's gave him hell last New Year's, and if he saw Mort, well and good; and if he didn't, it was too bad.

This time Eddie began to drink on the boat coming down from Knight Inlet. He had a certain brash charm and he became very funny. But many people who had laughed with him and encouraged him at the beginning of the trip wished later on that they had never given Eddie any encouragement at all, because by the time they were halfway down the coast Eddie had become far too friendly and had adopted them completely, still being funny, but tiresome now; his charm had palled and was not charm any more; and towards the end of the journey, by evening, as the boat steamed below the golden lights of the beautiful Lions' Gate Bridge and entered the harbour of Vancouver, Eddie was beginning to be hostile, and resented the less warm attitude of all his dear friends on the boat. When the boat at last docked it was all right, because people got away from Eddie, and, safe in the immunity of shore and darkness, they walked quickly into the night as if Eddie no longer existed. The brush-off.

It took Eddie some time and argument to find his suit-case. His suitcase contained his store clothes to wear in Vancouver if he ever got sobered up enough to put them on. He had a suit of very bright blue which he had chosen from amongst some other more conservative suits of clothes at the Army and Navy Stores, and an overcoat with a velvet collar which he had bought at a second-hand store on Cordova Street. When Eddie was sober and wore his overcoat with a velvet collar he did not look like a high rigger, bold and strong, magnificent among men, a rollicking Paul Bunyan of the Canadian woods, which he was; but like an imitation deacon, which he was not.

Eddie found his own suitcase and picked it up and stumbled along in the lighted dark in the rear of the smartly stepping crowd off the boat who so soon vanished out of his sight intent on their own business, weighed down, too, with hand baggage or packs. He knew that he was rather but not quite tight, and this decided him not to go to Mount Pleasant and stay with his friends Mr. and Mrs. Ole Almquist to whom he was always welcome when sober, but to go along Powell Street to the Regal Rooms where he often stayed and where he knew a guy who knew a guy who could get him some bottles of good rye any time he wanted.

Eddie reached the Regal Rooms all right, and met there a couple of friends, and after they had slapped each other largely upon the shoulders they went on to make a night of it, and so it was that in the early morning they all helped each other to bed, aided by the proprietor, and they all slept in their clothes.

Eddie's friends Mr. and Mrs. Almquist, who had been notified by Eddie of his probable arrival, looked at each other at about eleven o'clock, and Mrs. Almquist said to her husband, "Well, Ole, I guess Eddie's done it again," and they waited no longer, but turned out the lights and went to bed. Mrs. Almquist lay awake for a while, regretting that such a nice fellow as Eddie should be so dumb, and then she went to sleep.

It was in the early afternoon of Wednesday that Eddie woke up and thought he'd better get up and put on his good blue suit and go out somewhere. He didn't feel so good and thought that perhaps Herman might not be feeling so good either, and first of all he'd better go and find Hermy and what about a little drink. So he took a bottle and went to find Hermy's room which was on another floor, and when he got there he found that Hermy had got up and gone out. He felt affronted and deceived by this action of Hermy's and so he had a little drink. He then remembered his blue suit and started back to his room. But because of his condition, he did not go back to his own room, all the rooms being very much alike, but went into another room, had another drink, lay down on the bed and went to sleep again.

When he woke up late in the afternoon he pulled

himself together once more and thought again of his bright blue suit. He got up and went again to his suitcase, but the suitcase was not there. Who had taken his suitcase? Eddie became very angry. It was a shame that a guy could not leave his room for two minutes without having his suitcase stolen off of him. As he stood looking down at where his suitcase was not, the thought came spinning into his head, righted itself, and straightened itself up and stated that perhaps he had never brought his suitcase to the Regal Rooms at all, but had left it on the dock. So he started down the stairs which heaved up and down at him and at last he reached the door. All this time he was talking to himself or somebody.

When poor Eddie (who three days ago was so fine and strong and knowledgeable and sober, shinning skilfully up the great firs and monumental cedars on the sloping shores of Knight Inlet) began to progress along Powell Street towards the docks, he found the going hard. He addressed the passers-by, but they, silent as fishes, swam noiselessly past and vanished. He spoke to them loudly, greeting them, telling them what he thought of them for passing him silently like fishes, and telling them that he had lost his suitcase. They did not care and continued to swim past him past him swimming past him. He beckoned and waved to them but they, suddenly multiplying to three or four apiece and then vanishing, neither saw nor heard him. They saw and heard him all right, but found it more convenient to appear blind and deaf to Eddie Hansen. As Eddie weaved along he discovered that one side of the pavement of Powell Street was no good. That was, really, the kerb side. The other side was good and there was something hard which responded to you by holding you up. That was a house or a shop. So tall Eddie travelled along, leaning against this something solid from time to time, and it was as he took his ease against The Fishermen's Book Shop and harangued the shadows that slid by him without caring that he had lost his suitcase, that he saw as in a wavering cloud the good face of his friend Mort Johnson.

Eddie lunged out awkwardly and seized Mort strongly by some part of him and a great gladness filled him, and before he told Mort about going down to the dock to find his suitcase, he pumped Mort's arm up and down and told him again and again how fine it was to see him; and Morty was just as glad to see old Eddie, his big friend the high rigger, Paul Bunyan of Jervis Inlet, good old Eddie, drunk or sober.

XII

Just before the moment when Eddie Hansen, looking with glazed eyes at the passers-by, suddenly saw looming up the pleasant sight of the face of his friend Mort Johnson, Vicky Tritt, on the other side of Powell Street, minced along on her way to her Wednesday evening service at St. James Church, wishing that she had not put on her good hat with a veil, as the rain had now begun to drizzle. The hat with a veil did not suit her as well as her everyday hat—no hat could be said to suit her—but the good hat was part of her going to church. Because Mrs. Ravoli had borrowed her umbrella, she had no umbrella with her. As Eddie leaned against the Fishermen's Book Shop, and Victoria May, mincing along on the opposite side of Powell Street, saw across the road a huge drunken logger leaning against the Book Shop and addressing the passers-by, they both converged upon a moment in the life of Morty Johnson whom Vicky then saw swaggering genially down Powell Street in the direction of this drunken man whom Morty had not yet seen. Victoria May slowed up and looked across at Morty walking with his easy swagger and roll, seeming very much pleased with things, and she thought Oh, Morty does look nice! and Morty was indeed a contrast, one might think, to the fair drunken giant who leaned against the shop making large gestures to no one in particular. Vicky slowed up, watching her cousin by marriage Mort

Johnson walking cheerfully along, looking full of contented thoughts, which he was. So Vicky saw Mort sober
approaching Eddie drunk and did not suspect a connec-
tion between the two. Then she saw Mort sober stop
dead in his tracks and hail the drunken giant, and the
drunken giant almost fell upon Mort, and the two of them
swayed about in a kind of ecstasy of greeting that looked
Vicky thought, for all the world as though they were
wrastling. She wondered if this friend of Mort's could be
that Eddie Hansen of whom she had heard Myrtle speak
so unfavourably. She then saw a kind of argument
develop in which both men talked at the same time and
each seemed to pull the other in opposite directions.
Mort seemed to try to urge Eddie back along Powell
Street in the direction—but Vicky could not know this—
of the Regal Rooms. But Eddie was stronger and, being
drunk, was impervious to argument, and so he prevailed
over Mort who seemed to give up arguing, and Vicky
saw the two men, Mort sober supporting Eddie drunk,
continue an uncertain course down Powell Street.
Naturally she did not know that they were going down
to the dock in order to satisfy Eddie about his suitcase, but
that was where they were going. Then she could no
longer distinguish, across the misty drizzly street, the
figures of Mort and his friend among the other people,
so she went on her way, hurrying a little, to St. James
Church.

St. James Church is a noble grey building, non-Gothic,
perhaps neo-Byzantine, which stands staunchly on the
corner of East Cordova Street and of Gore Avenue which
runs down to the near waterfront. Although not lofty, the
church rises above the surrounding shabby wooden

buildings of the East End, and, higher still, holds up against the sky an aery cross. The parish, whose name the church bears, once extended all the way up the coast and back into the hinterland. Now the church serves, in the East End, many people from all parts of the city of Vancouver. The church is flanked by two ancillary buildings of faintly Tudor dignity, which are not incongruous, but are complementary to the sturdy architecture of the church itself. Kitty-corner from the church is the Police Station through which are sieved many of the major and minor crimes of the city, and where dramas —ultimate, penultimate and ante-penultimate—fuse, coalesce, absorb, resolve or do not resolve, and disappear, giving place to others. The Police Station exhales a breath peculiar to itself. The church building dominates the Police Station building, and the aery cross rises above all; but the cross is not seen as often as you would think by people who continually pass by, and who look about or within themselves thinking of other matters. Church and Police Station face each other obliquely, and serve the people of the city.

Vicky hurried up the steps of the church, and, avoiding the welcome of a sidesman but accepting the hymn book and prayer book which he held out to her, she took her seat in the very back pew against the wall. She dropped upon her knees. This performance was physical, not mental although perhaps spiritual (who could divine?), and, having conformed, she looked before her with satisfaction at the focus of the grey church, at the altar.

The church, although barren of ornament, is not barren of beauty. It is cool, with a lovely austerity. There are six tall shining candlesticks at the altar. The candles are lighted. Seven small shining lamps hang suspended, their length of suspension forming pleasing curves which the eye follows gratefully and again follows. The shining lamps and their small ruby-shaded flames canalize the thought, the prayer, the dream. Then there is the large suspended crucifix, again aery; two plain pulpits; nothing more. The music accords with this, in pure and sweet enunciation. The services are ceremonial and also informal; man speaks to man; man listens; God speaks to man through man in easy words that Vicky can understand, although she does not always listen; but she dreams, her eyes following the line of the suspended ruby flames of the seven shining lamps—up, down, up, down, up, down, up. Vicky does not know what all the short ceremonial of the service signifies, but it satisfies her, and she is aware, quite humbly, that it signifies something, or Father Whitehead would not perform it.

On the evening when Vicky took her place, anonymous, almost invisible, in the very back pew against the wall, Father Cooper came down from the pulpit and stood amongst the people and talked to them. "Blessed," he said, "are the meek," and then he went on to talk about the real meaning of rare meekness, and why his Lord had said "Blessed are the meek." Vicky liked to see Father Cooper standing kindly there among all sorts of people, talking to them; but she had such a poor opinion of meekness (so near it was to herself) that she did not listen to Father Cooper's words, and her thoughts strayed to Mort Johnson who had gone off with Eddie Hansen (she supposed). She was a little afraid that Mort might get into some sort of trouble with Eddie who was acting pretty wild and was a big powerful man and drunk, and then oh poor

Myrtle, wouldn't she be upset at Morty; because Myrtle was so proud.

Benediction and the last hymn ended the short service. Vicky knew the hymn and joined in the singing with her voice of a small twittering bird, with the thin twittering voice of a chickadee, perhaps, that whispers and whispers in the trees. Her thoughts left Myrtle and Mort and Eddie Hansen and came back to Father Cooper who stood now at the door of the church and shook hands with his people. Vicky liked Father Cooper to shake hands with her; nothing was demanded of her in return for this handshake. Her seclusion was warmed by it and not violated. She went out into the dark lighted street where wet pavements shone. The rain had for a moment ceased. I will get back home before the rain begins again, she thought, thinking of her veil, and she hurried along, her head poking forward, as if she had an immediate appointment.

A block or two along Cordova Street she saw, under the street lamp, a group of men standing, talking. Others joined this group. Men questioned each other. What is it? Vicky prepares to go around and so avoid the group. All the people are serious. What has happened? Something has happened. As Vicky skirts the group of people talking under the street lamp she hears a man say "Not Mort Johnson!"

Another man turns to him and says "Yes, the name was Mort Johnson."

Vicky stands still and listens to the men talking and questioning together. She then learns that Mort Johnson is dead.

95

XIII

IN WHAT good humour Morty made his way out to Burnaby to the nurseries to see if old Cameron had a job for him. This was the kind of job that he liked, something reg'lar but not too reg'lar. The one catch, he knew as he bounced along in the interurban railway, was that some years ago he had worked at these nurseries and had been fired by old Cameron for being lazy, negligent and incompetent; not grave faults perhaps, but faults which enrage a competent and industrious employer. Still and all, Morty questioned whether old Cameron would really remember him, as old Cameron had hardly seen Morty and had dealt with him through intermediaries. So all of this did not trouble Morty very much as he bounced along through the outskirts of the sprawling city of Vancouver and looked out of the car windows at the soft grey day, day soft and damp and enervating, air opaque and lethargic, holding promise of rain. The handsome mountains which line the northern sky of Vancouver receive the impact of bodies of air travelling across from the Pacific Ocean, down from the Queen Charlotte Islands, down from the Aleutians, and these bodies of air, striking the handsome mountains, grow heavy, and sullen with increase; they break, and the rain falls and falls, and newcomers from the bright prairies wonder if they won't go back home if there's one more day of this rain, but oldtimers of Vancouver, though a little weary of the rain, know always that when a glorious day breaks on the green ground and on the mountains, this rain will be forgotten in the brilliant air. Mort was nearly an oldtimer, and the rain coming soon didn't bother him, and the thought of old Cameron didn't bother him much, but the need of a job and some money in his pocket bothered him a little. He rather hoped to see out there a friend of Mrs. Emblem's, by name Mr. Mottle, before he ever came up against old Cameron, because Mr. Mottle knew Mort under the most favourable of circumstances and would certainly put in a word for him with old Cameron. Mr. Mottle was very respectable and was a sort of caretaker out at the nurseries.

Mort's acquaintance with Mr. and Mrs. Mottle was social and slight. They were in Mrs. Emblem's set and were often quoted by her, and before Mr. Mottle took the caretaking job away out at the nurseries, Mr. and Mrs. Mottle had been members of Mrs. Emblem's Bridge Club, although they only played whist, which they preferred— whist being optional at the Bridge Club. They were conservative people, not quite as dashing as Mr. Thorsteinsen and Maybelle Slazenger with whom they had a chatting acquaintance. The Bridge Club was a very nice place for Mr. Mottle in particular because he was a male gossip, passionately inquisitive, and the Bridge Club presented opportunities for making one's way from person to person, collecting irrelevant data about these persons and about the other members which was at once transmuted into significance by Mr. Mottle and by Mrs. Mottle too, and was passed along, instantly becoming news. Mr. Mottle was also devoted to disease and the discussion of disease, not so much in the abstract— although he enjoyed that too—but with reference to

A's kidneys, B's liver, and C's guitar of the stummick; thus he romped merrily amongst his friends' organs, publicizing them on the way; Mort did not know all this, as he was not what you would call well acquainted with Mr. and Mrs. Mottle, but he had met them once or twice when he was with Myrtle at Mrs. Emblem's place, and had also hung over the fence at the bowling green and had encountered Mr. Mottle doing the same thing on more than one summer evening. So that although he did not know Mr. Mottle at all, he felt that he knew him very well and auspiciously, and that Mr. Mottle would be bound to recommend Mrs. Emblem's nephew-by-marriage to old Cameron as a desirable gardener and as a man of excellent character. The job was as good as his. What job? Any job.

Mort got off the interurban car and walked the five or six blocks down the rough irregular road bordered by half-cleared and uncleared land which led to the nurseries. He looked about him appreciatively. There to the north where opaque clouds hung were, of course, the invisible mountains. Burnaby Lake lay not far away. In this depression of a country of hills and wooded ridges which lay near yet remote (it seemed) from Vancouver, the sun, when it shone, poured down its warmth; the land was well watered; the nurseries, with the good brown soil and the long rows of now decimated green, with the potting sheds, the long greenhouses, a few shacks, stretched in earthy richness. The tempo of slowness and peace was another exhalation of the land, like the earth and humus smell, and the faint and pleasant rotting odour of manures. Unlike the Chinese vegetable gardens which lay far away beyond South Vancouver on the River Road and on the delta islands of the Fraser River where the cultivated ground gave evidence of fierce unresting meticulous physical exertion, the nurseries in Burnaby displayed an easeful life in death of the soil. The very sight of the Chinese vegetable gardens—where a few active small men worked incessantly early and late, planting things, transplanting, cultivating, with an arithmetical calm ferocity and industry—would have repelled Morty in search of a job. He would regard slightingly, as one superior, the small expert Chinamen, squatting, under their wide hats, through the hot summer day, living their hidden Oriental lives of great frugality in adjacent shacks. Here after long days of planting their vegetables with elegant horticultural geometry—long rows radiating, spinning, crossing and recrossing to the river's edge, green against brown—they gather in earthy monastic conviviality and eat their rice and fish and pork when the day's work is done. Morty would have seen in the rich Chinese truck gardens little beauty, only a hard repellent toil, good enough for Chinks but not for him; but here, as he strolled in at the gate of old Cameron's nurseries, was the kind of work whose doing or evasion he understood.

I will mooch about a bit, he thought, not wanting to hurry things; so he mooched. Anyone interested in plant nurseries would at once know that work was being done, the slow work that tends flowers, shrubs, and young trees. Anyone unfamiliar with plant nurseries would think the place deserted and the work at a standstill. So Morty mooched, not much wanting to see old Cameron in person—yet—but thinking it better to find Mr. Mottle first, and so approach old Cameron by the Mottle avenue. No Mottle in the greenhouses or in the gardens, so Morty

99

opened the door of a shed that might be—and was—an office, and looked in. He was a little apprehensive of seeing old Cameron but, fortunately, there was only Mr. Mottle doing nothing in particular.

"Yes?" asked Mr. Mottle.

Morty took off his hat. "You wouldn't remember me perhaps, Mr. Mottle," he said frankly and engagingly, "but my name's Johnson, Mortimer Johnson, and Mrs. Emblem is my wife's aunt. I seen you at Mrs. Emblem's place and down at the bowling green if you remember."

Mr. Mottle at once held out his hand. He wore a hat and kept it on. He was very much pleased to see Mort and asked him how Mrs. Emblem was and said that he and Mrs. Mottle was only talking about her the other day, and how in winter evenings they'd missed the Bridge Club living out here, and how about going outside. So they went outside, and there was a box and there was an upturned barrel, and Mr. Mottle sat down on the box and Mort sat down on the barrel and Mr. Mottle took out his pipe with a spurious air of leisure that suited Mort well, and, encouraged by this, Mort rolled one, and they settled down to a good talk—Mr. Mottle the beneficent elder man of affairs and Mort not young, but younger, and of an engaging candour and attention. Mort left the conversation to Mr. Mottle, thinking that the job part could come later. Into the sounds of Mr. Mottle's speech crept, sometimes, but not regularly, echoes of his English boyhood. He was a friendly man, and, as I say, a male gossip, and always ready for a talk at his ease like this. It appeared that Mr. Cameron was away but might be back by six, or he would phone, and he—Mr. Mottle—had to stick around.

"And how's Mrs. Emblem?" enquired Mr. Mottle. "She's a fine woman, a very very lovely woman. She going to marry old Thorsteinsen? My wife—Mrs. Mottle— she says he's well fixed. She says he's got a homestead in Saskatchewan and he don't *have* to sell Fuller brushes. But you show me a man who's well fixed and chooses to sell Fuller brushes at *his* age! You tell your Aunty all that glitters isn't gold and that goes for old Thorsteinsen's front teeth. I seen him have a little money on the game under the table at the Bridge Club, but that doesn't mean a man's got money in the bank because he's got it under the table. She'd best be sure how he's fixed first. I said to Mrs. Mottle you tell Mrs. Emblem to hold off of Thorsteinsen where Matrimony's concerned until she finds out. He's okay for an evening, but for marriage he's too flash. You tell her. How's your wife?"

Mort was just about to say that Myrtle was fine but as that seemed a conversational dead-end he said, "I'm kinda worried about her, she's not so good."

Nothing could suit Mr. Mottle better than for Myrtle to be not so good. He lowered his voice, leaned towards Mort, peered into his eyes and said with intensity—this being exactly the kind of conversation that he liked—"What's her trouble?"

"The doctors don't seem to know," replied Mort, hedging.

Mort's angel, on hearing Mort say this, became extremely irritated. It buffeted Mort, or his id (or psyche), and said sincerely For God's sake why do you have to make up things like that? Isn't the truth good enough for you? And the id (or psyche) answered Sh, this is the way I like it, and so Mort continued "No, not a one of the doctors seem to know."

"Doctors . . .!" exclaimed Mr. Mottle. "You're telling *me*! Doctors . . .!" He lowered his voice further and looked around as though doctors might be creeping up through the shrubs, and said "There was a prominent doctor come here for seedlings last spring—wallflowers it was—and that doctor he was the stoopidest man I ever see and if I told you his name you'd be surprised. No int'rest in 'elth! No int'rest in medicine! Only wanted 'is wallflowers and get away. That's all '*e* cared about. I could of told 'im more in fifteen minutes than ever '*e* learned in college. Exhibited no int'rest. Well, I said to Mrs. Mottle, there's doctors for you!" Mr. Mottle, foiled and still smarting, had a better audience in Mort who had plenty of time and no convictions about medicine, and was ready to agree with anything that Mr. Mottle might say, especially as he wished to ingratiate and endear himself and so to establish himself by good report from Mr. Mottle with old Cameron, who was inclined to be tough with you. So Mort continued to sit on an upturned barrel and look respectfully at Mr. Mottle and encourage him with his kind brown eyes, and nod, and say emphatically "Sure," and "I'll say," and Mr. Mottle read admiration in the brown eyes, and went on expounding and Mort went on thinking Where's old Cameron.

"I'll tell you," said Mr. Mottle, "what's wrong with your wife. I'll tell you just what's wrong with Mrs. Johnson. It's the colin." He had neither seen Myrtle nor heard of the nature of her complaint which was non-existent, but that was of no consequence to him. "Tell her from me. You tell Mrs. Johnson to flush the colin and she won't need to have no truck with doctors."

"Thank you, I'll tell her, Mr. Mottle," said Mort respectfully, wondering Who the devil's Colin?

"You see that man," continued Mr. Mottle confidentially, "that feller going along there with a sack of fertilizer? Pore feller, 'e can't 'ardly carry it. You wouldn't think 'e'd been a passionate man in 'is day would you, but 'e did used to. What d'you s'pose is wrong with *'im?*"

Mort looked at an undersized man who bent beneath a small sack which he carried on his shoulders as he trudged beside a long furrow of good brown soil.

"I wouldn't know," he said. The man might be elderly, or lazy, or have corns, or rheumatism.

"Well, what would you *think?*" insisted Mr. Mottle. Mort thought.

"Rheumatism," he suggested.

Mr. Mottle smiled omnisciently, pulling down his lips, and shook his head from side to side.

"Wrong," he said. "'E's got a tapeworm."

"You don't say," said Mort, and he looked with more interest after the unwilling host of the tapeworm, who continued plodding down the gardens.

"Did the doctor say?" enquired Mort.

"'*Say*'! No doctor didn't need to 'say.' I took one look at 'im, and I said Tapeworm. Might have two for all you know," said Mr. Mottle knowledgeably and proceeded to his climax which usually interested people. "I s'pose you didn't know I'd had the tapeworm? Well, I did. You can't tell *me*. Went to prett' near every doctor in Canada and U.S.A. Couldn't do nothing for me till I went to a

feller here and he delivered me of two tapeworms head
and all. A yard long apiece them two reptiles was if they
was an inch. I regret I never kep' them two reptiles but
they sure were a spectacle for any museum. And now
look at me!" Mort looked at him. "If I'd known enough
then to flush the colin I'd never have had 'em." Just as
well as it was though, for Mr. Mottle had the memory,
and retrospectively the reptiles gave him a great deal of
pleasure, and were well known to all his acquaintances.
Mort was pleased, too, but was beginning to get restive.
He began to talk of the job.

"You wouldn't want to *live* here, or would you?" asked
Mr. Mottle. "There's two old shacks and me and Mrs.
Mottle took one and transformed it into an 'ome. When
Mr. Cameron's brother-in-law seen it 'e said 'Well, Mr.
Mottle, that is indeed a transformation.' If old Cameron,"
he became familiar, "took a fancy to you and if I recommend you he's very liable to take my say-so and if there's
a job coming up which there is for a man who's a good
potting shed man and would see to some of the firing
and you and your wife wanted to live here and not come
traipsing out at all times, old Cameron'd let a man have
that other shack and do it up for himself rent free. Like
to come along, and I'll show you." Mr. Mottle got
slowly up from his box and Mort arose from his barrel
and the two of them proceeded down a path, Mr.
Mottle going at his rather aged pace and Mort walking
behind.

There stood on the confines of the nursery garden three
shacks near together, relics of old schemes and old
abandonments. One had caved in, one looked as though
it might cave in, and one was a natty painted dwelling of

white and blue. Mr. Mottle and Morty stopped and regarded these.

"You wouldn't believe," (and you wouldn't) said Mr. Mottle indicating the shacks with his pipe, "that me and Mrs. Mottle transformed this 'ome you see before you from a shack prett' near as bad as that one there," and he pointed at the middle shack whose door swung half open, repulsive home of bats and spiders. "Old Cameron said Go ahead, and will you believe me it only cost us the paint and some finishing nails and I cut the cedar shingle in the bush with a shake knife and picked up a bit of stove piping laying around the furnace house and a bit of two-by-four laying around the carpenter shop and we brung our things out and here we are snug as bugs and rent free. That's the way, young feller. And there's no reason but what that other shack—not the one that's fell in—wouldn't do the same, if you're handy. Cost you nothing or near to nothing. You and the wife handy?"

Mort assured Mr. Mottle that he and Myrtle were handy and you couldn't beat Myrt for fixing things up, there wasn't anything she couldn't do, and so Mr. Mottle and Mort stood and regarded the smart little home, product of the undoubted handiness of Mr. and Mrs. Mottle, and also the residence nearby of bats and owls, and their two minds were occupied by two different illusory visions. Mr. Mottle had a vision of Mort and Myrtle, handy and neat as the Mottles, quickly transforming by their industry the melancholy and dilapidated shack into a trim and simple two-room residence like their own, and then how nice to superintend and advise and boss and own this nice feller to whom he—Mr. Mottle—was taking such a fancy, and in the evenings how nice to visit back and forth with Johnson and that refined looking wife of his, and it would be company for Mrs. Mottle who found life at the nurseries a bit dull without her friends and the Bridge Club, and in winter evenings a good game of whist. And in front of Mort floated the illusory vision of the melancholy and dilapidated shack transformed without any effort on his or Myrtle's part to the twin of Mr. Mottle's house, white with blue trim, and a pleasant easy steady job of stoking and potting, and him and Myrtle getting in to a show whenever they wanted in the evenings and not too much of Mr. and Mrs. Mottle. He had a presentiment that one could come to be owned too much by Mr. Mottle.

"Now we're here you better come in," said Mr. Mottle, and they went into the neat and linoleumed interior of his home and had a bit of bread and some cheese and some Postum because Mrs. Mottle was away and Mr. Mottle wasn't such a hand at making coffee and you couldn't 'ardly tell the difference.

"Mrs. Mottle shouldn't a went to Calgary but nothing would do," said Mr. Mottle. "She shouldn't be travelling around. She's a real liability to the railroads, she is. Mrs. Mottle's got a heart," and he looked seriously at Mort.

"Is that so," said Mort, "tt tt, that's too bad!"

"Yes, sir, Mrs. Mottle has a heart," said Mr. Mottle, "but her younger sister was took sick in Calgary and nothing will do but she must go. She's got trouble somewheres around the juggler, her sister has. They *call* it goitre, but it don't sound like goitre to *me*. *I* think . . ." and he whispered to Mort.

"Oh, yeah, sure," said Mort, nodding. "Sure."

When they had finished the Postum and Mr. Mottle had washed up and put away, and again the little home was as neat and unattractive as a pin, they decided to go back to the office, because old Cameron didn't like to ring up on the phone and no one there. So then they sat around and talked in a desultory fashion and it was quite late, about six o'clock, before the telephone rang to some purpose, and it was old Cameron.

"Yes, Mr. Cameron," said Mr. Mottle into the telephone.

" . . . "

"Yes, Mr. Cameron."

" . . . "

"Yes, Mr. Cameron."

" . . . "

"No, there wasn't. He never called up."

" . . . "

"I'll be sure to tell him . . . sure . . . hold them back . . . don't let him send them . . . deliver the spray . . . and oh, say, Mr. Cameron, there's" (voice lowered) "a nice feller here looking for a job. If I may suggest, just the feller to take Tompkins' place if Tompkins goes . . . yes, experienced . . . no, he wasn't fired . . . he just finished a landscapin' proposition up in West Vancouver and him and his wife would like to move out to Burnaby . . . yes, I know him well . . . known him for years . . . aunt's an old friend of me and Mrs. Mottle . . . no, no . . . sure . . . I told him . . . no loafing on the job but he's not that kind, Mr. Cameron . . . no . . . very good . . . I'll tell him . . . and lay an order for ten more sacks . . . okay, Mr. Cameron." And old Cameron rang off and so did Mr. Mottle.

"There, you heard me; he says to come around Monday and he'll see you and I'd say the job is as good as yours," and Morty thanked Mr. Mottle and thanked him again and as soon as it was decently possible to leave, he left, and walked down the rough irregular road bordered with half-cleared and uncleared land which led to the interurban car.

Morty sat on the interurban car and as he looked out of the window he did not see bush, small houses, bush, more bush, and drizzly grey mist sliding past. He saw himself and Myrtle settled without any trouble in a natty small home of their own, in a non-exacting and agreeable job, and in the perpetual sunshine that always surrounds one's most indulgent dreams. As he approached the city boundary his dream was spiked by the thought of the possible non-concurrence of Myrtle. Incredible as it would seem to most people that Myrt might prefer the two slatternly rooms at the top of the house off Powell Street and the proximity of the movies and Irma Flask to a neat home of one's own contriving and steady work in the country, it was none the less possible. However, Morty turned his mind away from anything as uncomfortable as argument with Myrtle, and as he got off the interurban car and walked towards and along Powell Street he was not really walking along Powell Street at all on a drizzly evening, but was idly basking in the sunshine outside a white cottage with blue trim on the windows, and Myrtle was inside the white cottage making coffee not Postum. He did not see, on the other side of Powell Street, his wife's cousin Victoria May Tritt who had paused to look at him, but his eyes picked up the tall figure of a drunk who lolled against the Fishermen's

Book Shop and gesticulated slowly and largely to the passers-by. His eyes informed his wandering mind that for gossakes if it wasn't old Eddie; and so the moments of Mortimer Johnson and Eddie Hansen and Victoria May Tritt converged and met outside the Fishermen's Book Shop. Morty quickened his steps. It *was* Eddie. Well, for gossakes.

The white cottage with blue trim vanished from Mort's mind as he fetched up with old Eddie the silly old fool drunk there on Powell Street, and at almost the same minute Eddie became aware of Morty, and the handshaking and wrestling began to take place which Victoria May witnessed as she stood still on the other side of the road. Other people witnessed it, and all this to-do occasioned the turning aside and going around of passers-by who did not necessarily wish to become involved in the affectionate greeting of two old friends or drunks. Eddie and Mort swayed to and fro, talking at the same time, and Morty thought it would be a good thing to get old Eddie to turn around and go back with Morty to the Regal Rooms where Eddie stayed; but Eddie thought that it would be a good thing to get old Morty to go along to the dock with him and see if they couldn't find that suitcase of Eddie's down there. And because Eddie was stronger, and drunk, and impervious to argument, and because Mort was so glad to see Eddie, drunk or sober, that he'd do anything to oblige, they set off, clasping each other, in the direction of the dock; and Victoria May, who could no longer see them for the crowd and the mist, hastened on her way to church.

Morty felt some kind of protective feeling for Eddie

drunk. He had never come across Eddie drunk before. He had got drunk *with* Eddie, which was quite a different thing, and did not engender a protective feeling. But now Morty, sober, with a fellow-feeling for Eddie (high-rigger, swell fellow, good old Eddie) drunk, shepherded and steered and protected Eddie although he had no confidence that they would ever find the suitcase on the dock—but, just to oblige, he did this; and it was a good thing he'd happened along, because by the time they reached the dock it was quite dark and the rain made the visibility very bad and goodness knows what would have happened to Eddie the old fool crossing the street if Morty hadn't been along to take care of him. Mort, I wish you to understand, was very very kind to Eddie, and almost gentle with him, if anyone can be gentle with a high-rigger who measures over six feet and is drunk.

By the time they reached the place at which you turn off to go down to the dock—and their progress had been slow—the street lights were all on, and there is nothing like street lights for announcing the arrival of night. It was unquestionably night. A light shone in an office where the Company's dock watchman was on duty. But as the watchman had gone into the lavatory for a moment, he could not and did not see the wavering arguing figures of two men, one tall and one shorter, cross the beam of light that fell from his window upon the wooden planking of the dock. He did not see the two men advance onto the dock. If he had, he would have gone out and shouted Hey at them, and found out what they were doing there, and turned them back if he could. But as he was in the washroom, no one saw Eddie and Mort walk together along the dock in the direction of a faint high light at the end of the dock, both of them fairly contented, yes, *very* contented in their own mutual company. It did not occur to Morty to be nervous of Eddie's safety on a dock when he was drunk, because Mort knew, if he had happened to think of it but he didn't, that Eddie had teetered about on half the docks and wharves of the logging camps of the coast of British Columbia and had never fallen in yet and never would. So Morty did not accompany Eddie on to the dock with any idea of protecting him from falling in—trust Eddie—but for the pleasure of being with him and because when they did not find the suitcase—and they would not—then Morty would go with Eddie back to the Regal Rooms and see him to bed. And next day he would go back and visit with him. He really did not think of Myrtle at all, and anyway he literally had his hands full, clutching hold of two hundred and forty pounds of old Eddie.

Eddie, whose head was clearing a little, had a lot to tell Mort about the fellows they both knew who used to be up at Jervis Inlet and especially about a very very funny guy called Mike Jerkin who was now with Eddie at Knight Inlet who had a stammer which he used to exploit when he got in wrong with people and whom Eddie could take off to the King's taste; and Eddie broke away from Mort and acted out Mike Jerkin the time the moose got into the cook-house. By this time they had reached the end of the dark and meagrely lighted wharf and had for a moment forgotten about the suitcase because of Eddie telling in a very drunken way—but still funny— about what Mike Jerkin said to the moose, when Eddie took a lunge in his story and stepped off the dark wharf into the dark night and fell with a tremendous splash into the dark water which closed over him and only a dirty spangly light moved on the surface of the water, although there were signs of commotion beneath.

XIV

EVERYTHING in the world narrows down now with horrid immediacy and intensity to only Eddie struggling alone down there in the dark and churning up the spangly water and clawing the empty water in panic haste because he cannot swim, and only Mort crouched alone up there in the dark . . . in the sky it seems . . . his arms extended, looking down into the high tide water under the dim light at the place where Eddie churns his way up to the surface of the water. Everything in the world vanishes, gives way, all laughing and story give way to Mortimer's terror as, crouched with his arms extended as if frozen there, he sees the dark agitation of the water with its dirty spangled light and then he sees the white face of Eddie, staring, unrecognizable in its surprised fear, rise for a moment above the indifferent moving water. And at the sight of this white patch of face turning, choking, shouting, covered again, sinking again Mort is vicariously in Eddie there; he is Eddie, struggling there. And he moves, and is released, and shouts, and does not know that he shouts and shouts and looks wildly around and runs wildly around and comes back for anything. Is that a rope yes it is a coiled rope. And he throws the end of the rope and it misses, and he leans far down and takes a good purchase on it and throws it again to poor old Eddie Mort Eddie who is going to drown sure if Mort doesn't do something quickly but I don't have to jump in do I Myrtle do I Eddie no no I don't have to jump in do I: and he sees again the ghastly face above the water. And the rope because it is not attached and has no purchase runs smoothly out and falls into the sea, and so because Mort has no real purchase, he falls into the sea, and Eddie who is strong, and is dying, and does not wish to die, seizes hold of Mort, and the empty water slides through Mort's fingers, and he seizes Eddie and they fight there, choking, grappling, the two good friends, in the dark water . . .

. . . but have to live and is drowning me God God what a fool blasted fool me Myrtle kitchen me Myrtle bedroom I mighta been there now little white house what white house Myrt God fool Eddie . . . bitterness despair anguish dreadful tearing anguish. And the water suffocated his eyes and blinded his lungs and Eddie held him tangled with hands and arms and legs and the agony grew and grew and at last diminished and ceased and Mort and Eddie in their loosening embrace sank uselessly down through the dark water and became both of them drowned men.

Woe for Mort. Woe for Mort's angel speeding away with an inaudible cry.

XV

UNDER the street light the small group of people which became added to, person by person, until it was a crowd, discussed and elicited and exchanged information and opinions until facts seemed to be established and passed around that two men had been drowned and one was Mortimer Johnson who was a Vancouver man and lived up there off Powell Street and the other was a big fellow who looked like a logger and that they were drunk. People had seen people who knew Mortimer Johnson and had seen the two men wrastling on Powell Street, and some men coming away from working late at the freight shed had seen them going along onto the dock together and had mentioned it at the time hadn't they, because one said that that was Mort Johnson because he saw him every day. And the night watchman, although he hadn't exactly seen them go onto the dock, had heard something, and he went out, and listened, and there was someone shouting and shouting, and he was sure he saw someone at the very end of the wharf, and he ran back and got his torch, and he went down the wharf, and no one was there but there was something happening in the water and he moved his torch light about over the water and there was a hat; and a rope that he had meant to put away had gone; and he got scared and took out the rowboat but he couldn't find anything but the hat— that was the watchman's story. And then when the police came they checked on everything and made further enquiries.

Having discussed all of this with solemnity, and some relish, and some awe (because death was so near in time and space), the crowd lost interest and melted away, making remarks, and left only Victoria May Tritt who at first couldn't believe that Myrt's husband Morty was dead because strangers said so. But as she stood there really stunned, she saw again, as in her mind, Morty approaching the big logger, and Morty and the big logger eventually going off down Powell Street, Mort sober and the logger drunk, and this scene which she had beheld bore witness to her that what the strangers standing under the street light had said must be true, because how could they have made it up. It was so clear in her mind that Morty was sober when he walked down Powell Street that she did not realize, however, that the people assumed that both men were drunk, and that was why they fell in and got drowned. She came to herself, as they say, and was very unhappy and was consumed with sorrow that Morty had died, not an hour since, and how would Myrtle bear it because they were such an ideal couple. She thought she had better go and see Myrtle because she herself had seen Morty so well and happy just a very little while ago and she must go and tell Myrtle that, and perhaps she could do something for her. But what could she—Vicky—do for anyone; she did not know what you do when your cousin's husband has just been drowned and your cousin's heart is broken, but you must go to her just the same. She was so stricken and so sorrowful that she did not feel shy in the ordinary way. But this was an extraordinary thing that might make anyone not know just what to do even if they were much easier about things than Vicky. Even Mrs. Emblem, for instance.

Vicky went on through the damp night and was vaguely aware how melancholy, how desperately sad life can suddenly become which was a few minutes ago all right, and happy—almost—and that people couldn't stop doing things, somehow, that ended like this; and you didn't know it would happen and so you couldn't stop them. She went on until she came near Myrtle's place, and as she approached the entrance she saw two tall policemen walking away together in the way that policemen walk and she was sure that they had just been up and had been telling Myrtle. The policemen had indeed just been telling Myrtle. They disliked telling her, and had done it as kindly as they could and one of them had ascertained the name of a woman friend from her and had gone down and telephoned her friend Mrs. Flask to come to her, and Mrs. Flask was out but her mother would get her right away. Neither of the policemen liked Myrtle when they came away, although they had gone there prepared—as human beings—to feel solicitude for anyone who was about to receive shocking news. And now they walked away reflectively, in their swinging dignity, both of them reflecting as fellow-husbands, not as policemen. One of them then said without enthusiasm ". . . boy oh boy . . ." and the other responded ". . . my gosh, when you see some women . . ." They remained reflective fellow-husbands in silence to the end of the block although still looking like policemen, and then turned down on their road back to the Police Station which was not far away. Myrtle had shown herself very nasty.

She was now sitting at her kitchen table. Her arms were resting akimbo on the table and she looked sullenly downwards. You could not see her eyes, but you saw on her fine eyelids—swollen and purplish now—not sorrow, but rage and scorn. You saw rage and scorn and hate as plainly on those dropped eyelids as if Myrtle had looked up at you with rage and scorn and hate in her pale eyes . . . It had been like this. The two policemen had first appeared at her door, and had come in, and had told her that there had been an accident. An accident to her husband. And upon her challenging look and word they had then told her that her husband Mortimer Johnson was dead. Myrtle had gazed with apprehension, with disbelief, with horrified belief, and then with the unwilling acceptance that what these two tall uniformed men said was true . . . that Mortimer Johnson . . . that Morty . . . was dead, and she had burst into tears (unfamiliar tears, for when had Myrtle wept?). She sat down at the table and again questioned them through her tears which rained down because she now saw Morty kind, easy, debonair, her husband whom she owned . . . part of her life . . . whom she had left this morning playing with the kitten . . . going out, he said, to see old Cameron and get a job. Was it an auto? I'll bet it was an auto. No, they said uneasily, her husband was drowned. What was he doing, she asked, startled, jealous, what was he doing to be drowned? He was on a dock, they said carefully, he was on a dock with another man. What man . . . why were they on a dock? Both men were drowned, they said, pitying her. What man, what man? asked Myrtle. The other man's name was Hansen, he was a logger from up the coast. Then they were drinking; had they been drinking? Well, yes, they seem to have been drinking.

Gone was the thought of Morty kind, debonair, easy, and in his place was the idle lying drunken loafer who had so deceived her time and time again. And after all that had gone the night before Mort—the no-good loafer— had hunted up Eddie Hansen, when he said he never seen Eddie Hansen, and knew how she felt about Eddie Hansen, and there he had hunted him up instead of coming home to Myrtle, and had got drunk with him, and they had gone fooling on the wharf, and had fallen off, and had got themselves drowned. She hated Mort so much for this that if he had then appeared, she would not have welcomed him back to the living; she would have reviled him; she might have struck him. For *her*, Myrtle Johnson that was Myrtle Hopwood, to be now an object of pity as a woman whose husband was no good, and had died a drunken death in poor company—for her to be exposed to this by Mort Johnson who had deceived her, and had gone out, and had sought out that drunken souse, and had drunk with him and had died with him—all this was not to be borne by Myrtle, but it had to be borne. And she changed. Under the eyes of the two policemen she changed from a woman bereft and weeping for her husband to a woman who regarded her husband—only just now dead—with hate and scorn. And as the two policemen listened, Myrtle poured out her pride and her venom, and became established in her mind as a woman deeply wronged by Mortimer Johnson.

And when the policemen had gone, and Myrtle was alone, she laid her head on her arms upon the table, and wept—not for Morty her husband, but for herself who would now be exposed to the pity of Irma Flask ("*I always knew . . .*") and the pity of Mrs. Emblem ("*I could have made a real man of Mort Johnson . . .*"), and she forgot that Mort had ever been her kind and foolish lover.

Such was the devious working of Myrtle's mind that when she raised her face all swollen and ravaged with weeping, she had forgotten the physical fact that Mort lay—somewhere—drowned, and she thought only of herself as uniquely wronged, and, if she held her head high enough, uniquely to be pitied yet held in esteem as one superior to other people not so wronged; and the assumption of this rôle began to assuage a little the torment of her mind. Settled, then, in her pride and in her resentment, she now sat, weeping no longer but looking sullenly down with her resentment heavy on her eyelids. The kitten, finding itself neglected and no longer fondled but pushed impatiently away, returned to its little place under the sink, and Myrtle remained sitting, waiting for Irma Flask, ready, before Irma could speak, to vent her pride and her resentment, but not her grief for she had only hardness now for her once dear silly lover.

Victoria May Tritt hurried past the policemen, looking up at them but unnoticed by them, and then she hurried up the stairs, and, transformed beyond herself by death— another's death—and by her own compassion, she opened the door at the head of the stairs, entered the room, closed the door, and stood against the wall, looking with great pity at Myrtle who raised her heavy lids and gave Vicky the full value of her sullen look. Vicky stood and looked sorrowfully at her cousin and her whole awkward little body was instinct with compassion as she stood leaning forward a little, with helpless hands outstretched and head tilted forward, and eyes—so colourless—lit now with dark pupils. How sad she stood, sadder by far in her estimation of her cousin's loss than her cousin, sitting at the kitchen table with anger growing cold.

"Oh, Myrtle . . ." said Vicky, " . . . you heard . . . oh, Myrtle . . . poor Morty!"

Myrtle's slight inverted smile as her lips turned downwards appeared on her stained face as the travesty of a smile, and she said to Vicky in a bitter echo "Poor Morty! . . ." and then she told Vicky what had happened, and what Mort, so dying, had done to *her*, and the pupils of Vicky's eyes grew darker and larger and her look changed as she listened. You would not have known her, I think.

"Stop it, Myrtle Hopwood," she said sharply, "you stop it. What you're saying isn't true . . ."

"I'll say it's true," said Myrtle, greatly surprised.

"What you're saying isn't true and you to think such a thing of Morty and him gone!"

"I don't need you to tell me what to think," said Myrtle looking obliquely at Victoria May with great scorn. "I seen the police and . . ."

Vicky leaned forward like an awkward little prize-fighter. Her thin arms were bent and her weak fists clenched ineffectually over her thumbs.

"Listen to me, Myrtle," said Vicky impetuously, with no fear in the world. "I seen Mort coming down Powell Street when I was going to service and he was no more drunk than . . . than *you*! And I seen that logger, that Eddie, and he was drunk, and I seen Mort come up with him and Mort was sober, like he was coming off work, and Mort looked kinda surprised and Mort took a holt of this Eddie and tried to make him go away but this Eddie he took a holt of Mort and pulled Mort and short of having a row, Mort went along and guided this Eddie." Vicky stopped and she was breathless because she had never used up so much breath in one speech before in her life.

But Myrtle, now established in the darling imaginings of a woman uniquely deceived and meet to be sympathized with, listened without satisfaction to Vicky. Vicky gazed at her cousin in the silence that followed and then she told her tale again, with vehemence, as if Myrtle were deaf, and Myrtle looked grudgingly and consideringly at her. And Vicky, who knew nothing of married love and married hate, of married joy and married fury, saw with a dawning understanding the dreadful thing about Myrtle Johnson—that she was content to have Morty die as she then thought he died; and that she did not much wish to believe what Vicky told her; and Vicky dimly apprehended that Myrtle in her self-love did not intend to cease being wronged by Morty in his death.

Vicky's eyes were like black stars. "Oh, Myrtle," she cried, strong in what she had seen, "you're a wicked wicked woman!" And then she told a lie, and how easily it came, from the depth of the life that she lived in her dreamings and her imaginings and the newspapers which were her fairy tales and the movies which were her other life. "When Morty died the death of a hero!"

"Hero!" repeated Myrtle, surprised.

"They was a man," continued Victoria May, still bending earnestly towards her cousin, "they was two men and they was talking to some people on the corner of Cordova when I come out of church and I heard them say Mortimer Johnson and I stopped and listened and one of the men—I'd know him again—was telling them how he was coming off work and he heard someone shouting and he ran and before he got there to the end of the wharf he seen a man and it was Morty and Morty took a dive off of the end of the wharf. He put his hands like So," said Vicky, living in her invention, and putting her two palms together as she seemed to remember divers seem to do, "and he took and dove right in after Eddie Hansen. And the man said He sure died a hero's death and all the people he was talking to said so too, and that was why I come along . . . I thought you knew . . ." and Vicky stopped, having invented her story with such surprising ease that she was ready to believe it herself. "Myrtle," she continued solemnly, "you're the widow of a hero!"

So great is the power of the spoken word that Myrtle, blinking, began to see herself not as a woman deeply wronged forever, but as the widow of the hero Mort Johnson. Vicky, watching her intently, repeated "The man said Morty put his hands together and then he took and dove into the water, and they was almost gone by the time the man—they was two men but one talking—by the time he got to the end of the wharf, because that Eddie he took a holt of Morty and pulled him under."

Something grew warm within Myrtle and she saw the simple picture of Morty putting his hands together and diving in to rescue Eddie Hansen and she became, as Victoria May had said, the widow of a hero, and she became proud of Morty, but prouder of herself for being the widow of a hero. Vicky, seeing what she had achieved, expelled a long breath, and relaxed. How simple it had been!

"Maybe I'd get you a cup of tea, Myrtle," she said, in her usual diffident tone. The kitten sprang onto Myrtle's knee and mechanically she stroked it, looking not at Vicky but at Morty who dived off the end of the wharf, and now would never come back, and how terrible it was, and so she was the widow of a hero; and that was how Mrs. Emblem and Irma Flask found her a few minutes later when they came hurrying hatless into the room. Mrs. Emblem coming into the room infused it with consolation. She did not seem to see Victoria May but came straight to Myrtle and bending over embraced her saying "You poor thing. You poor poor thing," and, bending, put her soft face against Myrtle's changed face and kept it there in silence, weeping a little.

"When Mom phoned me I phoned Mrs. Emblem right away and we come over," said Irma Flask. "Say, isn't it the awfullest thing!"

Mrs. Emblem with her arms around Myrtle and her face against Myrtle's face thought out of her own experience It's bad anyway, but when a husband dies drunk I guess it takes everything that might be sad or kind right away, and I don't know what to say to her; and so she continued to hold Myrtle in silence.

But Irma Flask said, taking off her coat, "I said to Mrs. Emblem, if it hadn't a been that they was drunk . . ."

Myrtle shook herself loose from her aunt. "Who was drunk?" she demanded of Irma Flask.

"Why, Morty and Eddie!" said Irma Flask. "The policeman said!"

"They're crazy, that's what *they* are, those cops," said Myrtle contemptuously, "and if you or anyone else dairse go around telling lies about Morty, Irma Flask, I'll have the law of anyone, I certny will." Irma Flask, who had come to comfort Myrtle in her own peculiar recriminatory way, was silent and surprised, and so was Mrs. Emblem, waiting.

"You tell them, Victoria May, you tell them," urged Myrtle, and Victoria May, afraid of Mrs. Emblem and of Irma Flask, but more afraid lest this new truth which she had made up and which had become essentially true might in some way fail, began her recital again; and as she recited she lost her fear in her vivid imagining of Morty's death.

She stood there, her plain face different (thought Mrs. Emblem), and recited, and the three women watched her and listened.

As Vicky told her story, she looked directly at Mrs. Emblem who was the one, she felt, who must believe her. When she came to the conclusion of her recital, the picture of Morty's dive from the wharf was so real to her that she herself was deeply moved by it, and the sight of Vicky with her simple tale and her simple tears also moved both Mrs. Emblem and Irma Flask.

As Mrs. Emblem looked at her sadly and in surprise, she accepted all that Vicky had said, as true. Even if she had in her mind questioned Vicky's story (which she did not), she would have told herself that it had to be true, because Vicky was too simple, too honest, too frightened, too stupid—perhaps—to tell a lie, and so she would know that it must be true.

"And what did you do then, Victoria May? Didn't you think to ask the man who he was and get his name?" asked Mrs. Emblem.

Vicky shook her head. "But I'd know him anywheres," she said.

"Well, for goodness' sake," said Irma Flask, "why didn't you ask him his name, so's you could tell Myrtle?"

"I dairsent, I was scared to," said Vicky humbly, and this was so probable that the whole fabric of Vicky's story was complete.

"Well, Myrtle," said Irma, "it's certny just *terrible*, but you must feel awful proud!"

"I certny do," said Myrtle, and her face resumed at least its calm.

"Irma," said Mrs. Emblem, "you fix up the stove and I'll make a pot of coffee right here on the gas, and you sit right here in the rocking chair, Myrtle honey, and then when you've had some coffee, you lay down and have a good night's sleep, and I'll stay the night and Irma can go home . . . I don't have to lay down . . . I can sleep just as good sitting up in my slip in the rocking chair . . . And Vicky, you run along home, you can't do anything here," added Aunty Emblem kindly, thinking That poor little queer thing, it's no use *her* staying, she'll just be in the way. So Vicky, whose courage was leaving her, became herself again, and, standing there awkwardly, looked at her cousin whom she had lately dominated, and tried to tell her how sorry she was, and failed, and said inadequately "Well, Myrt . . . I'll be seeing you . . . one of these days . . . well . . . goodnight all," and she turned and went out of the room and down the stairs and into the dark street where the air was so pleasant, and the heavy rain refreshing, and they forgot her.

The room which she had left soon became heavy and saturated with abundant feeling welling up and overflowing, and with repetition, and sentiment, and reminiscence, and indictment, with cups of coffee, and enveloping sympathy, and lavish emotion, and, before Irma Flask went home, Myrtle was established as the grief-stricken widow of Mort Johnson who had been a hero, and as the eternal detester of Eddie Hansen who had ended her husband's life. And at last Myrtle went to bed solitary yet sustained, and she at last slept, and Aunty Emblem settled herself in the rocking chair in her slip with her coat round her shoulders, and, rocking a little, soon slept. Mrs. Emblem and the kitten, who had much in common, woke from time to time, wandered about a little to see that all was well, settled again and slept.

Victoria May, having no umbrella, walked in her rather mincing way through the now driving rain and the darkness and the occasional lights of Cordova Street along the black and shining splashing pavements where a few people were hurrying through the wet. Oh, she thought mournfully, my hat-with-the-veil will be rooned, and then she accused herself of poorness of spirit for thinking of her hat on such a night. Her exaltation had left her and had exhausted her. As she hurried along the dark wet pavements, life and time continued as usual everywhere under heaven with practised ease their ceaseless fluid manipulations and arrangements of circumstance and influence and spiked chance and decision among members of the human family—such arrangements as had caused Victoria May to be what she was; and had caused her that night to see Mort sober and Eddie drunk; and had caused her to force her small will upon Myrtle Johnson; and had caused her in one instant by means of a lie to turn Myrtle aside from her fury, and had thus enabled

Myrtle to become the widow of a hero, not of a louse, and so had enabled Myrtle to remember Mort with half grudging tenderness and with her best and sleazy love; and had caused her (Victoria May) to do Mort a great service by so establishing him in general reputation and in memory; and had caused Myrtle to esteem herself a woman not preferred—for one fatal moment—to that souse Eddie Hansen, thereby adding to the power of her eyelids by being a wife widowed and deeply injured by this non-preference; and thus had caused Myrtle to continue to dominate Mrs. H. X. Lemoyne and Victoria May and even Irma Flask—more than ever before—and sometimes by virtue of her cruel loss to dominate Mrs. Emblem; and still to be very lonely.

The once-felt blaze of heat that had so warmed Victoria May as she stood over her cousin Myrtle did not of course long retain its virtue; but in solitude—which was to say in most of Victoria May's waking and sleeping life—she was often to be sustained by the contemplation of that moment and of that scene which her memory came habitually to recall, to fondle, to admire, and to enhance.

She reached the back door which was her entrance, and found Mrs. Pavey from the basement taking in her wash in the rain and the dark, and blocking the immediate approach to the back door with her person and with her big laundry basket. Mrs. Pavey had forgotten her wash and had left it on the line while she and Mr. Pavey had gone to a show.

"My goodness! Look what I did!" said Mrs. Pavey under the small porch light to Miss Tritt. "Went and forgot my wash and it's all wet again and you can't leave a thing out at night nowadays not with all these sneak

128

thieves round the place. My land, isn't it awful!" she said in the ill-lit darkness, reeling in the line and taking down the sopping clothes and putting them hastily into the clothes-basket. "Was it a good show?" for Mrs. Pavey naturally thought that anyone who came in late had been to a show.

"It . . . I . . . oh . . . yes . . . " said Victoria May nervously, very much afraid of being talked to. She dodged in the dark around Mrs. Pavey and went through the doorway and on up the stairs to her room and to her night of amazement.

"Well," said Mrs. Pavey, incensed, "people might at least try to be polite to people!"

LILLY'S STORY

TO

JO, AND THOSE NEVER-FAILING FRIENDS

I

In the early part of this century there lived in the young city of Vancouver in British Columbia a large family by the name of Hastings. The head of this family was old Mrs. Hastings who was a widow, a saint and a mystic. With her lived her younger, elderly sister Miss Edgeworth, some sons and daughters, and two grandchildren. They lived in a big square red wooden house which broke smartly into decoration at the corners. The family had but recently arrived from England, and they had at once planted a garden which quickly flourished in the soil and moisture of the British Columbia climate which encourages weed and flower, tree and vegetable with almost tropical energy. At the end of this garden were low wooden buildings. The building on the left included living quarters of the Chinese cook and a trunk-room full of the trunks which accompany a large English family in migration and also the good English bicycle of Miss Edgeworth who though elderly was daring and would try anything once. She was therefore well fitted to be a pioneer. She had bought this English bicycle before she had learned to ride, and she had never been able to learn to ride it. However, since she felt it to be a shame not to use so fine a vehicle (the bicycle was too heavy, sexless in spite of its sex, conspicuous for its bulky accessories of bright metal) she used to walk it about the town in the day-time. Thus the bicycle became well known in Vancouver for its handsomeness, for its cussedness, and because it was always walked, not ridden. A result, on the side, was that the bicycle was never taken out at night because Miss Edgeworth never wished to walk it at night when it could not be seen. It became available, then, to un-authorized people who might wish to ride it at night, and, at last, an unauthorized person did.

Yow, who inhabited the little room opening off the box-room, was the Chinese cook of this family. He was a formidable Chinaman, tall, pock-marked, and with a droop of one eyelid which added cynicism to his already disillusioned face. Even in the house, when wearing his Chinese slippers, he walked with a proud and swagger-ing gait. His look was derisive. He admitted that, in China, he had killed two men, one slowly, one quickly. He also said that he had been beaten to within an inch of his life. All this may have been true. He could juggle the affairs of this family of nine people and have an extensive private life of his own on the side very easily, although the pressure made him bad-tempered. He kept the children in their place by means of the simple threat "I killem you!" He was insolent, a good cook, a clean and devilish servant, rude to the younger ladies of the house, hostile to the men, and he worshipped the venerable Mrs. Hastings, arrayed in her age, simple goodness and heavenly piety. He had indeed three passions. One was for old Mrs. Hastings who actually believed him to be a very good man which perhaps he was; one was for gambling; and one was for Lilly Waller, a white girl with taffy-coloured hair who worked in Chinatown, whom, in his dark mind, he called "my lady-friend". Lilly seemed indifferent to him, or perhaps she was cagey.

Washing up the evening dishes as with one swift movement, Yow used to walk to his outside room and transform himself. His real life now began, and the innocent Hastings family were left to their silly and mysterious occupations. When Yow went to his room he wore a white coat and apron and his hair was plaited in a queue which was wound round his head. When he came out of his room a few minutes later he wore a good black high-necked jacket with trousers to match of expensive material with a faintly brocaded pattern. His queue, lengthened by a plait of green silk, was looped up under his right arm. He wore Chinese shoes turned up a little in front and he wore a round black hat. He walked, swaggering out of his room, through the box-room where stood all the trunks and also the English bicycle, out of the gate and down the lane in the direction of Chinatown, headed for Lung Duck's place. Anyone coming down the lane would instinctively falter at the sight of Yow advancing like Lucifer.

When Yow arrived at Lung Duck's place which was in Shanghai Alley off Pender Street, he went through a narrow door and through several stale and dark passages. The Chinese noise grew greater as he got near the gambling room which was full of very potent cigarette smoke and other smells which announced a different world, a Chinese world. The room was crowded with grouped Chinamen. One could see them through the smoke, clustered around tables, squatted upon the floor, all talking loudly in Chinese shorthand. The police did not in those days interfere very much with their pleasures. Shanghai Alley was riddled darkly with gambling dens, one much like the last, all smelling vilely of some kind of smoke, all resounding with voices clacking like typewriters (much argument), no place in which to spend the night. But that is what Yow did for choice. He spent the night, or most of it, playing fan-tan amid the smoke and jabber, losing a little or winning a little from his cronies (no big stuff), and arriving back at his bedroom in the early morning, elated or black as thunder. This is how he spent his nights while the white family he served were sleeping blamelessly in silent rooms with the windows open and photographs on the walls. No wonder he was bad-tempered. He did not drink.

Just round the corner from Shanghai Alley was a restaurant—no, a joint—with Chinese characters on its dark face. Restaurants in Chinatown were not in those days called Mandarin Gardens or Pekin Chop Suey and so forth for the benefit of foreigners. There were Chinese customers, and there were Chinese characters, or none, on the windows or doors. The food was good. Sometimes there were dried fish or octopuses in the windows. They stayed there a long time and collected dust, as they were a symbol, not to eat, although probably no one would have minded eating them.

In Lam Sing's place, which was the place that Yow went to for a snack of real food, not white stuff, there were two white waitresses. One was the pale girl named Lilly Waller. She had a room down on Cordova Street, but on the night shift she worked at Lam Sing's. Yow watched this pale Lilly moving quickly and well. She had taffy-coloured hair, brown eyes and a pale mouth. Up went the straight line of her back, up the straight line of her neck, with the head set well. Her demeanour was not friendly. Yow watched her nightly taking her orders, balancing her tray, moving well and quickly and with indifference from kitchen to tables. He was mad over Lilly. He was mad over old Mrs. Hastings too. Two different loves. He loved Mrs. Hastings steadily, purely, and disliked all other white people on principle. His love for Lilly was a desire that consumed him, and in her indifferent way Lilly played with him. She was not fastidious. She was not vicious. She was no particular good and she had an inordinate desire for *things*. She was all that Yow wanted.

"You likee go vode-vil show? I takem you," said Yow one night.

"Say, who do you think I am? I don't go out with Chinks," said Lilly, fondling her hair and looking straight downwards.

Yow's eyes went obsidian. "You callem me Chink, I killem you," he said, making a threatening gyrating movement with his fist, as though he were going to do it with a corkscrew.

"Twenny-three skidoo," said Lilly indifferently.

"What for you tellem me skidoo," said Yow fiercely. "You not tellem me skidoo! I rich man. I plenty money. You look see!" And Yow took from his pocket all his wages, paid that day, and two dollars and sixty-five cents besides. He was lucky. The night before he could not have shown Lilly sixty-five cents. He was clever, too. He had waited till payday to speak to Lilly. Lilly did not answer, but looked at the money and then looked at Yow obliquely and walked away to another table.

Not long before Yow first spoke to Lilly, young Mr. John Hastings had brought his bride to the big house for a few weeks until he moved to Montreal where he had an unusually good opening. His bride was a beautiful young American girl from St. Louis, and in point of riches she was far out of the Hastings family's class. Her trousseau was of great size and beauty. It was impossible to find room for all her trunks in the house, and one trunk had to be taken out again and put into the box-room. Yow helped to do this. He had a ferocious neatness and shifted all the trunks about until the box-room looked orderly again. He had to move the English bicycle as well. This was the day after Yow had first spoken to Lilly.

When Yow had arranged the trunks to his satisfaction, he turned and surveyed the box-room. Out of the bride's big trunk hung a bit of lace. Things had been crammed in and the lid squashed down. Yow opened the lid of the trunk in order to put the piece of lace in, and there he saw piles of silk stockings, layers of lawn and silk night-dresses tied together with silk ribbon, layers of petti-coats tied together. He saw camisoles threaded through with pink and blue ribbons; he saw knickers with em-broidered frills at the knee. He fingered these things a little and he began to think. He took two pairs of silk stockings with clocks on, and then he closed the trunk. He turned round. The box-room light twinkled on the bevelled glass and the steel of the English bicycle.

Because of the extra work in the box-room Yow had been later than usual with dinner, which had annoyed him very much because he would be late at Lung Duck's. The night was already dark. In the small light of the box-room his eye and a half fell upon the shine of the bicycle. How simple the idea that burst full-blown. The bicycle was never sought and taken out after dinner,

which was the one time when it would be useful to Yow,
and at that time its owner, Miss Edgeworth, spent her
evenings conversing vivaciously in the house. He
yanked it out, wheeled it forth, led it into the lane, down
the lane to the sidewalk, and mounted, or tried to. It
was not very hard for a man of strength, for once get it
under control and the bicycle was as solid as a tricycle.
He established himself on the seat and began to pedal a
little, with a fierce sense of triumph. To begin with, he
wobbled a good deal, but the bicycle soon carried him
sweetly and steadily, with fewer and fewer stops, weaving
a little along Robson Street in the dark, down Granville
Street, along Pender Street to Shanghai Alley. He took
a sharp turn neatly at Shanghai Alley, drew up at Lung
Duck's, swung his leg across in the lordly way of one
who owns a bicycle, propped it easily at Lung Duck's
place and regarded it arrogantly with his hands on his
hips.

Chinese moved ceaselessly up and down Shanghai
Alley, which was ill-lit. One of the few street lights stood
near Lung Duck's door. The drifting stream of Chinese
halted, gathered, made towards and surveyed Yow's
unusual English bicycle which had not been seen in
Chinatown before.

"That your wheel?" in the Cantonese dialect.

"Sure."

"What kind wheel? Not all same nudder kind wheel."

"He American wheel," said Yow, who did not know
what kind of a bicycle this was.

"He look all same lady wheel."

"American man wheel American lady wheel all same,"
said Yow loftily.

The bicycle stood there alien and shining, surveyed and talked about by twenty or thirty Chinamen all at once at the top of their voices. Small Chinese boys crouched down and fingered the pedals and the corset-like laced cover of the chain.

"Skidoo," said Yow to them, and they skidooed.

"How much money?"

"Two hundred dollar," hazarded Yow.

The crowd grew. Everyone wanted to touch the bicycle. Yow saw that it was not safe outside so he wheeled it inside down the long passage and into the smoky gambling room. Gambling stopped in a desultory way and all the gamblers came to look at the bicycle. Yow was the only Chinaman in Chinatown to own a bicycle at that time and he didn't own one. Well, perhaps he did, for here it was.

At about half-past two Yow arose from where he squatted at his game, strode arrogantly to the bicycle and, with it, departed. He wheeled it along to Lam Sing's place, pushed open the door and wheeled it in. He had an instant success.

"That your wheel?"

"Sure."

"What kind wheel? Not all same nudder kind wheel."

"He American wheel."

"How much money?"

"Three hundred dollar."

Yow sat down near the bicycle. Lilly drifted over. Yow looked up at her pale face, her soft pink lips and her taffy-coloured hair.

"That your . . .?"

"Say, I got something for you."

Yow pulled out the two pairs of silk stockings with clocks on, and put them on the table. Lilly bent her head and her eyes grew wide. She had heard of silk stockings but she had never seen any before. She sat down at Yow's table. The lure was working. She fingered the stockings. Only the very very rich, she thought, Society people perhaps, or some real swell fancy women had silk stockings like these.

She looked up at Yow. "Where'd you get them?" she asked, her eyes large and brown as she for the first time looked full at him.

"I buyem," said Yow, blowing smoke through his wide nostrils. "You likee go vode-vil show?"

"Sure," said Lilly.

"You puttem on," ordered Yow.

Lilly sat down at the table and pulled up her skirt and petticoat. She bent over so that Yow saw only the top of her pompadour. Then he saw her leg. Lilly took off her shoe, pulled off her garter, rolled off her black woollen stocking, pulled on the long silk stocking, gartered it, stretched out her leg—shapely now—gazed long upon it and then looked up at Yow. She smiled a smile of pure happiness.

"You puttem nudder one," Yow ordered.

This time slowly, luxuriously, Lilly put on the other silk stocking. She curled her toes up and down, up and down.

"They sure look swell," she murmured.

"You allasame my lady-friend," said Yow rapturously and pulled Lilly down upon his knee.

"Say, you're sure you *did* buy them?" said Lilly. "I don't want no trouble with the police." Lilly had once had trouble with the police, and this trouble, rather than her rectitude, had made her a careful girl and nervous.

"Sure, I buyem my friend bringem New York City," said Yow.

New York City. The stockings acquired more lustre. The passion (which ruled Lilly then) for *things* mounted in her and her slight repugnance towards Yow melted and flowed into a liking for a giver of things and a potential giver of more things. Lilly was favourably disposed also towards the owner of a bicycle. Perhaps, she thought, passing her finger along the pattern of Yow's coat, he'll let me ride it.

As Lilly walked along to the vaudeville with Yow, she thought of the silk stockings and the bicycle, but chiefly about the bicycle, which Yow had left at Lam Sing's for safety. She swung her hips as she walked, just to show that she did not care at all about being seen with this man. But chiefly she thought about the bicycle.

At four o'clock in the morning Yow rode home on his bicycle. He stood it in its accustomed place. Then he went to the bride's trunk, opened it and began to choose. A nightdress, a petticoat, a camisole and a pair of knickers. He took a newspaper and made a smallish tight parcel. That night, when it was dark, he rode to Chinatown. Lilly now changed to the day shift, and at night she learned to ride the bicycle. Night after night, Yow took her a present. Lilly was ravished by the trousseau which became hers bit by bit, but most of all she loved the bicycle. She began to covet the bicycle.

Soon Yow, who had been unlucky at fan-tan, had nothing more to give to Lilly. The trousseau had stopped half-way down the trunk, where books took its place. Yow's pockets were empty. His infatuated pose of rich man was ended. He had nothing left to give but his bicycle. It was inevitable.

The evening was cold. The stars were bright winter stars. Lilly was now able to ride the bicycle, and she and Yow and the bicycle went together up the town, in the bright darkness and along Robson Street; sometimes Lilly rode, sometimes they walked the bicycle. Slowly, persistently, an intimation lighter than smoke invaded Yow in his infatuation. While Yow's passion was for Lilly, Lilly's passion was for the bicycle, or so it almost seemed. Yow was becoming only the agent of the bicycle. The tall Chinaman, the pale girl and the bicycle were noticed by a few people, but not by two policemen who, walking with acquired majesty upon another street, paced together towards Barclay Street on their way to answer an excited call from young Mr. John Hastings. There had been a robbery; much of his wife's trousseau was missing and so was a valuable bicycle belonging to his aunt. Family opinion had already convicted Yow, who had lately been excitable and unstable. In the privacy of her bedroom, Yow's Mrs. Hastings knelt beside her bed and with tears prayed for Yow and besought the Lord that this might not be so. "He is, dear Lord," she murmured with her accustomed reverential intimacy and passion, "fundamentally a good man. But this Thou knowest, O Lord!" Her petition did not avail, for the past cannot be undone and it was Yow who had indeed stolen the trousseau, and it was Yow who was now sauntering towards his room with Lilly Waller, while two policemen waited for him inside the box-room door.

"You stay my place tonight," said Yow, in the dark, cajoling. "I likee you stay my place tonight."

Lilly did not answer.

"What for you not come my place? I go your place, you tellem me you no like me go your place. You come, Lilly. You go home oily [early] before alla people get up."

"Maybe the folks'll see me," objected Lilly.

"They not see," urged Yow. "I go now look see. Nobody come nighttime my place. I takem wheel puttem box-room. I look see. You wait . . . I come tellem you. You come."

Lilly said stubbornly, "I'm scared of the folks."

"Lilly," Yow begged with a frightening tenderness, "you come! I givem you my wheel. You come, Lilly."

"You'll give me your wheel to *keep*?" asked Lilly warily.

Yow had a feeling of disquiet. "Sure," he said, "I givem you my wheel. You keepem. *Your* wheel."

"W-e-ell," said Lilly, "I guess I'll come."

By now the nearness of the house which they approached oppressed Lilly. Yow pushed forward but Lilly hung back. The immense respectability of the house breathed from its walls. Its rectitude spread over the dark garden and spilled into the shadowy lane.

"You wait here," said Yow protectively. "I takem bicycle. I puttem shed. I look see."

So then Lilly loitered in the lane beside dark laurels and Yow trundled the bicycle towards the shed. There was a sudden light, hoarse shouting, Chinese shouting, and the scuffling of men, a furious cry. Oh, it is the police! the police! They have him! Lilly crouched, turned, and ran.

Proud skilful dangerous Yow, poor fellow, what has he done? He has lost liberty, and the English bicycle, and old Mrs. Hastings, and he has lost Lilly, the pale slut who is running running through the dark lane, stopping, crouching in the shadows, listening, hardly daring to look behind her.

II

WHEN Lilly Waller was about eleven years of age, she sat
one afternoon in the sunlight on the steps of the cabin
and listened to her mother and the lodger quarrelling
inside the cabin. They were drinking. It went on and on
and on, this quarrelling about nothing, and seemed to
be part of their attachment to each other. Lilly accepted
this as she accepted everything else, without like or dislike or opinion, and she continued sitting there playing
with a small yellow cat, and paying no attention to the
talk inside the cabin until a fresh bout of quarrelling arose.
This time it was about something definite, and it concerned
her. The lodger, it seemed, was going away and Lilly's
mother was going with him. Lilly's mother wanted to
take the kid and the lodger would not take the kid. The
kid remained on the steps with the other young animal,
the small yellow cat, and was as little concerned for the
future as the yellow cat. Indeed the only difference
between Lilly and the cat in their apprehension of a
future was that some day, no doubt, Lilly would plan
for a tomorrow and the cat never would. But, at this
moment, their interest did not extend beyond the present.
So, when Lilly heard her mother swear that she would take
the kid, and when she heard the lodger swear that she
should not, and when at last she heard her mother say
she'd fix things up with Mrs. Case to look after the kid till
her pop came home, and then heard her pour injured

abuse on Lilly's pop, Lilly did not mind. But, so as to be out of the way of trouble, when she heard her mother and the lodger begin to stumble up towards the door, and the little cat heard too and leaped down and ran under the steps, Lilly got up and slipped behind the cabin and then she went to where she had hidden an apple and then she ate it and then she went over to Belle's place, and that was all.

Lilly remembered without interest her pop, who was working up in the woods somewhere, but she did not think about him. He, her mother, the sun and the rainy weather, school, eating, going to bed and getting up, were all of a piece and she accepted them as being all right. Only one thing in the small incident of her life disturbed Lilly and made her cry out in her sleep sometimes "The police! The police!" and made her mother yank her and shake her until she awoke and was quiet again which was Lilly's mother's usual method of treatment whenever Lilly required treatment of any kind.

It was less than a year before the departure of her mother with the lodger that Lilly was stopped on her way home from school one day by a dark young man who said "Say, kid, d'you want to earn a quarter?" Lilly stood still, and, protected always a little by an element of self-defence, looked at the dark young man, put her hands behind her back and said "What for?" The young man looked up and down the empty street and then he said "I got a present here for my anty. She lives at 320 Dupont Street—you know Dupont Street?—and I want to give her a sprise. You take this and ask for Nicky's anty, and if anyone asks where you got it you say a lady gave it you, but don't you tell nobody else about it." This sounded reasonable to Lilly who told her own kind of lies whenever they seemed advisable and told them very well, so she took the quarter and the small parcel and delivered it to Nicky's aunty on Dupont Street. She performed this errand several times. Sometimes Nicky's aunty was a blowsy woman in a dressing-gown and sometimes she was a dirty man in suspenders, and it was all the same to Lilly since no questions were asked. But there came a day when just as Lilly was handing Nicky's present to the fellow in suspenders, a big man stepped neatly round the corner of the verandah and took the parcel, and the man in suspenders, and several other people in the house, and Lilly; then two policemen who seemed to come from nowhere held them until a horse-drawn Black Maria came, and everyone was pushed into it and Lilly found herself jolting down to a place which was the Police Station. She was very very frightened inside the Black Maria with all those strangers. Lilly was bidden to sit on a bench in the Police Station while Nicky's two aunties and several other inmates of the house on Dupont Street were talked to and questioned by a sort of head policeman, and then were led away beyond a door, sullen or protesting.

Lilly was desperate with fright. She sat taut and still. She was a pale thin child with taffy-coloured hair. She had soft brown eyes. So habitual was her duplicity that she would gaze softly at you, saying nothing when she was deceiving you, and the eyes would grow softer and —but only if need be—they would fill with tears which, at first unshed, would gather and roll unchecked down her cheeks. Her lips were very pale. As Lilly sat alone on the bench she was a pitiful small figure, and indeed she suffered a great deal from this experience which was not

quite understood. There was a something which was partly
smell about the Police Station which frightened her very
much, and although the policeman who talked to her at
first and the man who talked to her afterwards were
kind, Lilly's spirit fled from them in terror. She lied to
them naturally, with experience, and without effort.
She said that her name was Maudie Watkins and she
lived on Davie Street down by the bay and had two little
brothers and went to the new school. She said that a tall
fair lady with a big hat with pink flowers had given her the
package to take to her aunty on Dupont Street. She said
the lady had given her a quarter and she had done this
twice before. No, she didn't know the lady's name. Yes,
she'd know her again anywhere if she saw her. And when
in the dark early evening a policeman took Lilly home to
Davie Street where she did not live, she ducked and ran
and hid amongst the lumber of some new houses that were
being built in the woods, and huddled, frightened, silent
as a bird, while the policeman looked for her, cursing.
He gave up the search and went on with rising annoyance
to find the address that Lilly had given him. He did
not find it, for it was not there. When night was very
dark indeed Lilly went home. Her mother asked her
where she had been and she said she had been at Katy's
place and they had been playing run sheep run. And
Lilly's mother had shaken her and said not to dare to
stay out so late again. And when that night, and on many
nights, Lilly had whimpered and cried in her sleep
"The police! The police!" her mother had shaken her
well. This seemed to be a good idea as Lilly always
settled down again. The affair with Nicky's aunty and the
police was a lucky thing for Lilly and made her very

careful, and thus she was saved a great deal of trouble later on.

The day after Lilly had heard her mother and the lodger talking about going away, Lilly's mother said to her, "I gotta go away but I'll be back in maybe a month. Your Gran's sick and I gotta go. I'll fix it so as you'll stay at Mrs. Case's place till your pop comes down from the woods and then you can come right back home," and she took Lilly by the hand and gave her a good yank and hurried across the vacant lots to the house of a neighbour named Mrs. Case who lived about two blocks away, keeping fast hold of Lilly, who sometimes had to run to keep up. Lilly's mother smelt of very strong drink but Lilly was used to this smell and did not observe it. Mrs. Case did.

When Mrs. Waller had knocked at Mrs. Case's door and Mrs. Case had come out, Mrs. Waller did a bit of crying. She still kept hold of Lilly. She said, "I feel awful bad."

Mrs. Case smelt the air and spoke coldly. "Izzat so," she said.

Mrs. Waller continued, "I certny had a terrible shock yesterday. My mother in Winnipeg's real sick and I gotta go right away and I gotta leave Lilly here it wouldn't be right to take her away from her schooling. She's a good kid and not a mite of trouble," she felt near her placket with her free hand and brought out some bills, "and you wouldn't be outer pocket if Lilly could stay here a week or two her gran'll be all right by then I guess. She's a good kid, aren't you a good kid, Lilly?" she asked, bending down to Lilly and giving her a shake. Lilly nodded. She was biddable always. She stood there silent, looking at Mrs. Case with her soft brown eyes, behind which she added up the situation. She knew that her mother lied; she did not regret her mother's going, things would go on all right; and though Mrs. Case looked too clean, she was a woman, and she was a woman who produced in Lilly an impression that was good and, perhaps, kind.

Mrs. Case looked at the child without speaking, and thought rapidly. She saw the pale and silent Lilly whose fair hair was a tangled mop and whose dress was slovenly, and she saw her soft brown eyes in which tears now welled. She looked too at the woman who had borne Lilly and with whom she lived, and she made her decision while the woman talked.

"Send her over tomorrow morning with clean on and clean to change," she said, and held open the door. She cut short Mrs. Waller's protestations and praise, and Mrs. Waller yanked Lilly down the steps and the door was shut. The air in the room smelled foul with cheap whisky. Mrs. Case threw up the window, put out her head and called after the departing mother and daughter "And mind you wash her head!" Lilly's mother did not turn round, but nodded violently as she hurried back across the vacant lots to the cabin.

Lilly settled down with Mrs. Case into a routine of cleanly living that was at first irksome. She learned a good deal about neat habits and appearance, and how to eat her food; she learned the forms of obedience and nothing about truthfulness. She even went to church sometimes, and neither liked nor disliked it. She did not steal because she feared the police; but she deceived Mrs. Case, whom she feared, when desirable and possible. She

and a girl called Matty Venn who was in a grade above
Lilly played hookey from school as often as it seemed safe.
These hookey days they spent chiefly in the big stores,
amusing themselves. Matty took to petty thievery and
shoplifting, but when Matty slipped things off the shop
counters Lilly wandered off and left her. This she did,
not because she had any particular dislike of thieving,
but from her strong instinct for self-preservation and her
desire to avoid the police. Following these days Matty
and Lilly would concoct notes for each other. The notes
began "Dear Teacher, please excuse Lilly she was sick . . ."
and ended "And Oblidge Mrs. Case." Or they began
"Dear Teacher I had to keep Matty home I had the asma
real bad all night as I am subjeck . . ." and ended "And
Oblidge Mrs. Venn." This, they knew, was the formula
of the mothers of the district and was the kind of thing that
the teacher expected and read on small dirty pieces of
paper each day, with concealed nausea. Since Lilly and
Matty were in different classrooms, the thing was quite
easy; it would have been an idiot of a school-teacher
whose suspicions would not have been aroused by the
frequent simultaneous absences from illness of two of a
kind in her own classroom.

When it came to deceiving Mrs. Case, things were not
so simple, as Mrs. Case was not very deceivable. Lilly was
a realist, and knew that a deceived Mrs. Case would be an
angry Mrs. Case, and then things might be uncomfortable
for Lilly, who liked comfort. Still, it could be done.

Weeks slid into months, and one morning a tall, bald
man in a rage approached the open door of Mrs. Case's
house, waving a letter.

"The damn bitch," he roared, "she run off with that

damn——" Mrs. Case stopped him in mid-rush. She stood there with her broom in her hand.

"You go home and wash your mouth out, Mr. Waller," she said, "and then you can come back here and talk to *me.*"

Mr. Waller stopped short. He felt his head which was bare and, turning hurriedly, he hastened back to his cabin feeling that, because he had not his hat on, he had been caught naked by Mrs. Case who after all was a woman, though nothing to look at.

Mr. Waller, whose ruling passion was not love, greed, duty or sloth, but simple vanity, was never seen without his hat which he wore well. Without his hat he was only a bald man with dark eyes. Hatted, he appeared as a tall lounging handsome man with a pair of bedroom eyes which caressed the female on whom he looked—always excepting his wife and daughter. And now, betrayed by surprise and anger out of his customary flattering grace, he had flung his hat upon the kitchen table of his cold and deserted home and, after reading his wife's abusive scrawl, had rushed, angry, hatless, bald and betrayed, over to Mrs. Case's house.

When Mr. Waller, dismissed by Mrs. Case, arrived back at his own house, he had cooled down and was able fairly to take stock of his position. His position was good. He found it very good. He was rid of a shrew and a slut whom someone else (poor fool) would now support; he had a grievance which he could thoroughly develop and enjoy; and he had no doubt of blandishing Mrs. Case into taking charge of Lilly who, at the age of twelve, thin, pale, quiet, and unresponsive, was likely to be a nuisance and a care to him. He thereupon unpacked and put on his good suit which he never left at home with his wife who would have sold it. He put on his hat before the small looking-glass, adjusted it a little this way and that way, composed his features and became a handsome man, tall, virile, debonair and satisfied. He walked again across the open ground that separated his cabin from the little house of Mrs. Case. He walked with his customary loose-limbed authority. He knocked, and Mrs. Case came to the half-opened door. "Come in," she said.

"Thank you, no," said Mr. Waller, who felt at a better advantage outside with his hat on, "I see you're a busy little lady this morning. But I wanna apologize, Mrs. Case, for the way I spoke this morning and I hope you'll make allowance. It isn't everyday that a man comes home expecting a welcome and finds his wife has deserted him and with a dirty low-life too. That woman," continued Mr. Waller, "has been a snake in my boosum. Times without number I've forgiven her but if she comes back after this I'll have the law. What I've had to take from that woman! I'll tell you . . ." and he developed the theme.

I can't stand here listening to this lump of conceit all morning, thought Mrs. Case, and she said drily, "I always heard you were a great man for the wimmun yourself, Mr. Waller."

Mr. Waller recovered himself, smiled deprecatingly, and looked down at Mrs. Case softly-like. "I know . . . I know . . ." he acknowledged reflectively, "but it's a *lovely* pastime. . . ."

There was a pause.

"Coss money," said Mrs. Case coolly. She was about to seize an advantage.

"Sure, Mrs. Case, sure. But the best things in this world come high. You gotta pay. You gotta pay," said Mr. Waller smugly.

Mrs. Case came quickly then to the point. "If you gotta pay, what about Lilly?" she said.

"Yair, what about Lilly. . . ." said Mr. Waller. "If I could find a nice lady, if I could find a real nice lady like you, Mrs. Case, to take Lilly, I'd pay reasonable and I'd pay regular. . . ." His eyes embraced Mrs. Case who was not impressed.

Mrs. Case thought It isn't just the money, and it is the money too. I can't seem to get near Lilly, not to know her, but what can she do, pore kid? He's just a great big nasty masher and a lady-killer and no kind of a pa for her at all and she's got no folks and I guess I better keep her. So she said, "If you'll send me twenty dollars the first of every month regular, I'll board her and dress her if she's a real good girl. But if Lilly starts giving me trouble or staying out late o' nights or going with bad company, you can take her right back or I'll send her to the Salvation Army. . . ."

"You're a good woman," said Mr. Waller brokenly but relieved. "It's a real Christian act," he said, seizing her hand (Is*zat* so, thought Mrs. Case) and pressing it warmly. "You'll get the money regular. Bless you for a good woman, Mrs. Case."

Mrs. Case received the money from Mr. Waller for several months, but before he was killed by the snapping of a steel cable at the lumber camp five years later Lilly had begun to give trouble, and to stay out late at nights, and to go with bad company. And when for the second time she had stayed out all night, she did not return, for

L

she knew that the door would be closed against her. And now she was alone except for the bad company she kept. No one had loved her, and she did not even know that she had missed love. She was not bitter, nor cruel, nor was she very bad. She was like the little yellow cat, no worse and no better. She expected nothing. She took things as they came, living where she could, on whom she could, and with whom she could, working only when she had to, protecting herself by lies or by truth, and always keeping on the weather side of the police.

She had taken and lost or left several jobs before she went to work at Lam Sing's place just off Shanghai Alley. There it was that she saw and coveted a beautiful English bicycle which seemed to be owned by the Chinaman named Yow, and so it was that Lilly found herself running, running in the dark with everything forgotten but the need to escape.

III

When Lilly heard the cries and commotion in the dark garden, she crouched, turned, and ran.

Running, stopping, running again down the dark lanes and alleys, and walking, tense and with quickly beating heart across the lighter streets, she hunted wildly within herself, doubling and twisting, for some means of getting away at once from the unexpected terror which had only a few minutes ago sprung at her and entangled her. She did not need anyone to tell her that her presents from Yow had been stolen and that she was wearing stolen goods at that moment. She knew it instinctively from the clamour at the box-room door and she feared everything for herself. She feared only for herself. She gave Yow no thought at all, save for the terror that he might set the police on her. When she reached the house where she lived, she hurried stealthily up the stairs to her room and collected with trembling fingers all the delicate garments that she prized so much and that she had owned for so short a time. She undressed hastily and dressed again in her own old clothes. Then, hardening her heart against the beauty and feel of silk and lace and muslin, she made up tight parcels of the garments which even now the bride was lamenting with tears and the groom with fury. She pinned the bundles as firmly as she could— she had no string and dared not look for any. She dared not make the parcels conspicuously large. She dared not take them all away at once ("the police") . . . ("*What have you got there?*") . . . the shadows in her room seemed to breathe and close in upon her ("the police") . . . as she crammed the stolen goods into the scanty newspaper she started at a sound in the street ("the police") . . . there was a creak on the stair (listen! . . . nothing, nothing) . . . and Lilly, breathing quickly, moving fast, felt and smelt the Police Station again in the very room. She opened each ramshackle drawer again and explored each corner. The room was clear. Not a trace. Now, if she could dispose of these bundles before the police should find her, she was safe. Safer still if she could get away.

Lilly turned down the gas, picked up two of the parcels, and crept down the stairs. She looked this way and that. There was no one in the streets. She walked quickly across Powell Street and then through a dark lane to a black stretch of vacant land which she traversed feeling her way in the darkness with her feet until she came to where she knew that there was a tangle of bramble and brush. She threw the parcels as far as she could into the thicket. Then she made her way back to her room, fearing with almost a stoppage of her wild heart that the police would be waiting for her there. If the Chinaman had not yet told her name, perhaps she was for a while safe. The police were not there. The gas still burned low in the room as she had left it. She picked up the two remaining bundles and looked quickly round the room Nothing remained now but the poor stuff that was her own. The room showed her to be innocent. The Chinaman— if he told—would have lied. She cared nothing for him. Ignorant girl, she thought of no other witnesses; she did not think of Yow's cronies, who knew each the other's business. She crept again down the stairs and stole out in the direction of the waterfront. She had thought that she would throw these bundles into the sea because the night which was not yet day was still darkish and no one would see her. But when she reached the waterfront she saw the small fishboats moored at the wharves and on the water. She knew that boats have eyes and ears and that a splash might betray her. Lilly's fear was stretched to any height of cunning and of self-protection. She thought quickly, turned and slipped back towards the little waterfront chapel on Water Street. She pushed the bundles under the crazy steps of the chapel. Then she stood up, drew a long breath, looked round about her like one hunted, and forced herself not to run but to walk home. Stopping at a sound, hiding once in an alley, she was sure that she was not observed from the street, for she saw no one. She climbed her stairs with her naturally light tread made lighter by fear. All was as she had left it. She was used to flitting. She must go. But she knew that if she went away owing money to her landlord she might be pursued and still would not be safe.

She took pencil and a bit of paper and with easy deception she wrote:

> "Dear Mr. Hocks they was a man came and said to go to my grampa in New Westminister hes sick and to meet him on Westminister Ave corner Pender and he take me in his buggy. I don't just know when Ill be back but I gess soon. Heres the rent
> > And oblidge
> > Lilly Waller."

She picked the money out of her purse, packed her poor things in her cheap valise and strapped it.

She put letter and money in an envelope, placed the envelope upon the dresser, gave a quick look round the room, and, the day now being reasonably light, left the house, carrying her valise. Lilly had never before taken a journey, alone or accompanied. Frightened and watchful as she was and aware of many fresh apprehensions, she bought a ticket to Nanaimo and then her money was nearly gone. No one seemed to notice this astounding and unprecedented deed. Lilly was just a tall pale innocent-eyed girl buying a ticket and walking onto the Nanaimo boat amongst all the other passengers.

She found a chair, pulled it to a secluded place and sat down with her valise close beside her. Not until the boat pulled out did Lilly's strung nerves relax in a fatigue that was physically painful. Dazed now by the night's quick events and with the unaccustomed freedom of sea and motion, she fell asleep.

When she awoke, the ship had reached the more land-locked approaches to Nanaimo and through her unaccustomed exhaustion there spread a new feeling of something light and oblivious, the consolation of sea and wind and strange wooded shores. She went to the ship's rail and gave herself up to the wind that whipped her face and to the slapping and curling of the water against the side of the ship, looking around her and feeling sorry now that she had slept throughout the journey. Lilly had never in her young animal life looked below the surface of things as they occurred, nor had she looked within herself. She was not accustomed to plan; she had gone unresistingly with things as they arrived to her. Now, a little triumphant but still wary, she experienced an unfamiliar instinct to plan her future. When the boat

docked just below the old tower, Lilly walked ashore with
the other passengers. She did not know whether Nanaimo
was larger or smaller than Vancouver, and she did not
know that it was a mining town. It was only a name.
She easily found what appeared to be the small main
street. She walked slowly, carrying her valise, down one
side of the street and up the other. She explored a little
the side streets. Then, satisfied, she walked quickly to a
small café, went in, sat down and ordered breakfast.

She ate her breakfast slowly, observing the proprietor
and the waitresses. Then, when she had finished and paid
for her meal, she went to the proprietor and, with a
timidity that was suddenly real, she asked him for a job.

The man looked Lilly up and down. He approved her
carriage, her stillness, and her soft brown eyes.

"Had any experience?" he asked.

"Two years, on the prairies," said Lilly.

"Willing to work four to twelve?"

Lilly nodded. "Sure," she said, "any shift you say."

"What's your name?"

"May Bates," said Lilly.

"Married?"

Lilly shook her head.

"Know any folks here?"

Again Lilly shook her head. "Just come in from the
prairie right now, this morning," she said.

"All right, you come along at four and we'll see how you
make out. Five dollars a week one meal a day and tips."

Four nights later Lilly went home with a dark Welsh
miner called Ranny Griffiths. It seemed the easiest thing
to do.

IV

THE year that Lilly lived with Ranny and worked in the restaurant was her first year of comparative stability. She did not much care for Ranny; he cared for her a little but he cared more for comfort; her life with him was a convenience to both of them. Neither of them thought of it as permanent, yet neither thought of bringing it to a sudden stop. Three months before Lilly left him, even before the birth of the child, she had wanted to go; but the habit of precaution which could in a moment turn to fear kept her, for the time, in what seemed to her to be something like security. On the Welshman's part there was no desire to hold Lilly. He would have broken with her at the first sign of possessiveness, child or no; and the time was coming when he would break with her, and be rid of her, before his wife should leave Swansea and join him in Nanaimo. But Lilly's very indifference and biddableness made him put off from week to week the rupture that must come. Because he liked Lilly well enough, and, later, because his decency would be shamed and uncomfortable if he left her at that time, Ranny let things be.

It seemed, now, as if new elements in Lilly, the drifter, came into being, or, perhaps, coalesced and formed a purpose. As the birth of the baby came nearer, Lilly's habitual wariness, which included a keeping of herself to herself, made her watchful of habits and appearances. With the emergence from unawareness there came, gradually,

an ambition, not for reinstatement, but for instatement.
In the crude alembic of Lilly's being, there was set up
some clumsy distillation. She would be respectable.
She did not use the word "respectable" in the discussions which she had begun to hold with herself, but the
feeling for respectability and the desire to be "like folks"
flickered and then grew strong within her. She became
thrifty. She grew mean. She who had been used to
spend her last cent on what she wanted, now scrimped
and hoarded. She knew that she would leave Ranny
after the birth of the child, but she did not intend to
leave him without money in her pocket. She would
demand a reasonable sum when she left, and Ranny
would give it, for he would be glad to be rid of her. She
deceived Ranny when necessary. She bought carefully,
and lied about the price of food. She kept the place neat,
she cooked tasty and economical suppers, watching and
improving on the cooking of the Chinese cooks in the
restaurant. Ranny had no complaints; he had never
before been so comfortable. Day after day slipped away,
and week after week, month after month. Lilly worked
at the restaurant as long as she could, saving her pay,
saving her tips, changing silver into bills, changing small
bills into large, keeping her money in a stocking which
was the only suitable place she had ever heard of. She
thought sometimes of the Bank, but, through habit, she
trusted no one. If I go to that Bank, she thought, and
tell them I want them to keep my money, the man will
ask me questions, all kinds of things, and I'll get into
Trouble; maybe I'd never get my money out, or maybe
if I wanted to flit, I couldn't get it out quick. So she
kept her bills in the stocking.

Sometimes, when Ranny gave her money for house-keeping and seemed churlish (thinking of his wife's passage and becoming restive), Lilly was tricky. She would lie about her wages (her brown eyes soft and childish); she would buy a thick steak with her own money; she would make a treat, "*my* treat"; she would, indirectly, make Ranny aware that she was not spending his money on the coming baby; she would make Ranny very comfortable; she would demand nothing from him; she managed him well, and he fell again to being contented, and Lilly put away another dollar or two.

She had not long been in Nanaimo before changes induced by this spiritual chemistry acting mysteriously through trivial happenings and her own inner physical change and need made her at first dimly conscious of the world within and beyond her; and later, cognizant of and dissatisfied with herself as a person. Ranny had nothing to do with it. Ranny was only a kennel into which a homeless worthless bitch crawls away from the rain, and out of which she will crawl, and from which she will go away leaving the kennel empty and forgotten. In the meantime she is dry and warm in this kennel and seems to be safe from whatever it is that she vaguely fears.

She walked down the street one day, this friendless one, and entered the grocer's shop which was occupied at that moment by the grocer and by two superior beings. Lilly closed the door with its cling-clang and stood aside and waited. The grocer continued to draw upon all his flattering attention and displayed it to two young girls who—as if the world with all time and perfection belonged to them, as they truly thought it did—smiled upon him and upon each other, and, laughing, conversed with Mr.

Soal (who was a man as well as the family grocer) in a flattering manner. Without consciously flattering Mr. Soal (for they practised their art almost by nature), they seemed to compliment him and his shop merely by being there, by being young and beautiful, and by having lately returned from school abroad. They talked to Mr. Soal, not about food but about London.

Lilly watched, at first with only a pallid curiosity, and then with new interest and admiration. In the small shops of Vancouver's east end, where Lilly was accustomed to buy her bread and sausages, such beings as these did not appear. She knew, without the passage of the thought, that these were not fancy women. They were something else. They were only girls of her own age, but between Lilly and these two assured young girls who did not need to live with Ranny Griffiths there was a remove as of continents and centuries. It was unbridgeable. It was intrinsic in her life and theirs that they were different beings. The girls were vivacious but not noisy. Their new sailor hats were tilted upon their shining pompadoured hair. Their cloth Eton jackets and long pleated skirts which all but swept the ground were a kind of disguise which attempted to transform their brilliant youth into maturity. They knew themselves to be beautiful, admired, dressed with mid-morning chic, probably the most important persons in the whole world, and certainly the most important persons in Nanaimo. They accepted this without vainglory but as their due. Lilly could not even understand the language that these young beings spoke, although it was her own.

"Oh, Mr. Soal," said one of the girls whose name seemed to be Eleanor, leaving London suddenly and coming to the matter in hand, "Mother asked me to ask you if you have any more of that Indian chutney. Daddy *adores* it. It simply *makes* a curry."

Indian chutney. Daddy *adores* it. It simply *makes* a curry. What was she talking about? This was a language unknown to Lilly. She stood there silent, aware of the girls as completely as they were oblivious of her, worlds apart across the grocer's store. She did not envy them exactly, but she was conscious of something bright and sure which these girls had and which she had not. She could not see what it was, nor touch it; but it was bright and sure, bright and sure. Lilly suddenly felt cheap and dusty.

Eleanor smiled engagingly at Mr. Soal. (I do believe she'd even practise on Old Soal, thought her cousin indulgently.) They said goodbye. Mr. Soal hastened to the door and opened it, bestowing his affable benedictions upon them. He had known their mothers for twenty years. Their bills were large and their credit was very good. He closed the door and returned to business. He seemed, now, to see the hitherto invisible Lilly. "And what can I do for you?" he asked in a modified manner.

Nothing, Lilly thought, can touch or hurt these two. No Trouble can come near them. Yet was she not wrong? Their smiles, their charms, London and Paris, could not protect them.

And now Lilly as she did her accustomed shopping watched for those two secure girls. She watched for their mothers and their friends. They shopped only in the morning, it appeared. And what did they do with the rest of the twenty-four hours (which was also Lilly's twenty-four hours) in that bright exciting world in which

166

they kept themselves? In a fumbling way she wanted
to become not so different from those bright and sure
ones. She did not know what to do. She observed them.
Oh, she thought, I could never talk like they talk and
look like they do, and she did not try; but still she
observed them and became dissatisfied with Lilly Waller.

As time advanced and Lilly's condition became more
apparent, her growing desire for this respectability made
her now compare herself, as never before, with the young
wives of the miners whom she saw—Mrs. Davies, Mrs.
Hughes, Mrs. Jones. She saw these young wives doing
their household shopping by day and sauntering through
the garishly lit street in the evening, hanging upon their
husbands' arms with a kind of proud and weary satisfaction. Lilly never appeared with Ranny now, and she
showed herself upon the street as little as she could. She
bought carefully and, staying at home, she sewed. She
did not want Ranny to marry her. She did not want a
husband but she longed—and by this time she longed
passionately—for respectability. She had never yet in
her life looked forward far into time. Now for the first
time she looked forward and she schemed. She did not
yet think often about her baby—that consuming passion
for her child came later. But the passion was being
prepared each time that Lilly saw a young wife wheeling
a perambulator whose respectability seemed now to have
an absorbing significance to Lilly. She began to lay her
plans with care. As soon as she was able she would take
the baby away from Nanaimo. She would go up-country
or up-island. She would take a position of complete
respectability. She would become a new person. Day

by day she studied the newspapers. With her finger on her pale mouth Lilly pondered names and a name. She chose. She would become Mrs. Hughes . . . Mrs. Evan Hughes . . . Mrs. Will Hughes . . . Mrs. Walter Hughes . . . Mrs. Walter Hughes. . . . She savoured that name. It was a good name. But she loitered over the names for days. Then suddenly and without doubt she knew her name. It was hers and she seized it. I'd best get used to it by myself, she thought. She would become Mrs. Walter Hughes. In her pictures of the future, as she sat sewing, she saw Mrs. Walter Hughes with her baby, at first unknown, then known, established and secure in some other place. As the child moved within her, Lilly lived two lives. She lived the physical life which rapidly advancing and changing days and nights brought with them; but, within, she lived the important life of Mrs. Walter Hughes who had by this time become the widow of Walter Hughes, as yet a shadowy figure.

She read, daily, as she rocked, the advertisements. Suffering cruelly, she forced herself to buy a wedding ring. She had no one to help her except Mrs. Walter Hughes, widow of Walter Hughes. She dared not write to any friend in Vancouver. She had no friend in Vancouver. She had no friend anywhere in the world except Mrs. Walter Hughes. She trusted no one and was quite alone. She at last forced herself to enter a pawnbroker's shop. She wandered about the shop, looking, feeling, trying. She saw some rings. She fingered them. "Looking for a ring?" asked the pawnbroker.

"I lost my ring and I don't like to tell my husband," said Lilly. She saw, or thought she saw, that the man smiled. The colour flowed under the creamy pallor of her skin.

"How's this?" asked the pawnbroker.

Lilly tried it. "I'll take it," she said quickly. "How much?"

The man charged her too much. She paid without question. She went home and put the wedding ring into the stocking where her money was. Mrs. Walter Hughes was now prepared; she was coming into being, and the pallid figure of Lilly Waller was receding into some part of Lilly's mind which Mrs. Walter Hughes will forget, if she is wise and lucky. And as Lilly Waller—so trivial, so worthless—recedes and vanishes like impalpable mist, there emerges another being, shadowy yet, whose memory is now evoked by Mrs. Walter Hughes. In the shadow is the respectable man whose widow she is; there is the supporting shade of Mr. Walter Hughes who, as Lilly sits and sews, takes handsome shape. She admires him. He belongs somewhere midway between her world and the world of Mr. Soal's best customers. He is respectable. The dead but newly created Mr. Hughes is now Lilly's protector, and before the dreadful day when Ranny was at the pit and she had to make her way alone to the hospital, Mr. Hughes was well known to her.

All this Lilly did alone with planned duplicity and in ruthless self-defence. She did it in the solitude and courage and emptiness and experience and inexperience of her tricky mind. Well, a girl's gotta live, hasn't she? What I mean is, a girl's gotta live. If you don't help yourself. . . . I guess I gotta right to be like folks. My kid's gotta right to have a chance hasn't he. He's got his rights like any other kid.

V

BEFORE the latter part of the last century, the well-wooded
and watered area on Vancouver Island known as Comox
was inhabited by the Comox Indians. Since then the
white man has come, and there have been wars in the
distant world which have, a little, fretted the peace of
Comox. Navy and Air Force have visited these shores,
and changed them. But when Lilly arrived at Comox
in the guise of Mrs. Walter Hughes, wearing her innocent
black and carrying in her arms her pretty baby, the
small village lay hidden and scattered along the green
and wooded contours of land that slope down to the Salt
Chuck—to the sea. The village of Comox looked down
on the estuary of the Courtenay River, and across at the
forests, and out towards the ocean where curved the sand-
spit. Into the estuary swarmed the great spring salmon
that fought their way in their thousands up the Courtenay River. Afterwards, Lilly remembered—but not
often—that in the grey of cold dawnings she had gone
with Major Butler in his rowboat. He had rowed out
into the estuary, and then Lilly had taken the oars, so
that he could fish. She had seen dimly under the slaty
sky of dawn the great forms of the salmon breaking the
surface of the slaty sea. How cold it was at dawn. How
hard she pulled on the oars against the slapping waves.
And she remembered how the indolence of Major Butler
had changed to a keenness; and how at last a fish had

struck and the reel had screamed and the line had run out, and Lilly, cursed at and rowing hard, had worked until at last Major Butler landed the fighting forty-pounder and turned to Lilly proud and beaming, ill-temper forgotten, demanding praise.

And Lilly's little daughter Eleanor Hughes remembered Comox, years afterwards, as the place where, slipping away from her mother and following a little path that led among long grasses and then through a belt of trees, she came to an open sunlit space. And there, in the middle of the silent open glade sat a great cat with beards on his chin and a strong tuft of hair on the end of each of his ears. He sat proudly in the sun, owning the world. The animal's large lambent eyes, each slitted with black, gazed into the forest. Then the eyes closed and the cat opened its mouth wide in a silent cry. The little child stepped out into the sunny glade, her arms by her side and her fingers spread. She stumbled and looked down. She looked up, and the great cat had gone. She had not heard him go, but the glade was empty.

And Mrs. Butler remembered Comox as the place where she had found peace at last (she thought), until Maurice got restless again and they moved on. And she always remembered the strange girl who gave her so much comfort, Mrs. Hughes who came with her baby, and, years later, went away as strangely as she had come.

And Maurice, her husband, remembered the lazy days, and the early mornings when sea and sky were mottled with the same slate colour and dawn crept up and changed the sea and sky, and in the cold dawning he plied up and down, up and down, and sometimes he won, and sometimes he came back with nothing. And he remembered

the summer days when he rowed about and about the
sand-spit, and when he tried for cohoe nearer the shore.
But a man like Maurice Butler cannot always fish and
garden, fish and garden, and he became restless, and that
—what was her name?—Hughes—girl sometimes irked
him. And then she went away and took the little girl with
her. And the memories of Comox lying green and golden
to the sunshine at the end of the trail, sloping down to the
shore, came, but not often, to all these people who lived
there and are there no longer.

As Lilly for the first time jogged along the country road
that wound from Courtenay to Comox, following what was
at that time a beautiful dead end in the green of the countryside and in Lilly's life a fair dead end where she and Baby
would for some time be secure, she was more aware of the
agitation within her than she was of the green beauty of
the unfamiliar fields that bordered the dusty road. Mr.
Meeker drove her in his buggy that had a contraption
behind the buggy seat for carrying his bread for delivery to
the Comox store. When it was known in Courtenay that
there was a young woman with a baby, and that she wanted
to drive out to Butlers' place, people surmised that she was
going to enquire for the position of Butlers' Esther who had
to go back to Scotland to be with her folks because her pa
was sick. Mr. Meeker of Meeker Bros. Bakers and
Confectioners was very willing to drive Lilly. Mr. Meeker
was very willing indeed, because he was a male gossip and
busybody, and the unofficial discoverer and greeter and
reporter of any newcomer arriving in Courtenay. And so
Mr. Meeker questioned Lilly, and Lilly, mistrustful as the
yellow alley cat, mistrustful as Lilly Waller who feared the
police, mistrustful as Mrs. Walter Hughes, a poor young

widow alone in the world, planned, and observed her
usual reticence, answering with care.

She held the baby at her breast, and looked either
straight ahead of her or down upon the child. Mr. Meeker
enjoyed jogging along the Comox road in the sunshine
with this slim quiet girl dressed in black sitting beside
him.

"You said you was going to Butlers' place?"

"Yes. Please," said Lilly.

"D'you know Butlers?"

"No. I never seen them."

"You know they're losing that Esther of theirs, then.
She's a good girl and a fine worker, Esther. Too bad she's
gotta go back to Glasgow and look after her pa he's sick.
She hates to go back and she sure hates leaving Mrs.
Butler. She thinks there's no one can look after Mrs.
Butler but her."

"Is Mrs. Butler nice to work for?"

"Sure, Mrs. Butler's real nice, she's a lady she is. The
Major's a nice fella, crazy about fishing, quite a bit
younger'n her. She's one of those people all the time
readin' in books. They're English, that's why they're like
that. Crazy about gardening, the both of them."

"Would it be a nice place for Baby?" asked Lilly
diffidently. Since Baby had been separated from her body,
she was more than ever a part of her. Lilly's whole body
and spirit which had never known a direction, were now
solely directed towards giving Baby everything that Lilly
could give her. Lilly never said to herself, "I want Baby to
have everything I never had." Nothing was relative to the
past. She said, instead, "Baby shall have everything I can
get her. Baby must be like folks." So Lilly must try to be

like folks, too. She must try hard. She knew that there were great gaps in her knowledge, and that in these gaps of inexperience she might fall, taking Baby with her. So she had to be watchful of question and answer.

Of course Lilly would lie (for Baby) if need be (as she had lied her own way along her life), and she would steal for Baby as long as she would not be discovered. She would rather not lie nor steal, because lying and stealing so often mean Trouble, don't they; oh, yes, they often mean Trouble. So Lilly would be so careful, so watchful, so silent, but she would find a place where Baby could grow up like folks. And now that this old man was driving her and was full of curiosity about her, she must answer his questions, because if you say nothing, Lilly knew intuitively, people begin to wonder, don't they. It's best to say something. As Lilly sat upright beside old Mr. Meeker, jogging with the slow rough motion of the buggy, dressed in her innocent black, holding her baby, looking both young and serious—as indeed she was—she prepared her case. The sun shone down on the old horse taking her time and flicking away the flies, on Mr. Meeker avid with curiosity, and on mother and child jogging into Comox.

In the meantime Baby, rocked by the moving buggy, soothed by the monotone of Mr. Meeker's enquiring voice, fanned by soft summer airs, woke and slept, woke and slept, and, waking, looked up at her mother's brown eyes with her own brown eyes half closed, half open, and slept again.

"You belong around here?" asked Mr. Meeker.

"No."

"Thought not. How long you been in these parts?"

"I been in hospital. . . ."

Mr. Meeker looked at Baby. "Oh," he said.

"Well, well. Looks like you'd seen a bit of trouble?"

Lilly nodded, and then she said, "Lost my husband . . . coupla months before Baby was born."

"You *don't* say!" exclaimed Mr. Meeker, who had guessed something like that from Lilly's garb, but wanted to know for sure. "You pore young woman! Kinda young for a widda, ain't you?"

"I'm not as young as I look." Lilly was ready for this one. "Mr. Hughes always said seemed like I'd never grow up, but I guess I will. Trouble ages a person."

"Sure does. Did you say 'Hughes'?" enquired Mr. Meeker. "Your name Hughes?"

"Mrs. Walter Hughes," said Lilly primly. She rocked a bit, patting Baby's little rump.

" 'Mrs. Walter Hughes!' You don't say! Well, well. So you're Mrs. Walter Hughes! Got any folks?"

"Got an older sister back in New Brunswick. Lived with her till I was eighteen and then when we was married Mr. Hughes and me come west."

"B.C.?"

"No, we come to the prairie . . . he . . . we . . . was trying to farm . . . and Mr. Hughes . . . he . . . " Lilly faltered. "It was a horse," she said.

Mr. Meeker, looking sideways, saw tears in Lilly's eyes. He cleared his throat.

"Now, now, don't you think no more about it, a nice young woman like you, you'll get over it. But it sure was tough, ve-ry ve-ry tough." Curiosity got the better of him. "Why'n't you go back to your sister and not come out here getting jobs on your own and you with a baby?"

Lilly swallowed hard, blinked, and said, "My sister and

me aren't good friends any more. I'd be too proud to go
back east. My sister was mad at me marrying so young.
She had six kids and I guess I helped quite a bit in the
house and she figured I ought to of stayed and not get married. But Mr. Hughes he said to heck with them and he was
bound we'd get married and come west and we got
married and my sister was real mad but my brother-in-law
he was kinda sorry for me and he said you go right ahead
and he gave me twenty-five dollars and not to tell my
sister." *There*, thought Lilly, and it was good.

The mare had slowed to a very slow walk. Mr. Meeker
leaned forward, holding loose reins. He nodded agreement
as Lilly talked. "I got a sister like that," he said, "she'd take
the back teeth out of your head she's that mean. Giddap.
Well, I sure hope you get this job. It won't be easy, you
and a baby. But if you get this job you're fixed. There's
not a place like this in the whole district. They're particular, they're particular, and they like things done nice,
but they're fine people, well fixed. Well, I'll set you down
right there, at the white gate. I wish you luck, I'm sure.
You come right over to the store when you're through and
wait around for a lift back."

Lilly got down from the buggy and stood holding Baby
and looking up at Mr. Meeker.

"You've been real kind," she said timidly. She did not
know how to thank him.

"That's all right, that's all right. *Giddap*," said Mr.
Meeker, and drove on to the store where he was able to tell
the company all about young Mrs. Walter Hughes who had
buried her husband who was killed by a horse in Saskatchewan and was going to work at Butlers' and how she
was a quiet-spoken young woman and all broke up about

176

her husband so recent and wasn't she wrapped up in that baby, he sure hoped she got the job and that Butler wouldn't bother her none. The talk in the store then resumed the endless discussion of how much older Mrs. Butler was than Major Butler; what was they doing in China anyway; Major Butler was in the Customs, why then he wasn't no soldier; he was in the Boxer troubles, but he didn't look like no boxer, too skinny; he was head of the Chinese army, they musta kicked him out; he was in the British Ambassador's office, well, he might be at that; seemed a nice fella; well, they minded their business and paid their bills; kinda funny coming way off here, maybe they wasn't married anyways. Discussions like this were pleasant in the long winter evenings and in the long summer evenings too and had the merit that they went on and on and never arrived.

Lilly, holding Baby firmly in the bend of her left arm, looked at the square white house covered with vines of which she did not know the name and banked with flowers which she had never before seen, and then she walked in at the gate, up the path, and rang the bell. The door was soon opened by a woman who, Lilly felt, was a commander, but not, she thought, the commander of the house whom she had come to see. The woman was fresh-faced, with an open expression which clouded when she saw Baby. She wore a black dress and a small white apron. As she continued to look at Baby her face hardened. Lilly was alarmed, and looked at the woman with the soft and touching look which had become habitual to her.

"Please, I've come to see Mrs. Butler about the place," she said.

"Come in," said the woman gloomily. She preceded

Lilly into a hall, opened the door of a room, and said, "Wait there. I will tell Madam."

Lilly stepped into the room and her lips were moving. Madam, they said silently. Madam. Madam. The labials made no sound. She looked round her at a room which seemed to her at that moment like a pool of mellow light into which she and Baby had arrived. She ventured to sit down on a high dark chair and arranged Baby against her soft breast.

Above the mantelpiece of a neat open grate in which no fire burned was a large mirror framed in gilt. Lilly looked wonderingly at this. Towards one end of the mantelpiece were two ancient pieces of Chinese pottery, a hound and a horse. The melancholy hound, of a fair Chinese yellow glaze, held his head lifted as if listening for centuries for a master who did not come. Each elegant rib showed finely below the skin. The blue horse, standing beside the yellow hound, grazed peacefully forever where no grass grew, upon the shining mantelpiece. The hound and the horse were reflected in the shining mirror which held the room as in a picture. Two hounds and two horses. Soft broken light lay on the walls and on the dark shining floor. Everywhere was light or a dark shine. Light and shade falling through large vine leaves moving outside the window made moving pools of light and shade in this yellow room. Lilly's gaze returned to the hound and the horse, creatures detached from ordinary living, motionless yet somehow aware, in a world of their own. I'd be scared to touch them, she thought, I'd be scared to dust them. She heard voices.

One voice was low and broke only occasionally upon a voice raised, distressed and a little angry. Lilly got up quickly and went to the partly opened door. Baby made fretty resentful sounds. "Sh sh then," said Lilly, patting, and listened.

"And me looking after you all these years, Madam, and leaving you with a young woman *with* a baby! You and the Major have no call to start having a baby in the house, Madam." *Madam*, murmured Lilly, listening.

The soft voice spoke but Lilly could distinguish no words.

The agitated voice broke almost into a wail. "I'd never have an easy minute, Madam, leaving you with a young woman with a baby. I'd as lief not go home and let Dad go hang as leave you like this! And how do you know she's respectable?"

There was a low laugh, and the owner of the quiet voice must have risen and moved near the door, for Lilly heard the words, "Now, Esther, Esther, you must trust me not to do anything silly. I must see the girl. No . . . I won't promise not to . . . now, *Esther!* . . ." and from the other voice "Oh, *Madam!*"

Madam. Lilly's lips moved, and she slipped back to her chair. The door opened. A woman came in, and Lilly rose to her feet.

Mrs. Butler always remembered Lilly as she first saw her, standing in the mellow light of the Chinese room, this tall fair girl in black with the primness of small white edging at her neck, and the widowhood of a short black veil from her black sailor hat, with the wide black sleeves of her blouse, with the taffy-coloured hair brushed high and neat under the hat, with her youth, with her creamy pallor, with her brown eyes soft with shyness, her agreeable snub nose, and her baby folded in a white shawl against her breast. Mrs. Butler melted from her prepared position of a lady about to interview a domestic to the warmth of a woman seeing before her a young widow with her child. "Sit down," she said, and smiled.

"Thank you, Madam," said Lilly. She heard herself say the word with great surprise. It was not difficult. *Madam.* She felt, rather than knew, that this word was a strong weapon that she would use to win this house from Esther for Baby.

"Let me see your baby," said Mrs. Butler and, coming close, moved the lacy shawl from the little face. The two women looked down at the sleeping face of Baby, at the dark lashes against the soft cheeks, at the infinite age-old marvel of the sleeping infant. They raised their eyes, looked at each other above the sleeping child, and smiled in their wisdom.

Lilly saw a woman of middle size, slight, with iron grey hair. She's ugly, thought Lilly as she looked shyly at the long and rather horse-like and bony face that is sometimes the curious beauty of an Englishwoman. No, she's not ugly, the girl thought again, she's different to me. She looks kinda nice. Yes. I want to be here. I want Baby to be near her. We gotta be here. Safe. Madam. I'll *make* her. I'll fight for this job. I'll beat that Esther. We're going to stay right here. I'm not going to take Baby to no dump and people talking talking. Madam.

"Are you . . . a widow?" asked Mrs. Butler gently in that voice whose quietness was unfamiliar to Lilly.

Lilly nodded. (How like a child she is, thought the older woman.) "Mr. Hughes . . . he was kicked . . . it was a horse . . . he died . . . a coupla months before Baby was born . . . at the ranch . . . and I couldn't stick it there . . .

180

we was way off out of town and no neighbours . . . and I come west . . . I couldn't stay there any more." Lilly blinked wet lashes.

"Have you no relatives?" asked Mrs. Butler very gently.

"I got a sister back east," said Lilly, looking down and then up at Mrs. Butler with the full impact of her innocence, "but," shaking her head, "I wouldn't go back to her . . . she never liked me marrying Mr. Hughes . . . she never liked him . . . and when she didn't like Mr. Hughes, and him . . . gone . . . I couldn't go back to her."

How true, how true, how sad, thought Mrs. Butler, looking with compassion at the girl.

"But I can work, Madam, and I'm good and healthy," said Lilly earnestly, "I can cook and wait on table and I guess I can clean house if you tell me how . . . Anything you tell me, I'll do. Madam, give Baby and me a chance! I want Baby to live here. She hasn't got no folks, and I want to bring her up the way Mr. Hughes would like . . . he was better than me, and his folks was better than me, and I wouldn't want to go to his folks because . . ." Lilly looked quickly around the room, at the mirror, at the yellow hound forever listening, at the blue horse forever feeding, at the curtains of strange yellow stuff, at the dark unfamiliar furniture, and back to Mrs. Butler.

"I don't want Baby to grow up common like me, Madam. I want her to grow up like Mr. Hughes's folks!" Mrs. Butler looked at the wily Lilly. How incredibly naïve the girl is, she thought. How simple.

"If you'll try us, Madam, Baby and me will do our best," said Lilly humbly, "and Baby isn't any trouble, she's not a cryer, and you'd never be bothered by her. You'll never hear her, Madam." And then Lilly did a very disarming thing. What with the two large tears, real enough, that trembled on her lower lids, and then rolled slowly down her cheeks, her little nose felt damp. She sniffed, and slowly wiping the agreeable snub with the back of her hand, she looked earnestly over the back of her hand at Mrs. Butler, like any child, and the thing was done.

And, said Mrs. Butler to herself, she calls me Madam, how strange! And to think that I haven't asked for references, or spoken of wages, but because she says Madam, and wiped her nose like that, and loves her baby, and is a widow, and wants to come, I know I'm going to take her. And I'll have to fight Esther . . . and Maurice too.

"That's a promise?" she said out loud, looking kindly but with authority at Lilly. "You can do the work, and the baby *won't* take too much of your time, and *won't* disturb us? What time off do you want?"

"Oh, I don't want time off, Madam, not while Baby's little. I can take her in the garden . . . or anywhere . . . on fine days when convenient . . . I want to stay right here, I don't want to go away, not while Baby's little."

I'll be safe here, thought Lilly. If I start going into Courtenay there's sure someone going to know me some day and then Baby's chances'd be done. I gotta keep away from people and stay right here oh for ever so long. I don't want no time off.

"What would you like me to call you?" asked Mrs. Butler.

"To call me?" said Lilly wonderingly. "Oh, just my name, just Mrs. Hughes, Madam. Walter . . . Mr. Hughes . . . wouldn't like anything else, I don't fancy."

Walter Hughes, Mr. Walter Hughes, what would Lilly do without you? In life you were nothing, not even a shade. In death you are the strong support of Lilly Waller and her pretty baby.

Later in the afternoon Mrs. Butler ended her description of her interview with Lilly by saying "—so, Maurice, I took her."

And Major Butler said, "So from now on we have to have a baby in this house because her mother hasn't got a handkerchief and blows her nose by hand," and grumbled accordingly.

His wife laughed. "All right, put it that way if you like."

"I didn't know before this that you liked babies!"

"Well . . . not collectively . . ."

But, four years later, Baby, who was now Eleanor, and a grave pretty child, had become the pet of Major Butler and trotted round the garden after him as he puttered about, or sat quiet in the boat while Major Butler pulled slowly on the oars. And she was the pet of the big dog and of the little dog. And she was the pet of Mrs. Butler who had nothing to occupy her but books, and flowers, and a little ill-health. And Eleanor was dressed in little smocked dresses ordered by Mrs. Butler from a place called Liberty's in London. And Lilly blended with her worship of the child a good deal of shrewdness and hardness, keeping Eleanor well in hand.

"Don't take Eleanor away, Mrs. Hughes, she's not bothering me."

"Oh no, Madam, she's been with you long enough. Come, Eleanor." And the grave little girl would go.

And Eleanor was growing up in a happy world of ordered calm and pleasure, and knew no other. Her mother told her sometimes about her father, tall and fine, who had been killed long ago by a kick from a horse. "Was it Farver's horse?" "Yes, Father had a lot of horses." "More horses than Major Buckler?" "Yes, more horses than Major Butler."

And now Walter Hughes, established firmly as almost a memory in the little daughter's mind, faded, and faded. There seemed no further need of him at present. He remained established in the past but the past was over. Lilly lived only in the long peaceful present and in her child's future. Walter Hughes' work was done and he might go. Lilly did not exactly discard him, but because she had never known faith in the living or the dead, Mr. Walter Hughes, no longer of any particular use, faded out, out, out, until he might some day be needed again.

VI

BY THE time Eleanor was six years old she had three gods and her mother. Her mother was not a god, she was simply an extension of herself. She had a slave, and she had a companion who refused to be owned and could not be coerced—the cat. Eleanor's gods were Major and Mrs. Butler and Leo, the big dog. As Leo sat upon his haunches looking majestically round him, Eleanor, standing, could look into his face, caressing his ears, and Leo suffered her. Her slave was a nondescript faithful little black and tan dog who could be dressed in doll's capes and hats, and would sit, miserably, in the doll's pram that Mrs. Butler had given to Eleanor. There was the shining house with books and pictures and stories and a yellow Chinese dog and a horse that must not be touched. There was the garden with grass and trees and flower beds and a vegetable garden and raspberry canes and gooseberry bushes that hid her as she stood. And there was Major Butler squatting down on the soil, planting and thinning, or reaching up to cut and prune, all in slow time in grey weather or sun, always with a pipe in his mouth, and nearly always with Leo and Eleanor and the little dog somewhere near, very busy about their immediate concerns, until Eleanor's mother would call her, and her world would change into being washed and sitting up at the kitchen table and eating her lunch like a good girl. And there was the sea, and the shore that she and her mother sat upon while the two dogs roamed about on their business, and Eleanor soon got up and ran about finding things. And sometimes the haughty cat, friendly for a few minutes, would walk behind them to the beach, and sit upon a log, and survey things, taking into its cat mind what of the meaningless sea and shore, and then would vanish into the meaningful woods and grasses. And there was Major Butler's rowboat, and fishing that was important and she couldn't go if she was going to be a nuisance. And she could be with Mrs. Butler for hours together, playing beside her on the floor, or listening to stories. But Major Butler was her number one god. There were other people who touched the rim of her world. There was Mr. Meeker who knew her when she was a baby, and drove into the store three or four times a week, and there were the people in the store, and there were visitors (but then her mother kept her in the kitchen beside her), and there was church sometimes when the clergyman came from Courtenay, and there were cobwebs in the church, such cobwebs, till her mother and the lady in the store gave it a good cleaning. And as Eleanor grew up into this life of happy order, her mother who had been Lilly Waller, grew into it too. And there was the sand spit, and on the sand spit the little cemetery where Eleanor loved to play. Among the blowing grasses eternally blowing on the spit were the small headstones, some straight, some leaning this way and that, and on the headstones were the names of Fan—a dog, or Tom—a cat, or Butty—a goat, or Poll —a parrot who lived to a ripe old age, said the headstone. And all these little animals and birds that lay buried with ceremony and remembrance upon the Comox sand spit had been pets or mascots of British men-of-war that had come up from the naval station at Esquimalt for target practice. Or at least, the little headstones commemorated some little animal who had died at sea—"Nigger the best cat the Warspite ever had". There were great names of ships and little names of animal pets loved by the seamen. Here lay a tortoise—or the name of a tortoise "lost at sea". Lilly would spell out the names—sometimes fading —of cat and dog while Eleanor played among the small headstones, lonely but not desolate, among the waving grasses on the bare spit. It was a pleasant place. And then they would see Major Butler rowing slowly towards the spit, and know that he had finished his cohoe fishing, and they would gather up their things and wait for him. Sometimes Mrs. Butler came too, but not often. And then it was teatime and the day was over, and while her mother got dinner for Major and Mrs. Butler, Eleanor must stay in the bedroom with her picture-books and toys. And by the time that Eleanor was nearly seven years old she had learned to put herself to bed, and often when Lilly's work was done she would go upstairs and find Eleanor asleep with the lost look of childhood—who shall describe it?— her softly curving arms thrown wide, among a litter of dolls. And the next day was like the last.

Lilly, who was matter-of-fact and in whom introspection, poetry, or contemplation had no place, who dusted books but did not read them, would at the end of the day straighten the bed, remove a surplus of toys, undress, go straight to bed, and to sleep. But sometimes even Lilly, looking down on the sleeping Eleanor, would think Can this be my baby? She's a lady, that's what she is. She's not common. She's better than folks, she's like she was Mrs. Butler's kid. I'm not so common neither as

I was. I guess I've learned a bit. Studying to watch and keep quiet, that's what does it. Baby, you're a sweet lovely kid, and you're my kid, and I done it. And Lilly never had to act, now. She lived and worked with no occasion to stand and look at her questioner with soft deceit while two round tears gathered and fell. Some people have flat tears. Lilly's tears were round, dewy and slow, but she never needed them now. Life was nice, full, and steady. She did not have to ask "And what next?" There was enough in the day's work, though never quite enough time, except the lazy times with the child, on the shore, in the boat, on the sand spit, and sometimes, on wet days, in Lilly's own precious room. A room of their own they had, her bed in one corner and Baby's cot in the other, and when the door was shut, and the rain beat on the windows, Lilly rocked and mended, and Baby was busy with her crayons—"Look, Mummy!" Security.

There had been a time when Maurice Butler became aware of Lilly. He saw her for what she was, a girl of no account but possessed by her baby. But because Lilly was young, and moved well and quickly, and because of her creamy skin, and taffy-coloured hair, and brown eyes, and the agreeable snub nose, and her non-observance of him, and some possibility lying waiting in her, his old familiar devil stirred in him. He tested her, to see if she would play. As he stood in the shadow of the passage taking his rod out of its case, Lilly passed and re-passed him. He blocked her a little as if by accident, and the girl stood waiting. He looked at her pleasantly as if considering and said quickly in that lazy voice whose quality was so immensely agreeable, "Do you know, young woman, you're an extremely pretty girl."

There was no answering expression on Lilly's face as she said flatly "That's what Mr. Hughes always used to say." That's done it, she thought, he'll let me be; once I let him start anything, Baby and me are out. Well, I'll be blowed, he thought, is the girl stupid or very clever, and he said heartily, as if continuing, "Yes, a pretty girl and a good cook . . . did you happen to see my landing net?"

"It's there," she said, pointing, and he could not tell whether it was a touch of scorn that he saw on her pale face.

Well, now he had tested her; but the girl was so stupid that he let her alone, irritated with himself that he could be stirred by anything so dull. But Lilly was not dull, and she said to herself The silly fool, what does he take me for? If it had not been for Eleanor she would have accepted his understood invitation, she would have played, she would not have spared Mrs. Butler—human relations were not Lilly's concern—there would have been Trouble, of course, but when Trouble came Lilly would have moved on. But because of Eleanor and security, she would not play, and Maurice Butler, irritated with himself and with the girl, was glad that she was too stupid to see that he had been, for a moment, such a fool, and now he had not lost face in his own house. And Tess was saved the same trouble all over again and what a damned idiot he had been ready to make of himself. Well—forget it. And it was forgotten, and Maurice Butler came to forget that he had ever reached for Lilly in the dark hall and Lilly who made no sign had nearly forgotten too, and Tess Butler had put aside the suspicion that Maurice seemed to be watching Mrs. Hughes—and were they to go through all that again? No, thank God she was wrong.

And life resumed its way, and nothing had happened, and every one was mistaken, and time passed, and Eleanor grew.

One day Eleanor and her mother and the cat's kitten came down to the float where Major Butler was untying the rowboat.

"Want to come?" he asked.

"Oh, Mummy, can I?"

"'May I'," corrected Lilly, echoing from habit Mrs. Butler although she did not know why, for "Can I" seemed good enough. "Yes if . . ."

"Well hurry up both of you and get in," said Major Butler, sitting in the boat and holding on to the float with his hand.

"But I want to take kitty to the sand spit for a treat she's never seen it," said Eleanor.

"All right, Hughesy, let her take it, but you be responsible for the kitten."

"I'll put it like this . . . see! . . . in my little bag," said Lilly, and she put the kitten in the bag and drew the draw-string so that the kitten's head and arms were out of the bag and the rest of her remained well pinioned inside.

"Oh look *look*, Major Butler, *look* at kitty!"

"You get into the boat now . . . *care*ful . . . that's the girl. You go in the bow, Eleanor, and Hughesy, you and the cat go in the stern . . . all set?" and they pushed off, Lilly bareheaded with her fair hair blowing, and Eleanor bareheaded with her two little pigtails and a fuzz of brown hair blowing round her brown face, and Major Butler in his old hat, and the kitten who suddenly stopped struggling and looked this way and that out of the bag with great wisdom.

They rowed slowly over to the sand spit. Lilly and the little girl scrambled ashore and the boat was soon moving off in the distance. On this glorious day the sky seemed higher and wider than usual. The vault was blue and of intense clarity. A large tumble of white cumulus lay motionless near the horizon. Always on the sand spit a breeze blew. Sometimes, when skies were grey and the wind was keen and bitter, the sand spit was desolate and the little headstones added to its abandoned loneliness. But on this fair day of summer the fresh loveliness of the place with a light breeze blowing brought to Lilly one of those perfect moments of time that seem to last forever but do not last forever, and are so fleeting that they make some people afraid.

Lilly lay face downwards on the grass, lifting herself on her elbows and keeping watch on the little girl who ran and stopped among the grasses, gathering sea pinks, and on the kitten who crouched and sprang and played close by—two innocent creatures and Lilly in the wind and the sun. Lilly's glance playing idly over the grasses was caught by a vigorous small movement. A large robin was pull—pull—pulling at some object on the ground. Lilly raised herself a little so as to see what the robin was doing and at the same moment the kitten saw the bird. The robin had found a small garter snake, thin and quick as a whiplash, and with great industry was trying to pick it up and carry it off. The little snake slid, coiled, lashed out, and the robin gathered it together into folds and tried to rise with it. The folds were too big and the snake uncoiled. The robin tried again. And again. And again. Lilly, sitting up now, watched this small battle on the sand spit. The kitten became transformed to a ruthless hunting cat and flattened its belly to the earth, stretching out paw after predatory paw, moving forward towards the robin.

The robin's trying to catch the snake, and the kitten's trying to catch the robin, thought Lilly, and she reached out restraining hands and held the kitten, because she wanted to see what the robin would be able to do. The little garter snake twisted and twisted. It was the only jewelled thing upon the scene. The kitten wriggled free of Lilly and bounded into the grass; it lay there quivering, pointed towards the robin and the snake. Then the kitten resumed its slow predatory crawl, starting and stopping. A dark shadow appeared from the sky. It fell upon Lilly and moved smoothly over the grasses. Lilly looked up quickly at the eagle that circled low above them. The kitten! It sees the kitten! she thought. She scrambled to her feet. Then, shading her eyes she looked almost into the eye of the sun and saw close and plainly the notched blackish wings and wide white tail of the great bald eagle circling low round and round without motion of wings. Eleanor stood among the grasses, looking up. "Oh, Mummy, it's a neagle!" Lilly caught up the kitten and ran and drew Eleanor to her.

The kitten did not see the eagle whose shadow had now twice passed over it. The robin did not see the kitten who had lain quivering from nose to tail not five feet away. The eagle did not see two enemies who now assailed him from the rear. From the sky swooped a gull and from the fir trees on the near shore flew a crow; white bird and black bird, inveterate enemies of the eagle, came to beat him away from their homes and children. Lilly held fast the kitten who lashed its angry tail. At this moment the robin, successfully gathering the snake together in two loops, rose heavily and flew low and away, unaware of kitten or eagle, woman or child. The battle now remained between the two birds and the eagle. The hunt of robin for snake, cat for robin, eagle for cat was over. (Everything after something, thought Lilly.) With harsh cries the white and black birds beat about the great and ancient bird's flanks and tail, manoeuvring quickly. The eagle could not swiftly turn, and continued its majestic soaring at quicker speed. The gull and the crow beat about its tail crying loudly until it seemed to Lilly that the crow was exhausted. It flew to a spindling broken tree while the gull continued the attack. Then the crow returned, followed by more crows from the fir trees, and the seagull flapped away towards the shore, ejaculating from time to time as sea-gulls do. The crows beat violently about the rear of the eagle who retreated, still circling, and became somewhere invisible as eagles do. The crows returned, praising themselves loudly, as crows do. The hunt was over and only the small garter snake had perished. Around and about among the grasses a myriad invisible hunts went on. I wisht another grown-up person had been here to see that, Lilly reflected, still looking into the distance, that was the queerest thing I ever did see in all my life. She felt uneasy . . . seems like everything's cruel, hunting something.

Since the cycle which she had just been watching created little philosophical stir in Lilly beyond this faint uneasiness, she lay down again upon the pleasant softness and scratch of the green and dried grasses and began to think. This is a lovely afternoon, just too good to last, but I do wish to goodness he'd come; we gotta go up to the store, and that roast'll take a good hour and a half and She's gotta have her supper and She'll be wondering. (The first "She" was Eleanor and the second "She" was Mrs. Butler.)

Eleanor now had taken the kitten to the grave of Nigger the best cat. She talked to the kitten who did not listen but continued to play her own little games with something or nothing. It was very strange that Lilly to whom the world of the invisible senses was closed should have given birth to this daughter who, when her day should come, would experience love and friendship and beauty, joy, sorrow and the poetry of experience. On such a day as this and in such a place Eleanor would—some day and days—be aware of the incorporeal presence in air, and light, and dark, and earth, and sea, and sky, and in herself, of something unexpressed and inexpressible, that transcends and heightens ordinary life, and is its complement. Without it, life is uninformed, and life in Lilly was uninformed, without poetry or ecstasy or anguish, with little divination in human relations, yet fortified by her child, and well fortified.

Round a headland came the boat with the oars tranquilly dipping. The boat slowly crossed the bright glistening path of the sun, and beached on the sand. They rowed to the village wharf and went up the wharf to the store, and there Lilly and the child waited while Major Butler talked to the storekeeper. There were strangers there today, visitors, and Mr. Meeker was there, talking, enquiring, and informing them with great pleasure as was his custom. They looked towards Eleanor.

"No," said Mr. Meeker, glad to oblige, "she's not

Butlers' child . . . yes, she does, don't she . . . well, I guess
Mrs. Butler gets all them cute little dresses from England, she's awful good to her, gives her everything . . .
no, she's the maid's child . . . no, she don't look it . . . sure,
that's the maid, Butlers' maid, a good one to work . . .
I nev-er thought . . ." and Mr. Meeker went on expounding what he never thought, and then Major Butler
finished what he was saying and turned to Lilly and the
child who joined him, and they left the store. "We'll
leave the boat for Bill," he said, "and walk home."

While Mr. Meeker gave detailed information to the
strangers in a voice that carried very well, Lilly's face had
remained the impassive face of one who does not hear.
But she heard. Something was set violently in motion
in her mind, and on the way home it became for the first
time blindingly clear that Eleanor was to be always and
in all places, "the maid's child". Sure, I'm a maid, what
of it, she said to herself defiantly; she was Mrs. Hughes,
the Butlers' maid. All right, I'm Butlers' maid. But I'm
Eleanor's mother. And Mr. Meeker's words opened
Lilly's eyes wide. Everything had been very well, very
well indeed, but Eleanor was growing to be a big girl
now, and soon she would be forever just "the maid's
child", and never a home of her own, and never a life
of her own. And with easy ruthlessness Lilly decided
instantly. We're going. We'll pack up. However much
she'll try to keep us, we're going. I'll find somewhere,
and I won't tell her till I know where. I'll read in the
papers, and when I see what I want, we'll go. I'll give
my fortnight else she won't pay me, and then we'll go.
Besides (and she beat up some anger in herself) they act
like she was their child sometimes and I won't stand for

it. And Lilly, who had left the house that afternoon
with her usual equability, and had lain half awake half
asleep upon the sunny grass with never a care in the
world, and had thought that life was perfect, and had
watched the hunt of bird and beast and reptile, came
back to the house alert, alarmed, hunted, and committed to a plan from which she would not turn aside.

Six years of living with the Butlers. Six—no, nearly
seven years of seeing how pleasant life could be for the
Butlers and for their kind of people. Seven years of Lilly
learning. Seven years of Eleanor growing into that life.
Seven years of Eleanor becoming a lady and like folks,
and now a revelation that Eleanor's life would be phony,
she thought, not real. It's a good start for her though,
she reflected, and now goodbye, we're going. I know a
lot more'n I did, and if I'm not a lady, my girl is, and
she's going to be, and I'll have done it. For me, I've just
got to watch and study to be quiet so she'll never be
ashamed. Little girls of six aren't ashamed of their
mothers, she reflected with practical wisdom, but little
girls of twelve can be, and big girls of eighteen can be too.
She mustn't never have any call to be ashamed of me.
We're going. I won't speak now, she thought. I'll get a
hold of yesterday's paper and see what offers, and every
night I'll get a hold of the paper before I put it away and
then I'll kinda know where I'm at. And so it was the same
placid equable Lilly whom Mrs. Butler, standing, watching for them, saw come quickly ahead of Major Butler
and the child, carrying parcels.

"You all right, Madam?" she called, and, smiling,
went to the kitchen, never hurrying, moving always well
and quickly. What should we do without her, thought

Mrs. Butler, I've got to be so lazy I'm almost helpless, and, looking after Lilly, she felt secure.

Lilly laid down her parcels, speeded up the fire, put in the roast, put aside the vegetables and set out Eleanor's tea. While Eleanor ate her tea, Lilly prepared the vegetables. Everything in the kitchen was neat, clean, and in order. Everything in Lilly's mind was neat and in order. Below the surface of her mind which was busy in routine, her new comprehension did not seethe and disturb her. It hardened. When she had served the accustomed dinner, when Eleanor was in bed, Lilly went out for a while into the summer dusk and examined this projected change of scene and life. Then she went upstairs and studied the advertisements for help wanted, from beginning to end. Downstairs Major and Mrs. Butler sat, secure, they thought; making flies for fishing, talking, reading, yawning, and then going to bed. Upstairs Lilly considered once more Mr. Meeker's talk, seeing again plainly all that it implied, and weighing again present security and comfort against Eleanor's future. She returned, confirmed in her decision, to the rattling newspaper. And Eleanor, murmuring sometimes, lay in the innocent abandon of a child's sleep which was the only thing that sometimes seized and tightened Lilly's heart as she looked at her.

VII

THE household went its usual way, and Lilly's purpose matured. At night in her room she pencilled tentative answers to advertisements, licking the pencil stub. She was afraid of making mistakes for she had had no occasion to write letters and did not know what to say. She expressed herself with rather more ease than she would have done seven years ago, and was able to regard her efforts more critically. She picked Mrs. Butler's torn-up correspondence out of the wastepaper baskets and scrutinized the letter-endings. "Yours" . . . "Always your loving . . ." "Yours sincerely" . . . "Respectfully" . . . "truly" . . . "devotedly" . . . Of the contents of the letters she cared nothing, but—as in life—she took what she needed, and left the rest. One night, as Eleanor peacefully slept, and Major and Mrs. Butler sat reading downstairs, unaware that their foundations were crumbling, Lilly wrote with care

"DEAR SIR

"For nearly seven years I have been housekeeper in a big country house with polished floors. I do all the cooking and washing and housework. I am a widow. I have a little girl. I do not need much time off. I am strong. I need good wages so I can save. I have given" (Lilly looked in the dictionary) "satisfaction.

"Respectfully yours
"MRS. WALTER HUGHES."

There, said Lilly, having read it again and again.

. Ten days later she went into the room where Mrs. Butler was sitting. Lilly had a duster in her hand. She took the frail limp duster as her only support, although she needed little support for what she was going to do. She knew what she was going to say to Mrs. Butler, but she did not quite know what she was going to do to her, and she gave that no thought. Performance of a duty well and constantly and with what appears to be affection over a long period of time generates a responsibility and obligation on the part of the server to the served one, and on the part of the served one to the server. Something unique has grown up, they find, between them. They do not observe it until stress or trouble comes, and then the tie is apparent; it is close and perhaps painful, and the obligation one to another is there and can seldom be denied. But Lilly was immune to this and, infused only with her passion for her child, she was able to undo the buckle that bound her to Mrs. Butler, let drop the band, and the dismayed Mrs. Butler was to be to Lilly as though she was not. I shall tell her we're going, she said to herself. And then she found that she could not easily tell her why. If I tell her what old Meeker said and how it started me thinking, they'll argue argue argue. "Oh Hughesy" she mimicked in her mind, "don't pay attention to silly old Meeker . . . Eleanor's as much a lady as . . ." no, thought Lilly, it'd be all words, and all the time Eleanor'd just be the maid's child and they know it, and they'd fight to keep me here for their own comfort. I'll not argue. I'll just say "It's time to go."

Gentle, placid, obstinate, Lilly stood over Mrs. Butler, and looking down at her with freshened eyes thought How coarse and grey her hair's getting. "Madam," she said.

Mrs. Butler looked up from her letters and smiled. "Yes?"

"We're going, Madam," said Lilly simply.

"Going where?" asked Mrs. Butler serenely.

"Going. Leaving. Going away," said Lilly, holding her duster between her hands.

Mrs. Butler's eyes widened and changed as a faint shock went through her. "Hughesy . . . what are you saying . . . you don't mean it . . . why . . . this is your home!"

"No it isn't, Madam. It's yours and the Major's home. We're going."

"But Hughesy . . . Mrs. Hughes . . ." said Mrs. Butler, incredulous, suddenly seeing before her a stranger in the place of the woman she thought she knew. "What has happened?"

"Nothing," said Lilly.

"Then why are you suddenly going?"

"It's time," said Lilly.

"Come now, Mrs. Hughes," and Mrs. Butler began to feel hurt, "you can . . . you should . . . at least tell me what has made you do this!"

"It's time to go," said Lilly stubbornly.

Mrs. Butler reflected—and hated herself for reflecting—how much she had done for Eleanor, and how much she cared for the child who was now to be removed, and how much she resented having been simple enough to think that all was well, while something, something—what?—had not been well. Had she been stupid? Had Maurice . . . what had Maurice done?

She spoke slowly. "Have I done something to hurt you . . . or annoy you, Hughesy?"

"No, Madam."

"Has . . . Major Butler done anything . . . that . . . has he . . . spoken sharply . . . perhaps . . . or . . . ?"

In the pause while Lilly thought, before answering, I'll be kinda sorry to leave the Major, he's real good to Eleanor, Mrs. Butler thought swiftly and with pain Oh, she's not answering directly. It's that! Is it Maurice again—and with this girl, this common common girl! And Lilly changed as she stood there from being just Hughesy, and a woman giving notice, to being a common common girl to whom Maurice had again turned as twice before, and had caused her—his wife—to suffer pain, and humiliation, and to forgive. And these affairs of Maurice's (so she couldn't hold him, it was clear, she need not deceive herself) came sharply in memory to her with the old sickening pang, not to be spoken of, ever, and hardly to be borne in memory.

"Oh no, Madam," said Lilly after the pause.

Mrs. Butler looked at her with pain and dislike. How much had happened to drive away this girl? Maurice, I can never ask you, and you will never tell me . . . oh perhaps nothing has happened, nothing at all, and I am cruel and unfair. And then memory sprang at her again.

"Have you nothing to tell me, Mrs. Hughes, no reason to give?" she said.

"No, Madam. Only it's time to go," said Lilly.

"Are your plans made, or are you just . . . going . . . ?"

Lilly hesitated, and then said "I'm going to be house-keeper in a country hospital, Madam. It's a good job and good pay."

Mrs. Butler's hope leapt. "Is it more wages you want, Hughesy?"

"Oh no, Madam," said Lilly. She was so evidently sincere that Mrs. Butler was chagrined. It was something else that now raised its head and struck at her. I'm very foolish, sighed Mrs. Butler within herself, to feel as I do. What has happened? A maid who has a child of whom I am fond has given me notice and will not say why. And I am shaken and disturbed and all my old terrors are awake again. I am not wise to seek below the surface. Poor Maurice. And she tried to assume, before her own eyes, the demeanour of the mistress who is parting with dignity from a maid whose work she respects, whose character she now has reason to doubt, but for whose frailty she must, as a superior being, have compassion. She must remain unmoved if she was to respect herself.

"Very well, Hughesy," she said, with a small smile, "we shall be sorry to see you go, and very very sorry to part with Eleanor, but you must do as you think fit. When do you want to go?"

"I think two weeks will do me, Madam," said Lilly suddenly after seven years.

"Two . . .!" echoed Mrs. Butler, startled, and then recovering herself. "Will you give me my account book . . . no . . . the third drawer on the left. Thank you." Re-established in a shaking calm and dignity by the third drawer on the left, Mrs. Butler scanned her account book with eyes that did not see, and Lilly, standing a moment, but dismissed, left the room. If there had been a battle, Mrs. Butler had won. But there had been no battle. Lilly was leaving, and had now proceeded another step on her planned way.

She went into the small yellow drawing room with the duster in her hand. Light fell in pools on the shining floor, wavering as the translucent vine leaves of that summer wavered outside the windows. The Chinese horse and the Chinese hound still stood timelessly upon the mantelpiece, reflected in the gold-rimmed mirror, and Lilly saw the room for a moment with new eyes, the eyes that say farewell, I shall not see you again . . . I am leaving you behind. The hound and the horse took upon themselves a changed aspect, the aspect of goodbye. This gave Lilly no pang. She proceeded to sweep and dust.

Mrs. Butler recovered herself and went out to find her husband in the garden.

"I have had a surprise," she said, and in order to be fair to him she did not watch him as she spoke. She looked over the hedge at the sea. "Hughesy says she's leaving."

"Leaving! What the devil . . . what's she leaving for?"

Oh, she thought, he *is* surprised . . . he sounds surprised . . . and she looked at him.

"She won't say. She just says 'It's time' and she won't say another thing . . . have *you* any idea, Maurice . . . what have we done? . . . I thought we were happy . . . I don't know . . . there must be *some*thing . . . but she won't say . . . she just says 'It's time to go.'"

Maurice Butler, injured as we are injured when we have given ourselves—the best gift we have—and the gift is disregarded, thought of the child that he had treated as his own, and of Lilly's mild acceptance. He thought, for a moment only, of his distant folly. He thought of his wife and of himself, indulged by circumstance and by Lilly, and he grew very angry.

"*I'll* talk to her!" he said.

"Well," said his wife, "do as you like about that, but it won't do any good, you won't change her and I don't think you'll get anything more out of her, and if you're angry it'll just make the last few days unpleasant."

"Well, if she's going to be unpleasant she can go at once," said her husband unreasonably, and, unreasonably, Mrs. Butler's spirits lifted. No, it's not Maurice . . . it's something secret of her own, the queer girl, she thought.

So Major and Mrs. Butler left for a visit to Victoria, where they had charming friends. They needed a change, one gets tired of the country they said, and in Victoria, also, one can more easily engage good domestic help than in the country. And Lilly, unperturbed, cleaned the house punctiliously, and then left Comox, and took Eleanor, and went to work in a small hospital in the Fraser Valley, where Mrs. Walter Hughes, the efficient and experienced housekeeper, had a cottage adjoining the hospital for herself and her well mannered and nicely spoken child Eleanor. In this way all the unpleasantness of parting was cleverly avoided. In Lilly's mind was no regret; in the minds of Major and Mrs. Butler was the resentment of those who have been betrayed ever so little; and in Eleanor was the baffling loss of her gods, with passing tears, and a memory that faded, until only the legends remained fixed in her mind of a lady who was kind and not pretty and of a big man whose voice and shadow Eleanor loved above everything and of the big dog and the small dog and the cat and the kittens—and wasn't there a china dog and a horse, yellow, that mustn't be touched, on the mantelpiece? Yes, there was.

Soon after arriving in the Valley Lilly gave Eleanor a

kitten of her own and the kitten established Eleanor as an owner. An acuteness on Lilly's part distinguished between Eleanor receiving generosity, even if it were given freely and without any smirch of patronage, and Eleanor enjoying the simplest of possessions in her own right. The days of accepting were over for Mrs. Hughes and her little daughter.

Lilly spoke sharply to Eleanor when the child forgot her accustomed manners or when her voice (soft like Mrs. Butler's voice and admired by Lilly) rose to the pitch of the schoolroom voices. She was intuitive, a little shy, but merry; she liked games and loved the new experience of playing with other children. She mingled, but did not excel. People noticed that little Eleanor Hughes with her shy yet responsive smile was a lovely child and not, somehow, like her mother's daughter. But—it was generally understood—her father, the late Mr. Walter Hughes, had been a man of very good family, from—vaguely—the Maritimes. He was superior in education to his wife who had been, as she said, only a country girl. But she was a nice-looking young woman of ability who became respected in the Valley and was soon appreciated for her trained quick efficiency by the Matron of the Hospital.

No doubt the child resembled her father and his family. Comments and queries soon died away, and Mrs. Walter Hughes and her little daughter gradually became Valley people.

VIII

Picture then Lilly and the child in the small cottage situated behind the little two-storeyed Valley Hospital. The cottage was of one room with a shabby fireplace, a bedroom, a washroom and a small kitchen. The place was clean but worn. It was furnished with left-over and handed-down furniture. The chairs sagged, the table and chest of drawers were scratched and scuffed, the carpet was an ancient drab. But when Lilly and Eleanor and their small baggage were within, and the door was closed, and Lilly, looking out of the window, saw the retreating form of the hospital Matron and knew that she and her child were in this home of their own, she experienced a joy that she had never known before. This most precious thing of four walls, roof, windows and one outer door was hers. She who had been homeless, had now a home, and in Lilly's eyes, this conferred a dignity upon her. Here was a door which Mrs. Hughes could close when the day's work was done, and behind which she could be at home. She looked into the bedroom where there was a large shabby double bed for herself and Eleanor. There was nothing to commend the room except that it was hers. Her room at Mrs. Butler's had been a better room, yet it was not Lilly's room in the sense that this small square uncompromising place was hers. A warmth of affection rushed from Lilly as she looked about her shabby house. It humanized her. She had learned enough from Mrs.

Butler (whom she had now so easily discarded) to know what she could do to this little place with pots of paint and some bright cotton. The Matron, returning to the hospital, reflected with a quizzical smile that the new housekeeper was a young woman of few words, that she seemed to know what would be required of her but it was impossible to tell what she thought of her living accommodation. The Matron had shown Lilly into the cottage with misgiving. There were no funds available for refurnishing and she was afraid that Mrs. Hughes might show dissatisfaction. Mrs. Hughes showed nothing, and the Matron could not have guessed what unaccustomed and melting joy overflowed Lilly as she entered for the first time her own home. That joy became as time went on a placid satisfaction and the mark of her freedom and her dignity. She was not "Butlers' maid". She was Mrs. Hughes, housekeeper at the Valley Hospital, who had her own house, with a front door that could be opened— or shut. And this little girl who ran about and pulled out the drawers that stuck so badly, and jumped on the bouncing big bed, was not "the maid's child at Butlers' place" any more. She was Eleanor Hughes, daughter of Mrs. Walter Hughes who lived in this little house.

These thoughts, unidentified but potent, flowed through Lilly. "Mummy, Mummy!" called Eleanor from the washroom, "there isn't a bath tub, Mummy, what'll we do?" The little girl saw with the unequivocal eyes of childhood never a bath in life again.

"Never you mind, Baby, we'll do," said her mother wrapped in her happiness.

Next morning Lilly, before beginning her duties at the hospital, took Eleanor to school, and the daily routine of their life began. The Matron relaxed as she discovered the trained perfections of Mrs. Hughes who moved quickly, neatly, silently. She took some credit to herself and had a proprietary feeling for Lilly and her little girl. She became, as years went by, Eleanor's unofficial godmother.

"Mrs. Hughes," she said one day, "I'm afraid you'll be lonely. How would you like to come with me to the Schoolroom party on Tuesday and get to know some of the people?"

Lilly hesitated. "I'm not fussy about people, Matron. I guess I'll stay home. When Eleanor's in bed and I've tidied up, it's kinda nice to sit beside the fire and look at the paper."

And then one day the Matron said, "Mrs. Hughes, I have an invitation for you. Mrs. Miller down at the store asked if you wouldn't like to go in and have a cup of tea with her on your day. She's seen you in church. She's a nice woman and friendly."

And Lilly said awkwardly "I'm not one for going to tea. I got Eleanor's school dress to give a good sponging and hang out. I guess I'll stay home." Lilly had never sat across a friendly table with a stranger and talked freely, for pleasure. And now it was too late to begin because there lay in wait for her the little pitfalls of speech and observance and she knew it. She was frightened.

I guess I don't talk very good, she said to herself, and now I never will. I don't feel easy with folks.

At the end of her day her habit was to sit down to a cup of tea with Mrs. Basko the cleaning woman before Mrs. Basko went home and before Lilly went across to her cottage and tidied up. Then how simple and easy the talk was.

"Those hot taps need new washers on," or "I don't
think much of that new cleaning powder," or "You
know that old man who came in with the leg? Well, he's
Andy's grampa in the drug store."

And sometimes in the evening the Matron slipped over
to the cottage and had some tea and toast with Lilly
beside the fire. Or the Matron took Lilly in her little
car and they drove down to the village and went through
the things in the store, because Lilly knew values. And
a few times the Matron took Lilly with her to a show in
the village because Lilly seemed to have so few diversions.
And the talk with the Matron or with Mrs. Basko or
with the farmer who brought the chickens, or with anyone else whom Lilly knew, was easy, because it was about
the world that all lived in, that is to say, about the
workings of the hospital, or about the village, and about
the people in the hospital or in the village. It was
enough. The world outside did not exist for her or, if
it did, it was of no interest or significance to her. Sometimes in the evening Lilly would turn, yawning, through
the newspapers, dwelling chiefly on the advertisements
of the moving picture shows or of the department stores.
These advertisements held only an entertainment value
for Lilly. She was not tempted to buy an evening dress
or a lawnmower or a linoleum rug. But these things held
a valid interest as against international or political or
artistic events which had no validity at all. Her eyes
slid over Persia or Co-operative or Symphony, to *Sale!
Specials Monday Morning!* or to crime. Crime interested
her, but only to the point of speculation in a chat with
Mrs. Basko who also liked crime.

It must be admitted that years passed before Lilly felt

secure in the Valley, and the reality of the edifice which she had built, of which Mrs. Walter Hughes was the culmination, wavered sometimes uncertainly before the pseudo-reality of what had really been her life. So there was a reason beyond her personal gaucherie that kept Lilly at home and watchful. When she and Eleanor had lived at Comox there was the good feeling of being at the end of a road. And so they were. This had given her an immunity. But the Valley was on a highway, people came and went, Vancouver was not far away. Up the Valley memory reasserted itself. When Lilly was invited to go to Vancouver for a day's shopping, she declined. When the Matron suggested that she should take a holiday in Vancouver, Lilly only said "I'm not fussy about cities. I guess me and Eleanor'll stay home."

Every other Sunday morning Mrs. Hughes took her little girl to church, and every Sunday Eleanor went to Sunday school. Although Lilly was satisfied to see her child having friends of her own, she was as careful as she knew how to be that Eleanor would not lose what she had learned from Mrs. Butler. She watched the child's habits and manners and, as for that, Lilly knew what good observance was in a child. But then, suddenly, something would puzzle her. Is Eleanor talking different? she thought. Is she talking kinda loud? She did not know what was wrong, but she felt that something was wrong which she could neither detect nor explain.

She would say sharply "Is that the way you'd speak to Her?"

"Her?" Eleanor would say, wondering. She had begun to forget the presence of Mrs. Butler.

"You know . . . Her . . . Madam . . . You don't sound

to me like you did when you was talking to Her. You should talk more quiet-like. What's the good of me bringing you here and you playing with the other kids if you're going to speak common."

"Well, Mummy . . ."

"You do as I say. You talk like you was talking to Her, and don't you forget. I don't want you shouting round like you didn't know any better."

That was how Lilly talked sometimes to her little girl, out of the fullness of her love and out of the strength of her ignorance and her set plan. To the Matron she said "Tell her, Matron, will you, if you hear her?"

In church they sat, mother and child, well mannered, joining in the service as they should.

Before Lilly lost her looks there was almost the affair of Mr. Meakins.

Mr. Meakins who was the Chairman of the Hospital Board was a member of the congregation. He was, it seemed, a congenital bachelor, and had been a bachelor for so long that he supposed himself—and was supposed— to be immune from the annoyance of love. Soon after Lilly and her little girl came to the Valley, he found himself in difficulties. Every other Sunday Mr. Meakins, sitting behind Lilly and her daughter, was increasingly aware of the slim young woman whose green tweed back he studied and of the child whose bright face turned so often with confidence up to her mother. The child would tug at her mother's sleeve. The young woman in green tweed would bend down, and with a quick serious smile would satisfy her little daughter and then return her attention to the service. This small action touched Mr Meakins. He invested Lilly with every good quality as he looked at her slim back fortnight by fortnight. He knew that this was the young widow who was the new housekeeper at the Hospital, of whom he had heard such good reports from the Matron.

"You're still satisfied with your housekeeper, Matron?" he said one day at the hospital after the Board meeting.

"Yes, but I'm still dazed, Mr. Meakins," said the Matron. "I ask myself what I've done to deserve her.

She leaves order wherever she goes. Nothing is too much trouble and I really think she's as interested in things going well as I am. When Miss Sands was ill she even went on the ward, and last week when Mrs. Basko couldn't come, Mrs. Hughes did her own work and Mrs. Basko's too. And she lends a hand with the cooking when Wong goes to town. She's a jewel."

"A widow, I think you said," said the Chairman.

"Yes. I think her husband died when the little girl was a baby. I gather she's always had to work."

"She looks very . . . ladylike," suggested the Chairman.

"Well," said the Matron carefully, "I'd call her a very self-contained young woman. She has some dignity of her own." It occurred incredibly to the Matron that Mr. Meakins seemed interested in Mrs. Hughes.

As Mr. Meakins followed the service Sunday by Sunday, his thoughts also followed or, rather, pursued the slim woman who sat in front of him. On the Sundays that Mrs. Hughes and her little girl were at church, Mr. Meakins looked at the straight back of Lilly Waller who was Mrs. Walter Hughes, and the turmoil in his mind increased and maddened him. He could not take his eyes from the form of Mrs. Hughes, and on the alternate Sundays, when she was not there, he pictured her there, standing, kneeling, bowed in prayer—what prayer? His blood began to tell him so loudly about this woman that he was afraid that people would see, that they would hear, and that he would betray himself. He had fallen in love with a green tweed back. He became sentimental, and he knew it. I'm crazy, he said to himself, and what can I do? can't get to know her, she's the hospital housekeeper, and in a place like this . . . and I can't marry her out of hand without knowing her. He pictured the girl in green and her little daughter in his square house. He made up his mind.

Blandly after church he contrived that he should pass by the young woman with the child. As if surprised he said kindly "Haven't I seen you at the Hospital?"

Lilly smiled faintly. "Maybe," she said.

"And is this your little girl?" asked Mr. Meakins.

Well, what do you suppose? thought Lilly.

"Yes," she said.

"And what's *your* name?" asked Mr. Meakins in a hearty and jocose manner of the child.

"Eleanor Hughes," the child said shyly.

"And how old are you?"

"Going on eight."

Lilly watched with eyes that told nothing.

Two words only he had heard from her and he was enchanted, but he was self-conscious and was afraid of becoming conspicuous.

"Well, good day," he said heartily, and moved on.

"Good day," said Lilly.

"Who's that man, Mummy?" asked Eleanor as she walked with her hand in her mother's hand.

"I think that's Mr. Meakins," said Lilly.

"Who's he?"

"He's the head of the hospital," said Lilly, and thought no more of it, but she was pleased that Mr. Meakins had noticed Eleanor so nicely.

Two weeks later Mr. Meakins steadily watched Mrs. Walter Hughes. She had filled his mind, together with the difficulty in which he found himself. Should he pay this woman open attention? How else could he get to know

214

her? If he paid her open attention the Valley would
buzz, whatever happened. If he found her to be other
than he thought, or if she refused his attentions, and
perhaps if she accepted them, the Valley would know,
and he would be laughed at. I must wait, he said to
himself. I must go slow. And still he watched Lilly.

Outside the church he chanced again—or so it seemed
—to be at Lilly's side (I can't even do *this* too often, he
thought uneasily). He gave her the briefest glance and
turned his attention to Eleanor.

"And how's my little friend?" he asked.

"Very well, thank you," said Eleanor looking up at her
mother as if to say "Is this right? Am I doing right?"

"Are you comfortable in your cottage, Mrs. Hughes?"
asked Mr. Meakins in the tone of the Chairman of the Board.

"Yes, thank you," said Lilly very low. Mr. Meakins
gave himself completely away by a look. Well, for goodness' sake, thought Lilly startled, but she remained out-
wardly composed.

"Would you let your little girl have a puppy, Mrs.
Hughes?" asked Mr. Meakins. "I have a spaniel pup
to give away."

"Oh, *Mummy*!" besought Eleanor.

"We'd have to think about it, thank you," said Lilly
primly. People passed them as they stood.

"Oh, Mummy, *why* do we have to think? Oh *please*,
Mummy!"

"Nigger mightn't like it," said Lilly. "Thank you.
We'll have to think."

"Well, you can tell the Matron and she will let me
know," said Mr. Meakins, determined to conduct his
courtship on the safest lines.

"Thank you," said Lilly again, letting her brown eyes rest on him, and taking in without illusion the compact form of Mr. Meakins, his reddish face, thinning hair, and the urgent moist look in his eyes which said as loudly as if Mr. Meakins had shouted "I'm mad about you." Well, the old coot! she thought in surprise. She was stunned. "Come, Baby," she said. She did not say goodbye to Mr. Meakins, but letting her eyes rest on him for a moment that said Goodbye and perhaps a little more, she walked on, with Eleanor turning and waving a shy hand to the Chairman of the Hospital Board who went his way, observed by several people.

"Seems like every Sunday morning I see Meakins hanging round that Mrs. Hughes," said Mrs. Miller.

"For God's sake, you women make this Valley into a regular goldfish bowl," said Mr. Miller. "Can't a man pass the time of day without you cooking up something!"

"Well, there's no call for you to swear coming out of church," said his wife. "I only said Meakins was speaking to Mrs. Hughes again."

After Eleanor was in bed that evening, Lilly put the question to herself. If I wanted to, I guess I could marry him, she thought, not right now maybe, but go along quietly and mind my own business and I could marry him. Lilly, sitting by her fire, considered. She weighed the matter coolly and found that she would not marry Mr. Meakins and that she could make that apparent to Mr. Meakins as easy as easy without making talk. If there was talk, it was bad for her and Eleanor. If there was no talk, she and Eleanor would keep on very well just where they were, staying quiet until Eleanor was a big girl. And then . . . Lilly's mind moved on to a new step. Well, time to think of that, but there'd have to be a new step. Right now, said Lilly to herself, disposing her forces like a general, we're best off here. It was all very well for the Chairman of the Board, thought Lilly, to fall for a girl he didn't know a thing about, and hasn't even talked to. Men do that, I guess. She thought erroneously, I guess men are a whole lot softer than women that way. If he made a fool of himself and tried to marry a girl who couldn't talk good or mix up with his friends, it wouldn't be good for me and it wouldn't be good for Eleanor. We're better right here, she said to herself again as she looked round the walls of her little room. And what and if he wanted to go to Vancouver! I couldn't say as I wouldn't go, but I don't feel safe going to Vancouver. Best keep out of it, and we'll go right on the way we are, Baby.

So the next day there were tears when Eleanor was told that her mother hadn't time to train a puppy, not now, and anyway Nigger the cat wouldn't like it. And Lilly, with her usual composed air, told the Matron that Mr. Meakins had offered Baby a pup, but that she, Lilly, didn't want no dogs around, and please to tell him. And thank you, she added. And two weeks later Mr. Meakins regarded Lilly in church with frustration and relief, and after church Lilly did not see Mr. Meakins anywhere near, and she walked home as usual, and even Mrs. Miller soon forgot that Mr. Meakins had twice running spoken to Mrs. Hughes. Lilly had been exhilarated, a trifle disappointed, satisfied, and, on the whole, pleased. Mr. Meakins had been titillated, consumed, frustrated, saved as by fire by Lilly, and was eternally thankful.

Having been thus for a time deranged by love, he married somebody else shortly afterwards.

In quick succession Lilly had two other invitations to change her station. The Valley being what it was, the Valley knew, and approved of this young woman who was devoted to the memory of her husband. Mrs. Butler's tweeds were cut ruthlessly into spring and winter coats for Eleanor. Lilly, wearing dresses bought at the village shop or chosen from the mail order catalogue, her hair destroyed by the permanent wave machine in the village, lost her looks. Only her erect, quick, graceful carriage reminded you of beauty, and, if she cared to look at you, her soft brown eyes. She became a dowdy, and unaware of it. Yet, on a second look, she was still the young Mrs. Hughes who had been driven down the dusty Comox road clasping her baby, and she was still Lilly Waller who had waited on white men and Chinamen at Lam Sing's café. Looking again at her, one would say "I remember you . . . wasn't your name Lilly Waller? Yes, I remember you, quite well."

Between the Matron and Lilly was that relation that exists a few times in some fortunate lives where there is mutual respect and affection and a real though limited pleasure in companionship, with which relative education has little to do. Lilly was ignorant. The Matron was a woman of some education, intuitive, quick-witted, practical, but with a joy in beauty and an unsatisfied aesthetic taste beyond anything that Lilly could ever know. She still stayed in the Valley where aesthetic pleasures were in part denied her because she loved the claims of her work and her people. She had become a personage in her own place. Not beautiful, hardly good-looking, she got on well with men and women. The Matron had come to mean to Lilly everything that Lilly respected or could wish to be. She was the only person with the exception of Eleanor for whom Lilly had ever felt any sentiment of affection. On the Matron's part, Lilly's solitary condition, her independence, her uncompromising devotion to her child and to her work, aroused the older woman's protection and, perhaps, her curiosity. Where I love, I meddle, mused the Matron, and she did. She loved the child, watched her, and corrected her. She meddled. In fact, Mrs. Butler's influence, fragmentarily, survived in the Matron.

X

WHEN Eleanor had grown to be nearly seventeen, her mother fell unbearably in love with a man named Paddy Wilkes.

The Matron thought of Paddy Wilkes as the handy man and called him our engineer. Other people called him a janitor. He was a tall fellow with a well-shaped well-brushed head, strong arms, a harmless roving eye for all women, and he was married. Lilly had worked near him year after year; he had mended Lilly's taps, built her shelves, made all the small repairs that her quick eyes saw were needed; he had long ago tried Lilly out for a mild flirtation and she had ignored him and Paddy had said to himself "No dice"; and during all this time Lilly had not cared at all for him.

And now that her young prettiness had gone, and she had settled into a life of custom and, perhaps, security again as year followed year, Lilly allowed her cloak of self-protection to drop from her. What influences or arts contrive to make men and women lose their hearts and their heads? Perhaps it was the weather.

During that famous hard winter when fresh blizzards of snow continued to clog the roads of the Valley and thaws followed snows and frosts followed thaws, there were many accidents and there was too much illness. The little hospital was almost isolated; it was difficult of access and still it was overcrowded. The small staff was depleted, communications were interrupted, supplies were a constant worry and hazard, and it seemed at last that only the Matron and the housekeeper and Paddy Wilkes— who never left the place—working together often for twenty hours a day, kept things going. When the last thaw came, the Valley seemed to draw a long breath and look about at the ruined roads, caved-in shed-roofs, the acres of split and broken fruit trees, and the dead vines. Farmers and storekeepers, road men and river men, the gardener and Paddy Wilkes began the work of repair, and, as the air softened and spring and buds and birds appeared all over the Valley, the hard winter was miraculously forgotten except by those who had suffered most.

Now that the sense of continued crisis was over Lilly relaxed, and found that the new close bonds had loosened and that the former working relations were re-established. Something had gone. She was very tired, but she missed the crisis and the urgency and the drama (if she had known it) of human need. Yet something beside fatigue had survived those six weeks of strain. Her relations with the Matron who had so much depended on her had become intimate, and she had begun to care for Paddy Wilkes.

Now, each day, she looked for him, she needed him, and he who had seemed to be almost hers was not hers any longer. He belonged to nobody, to everybody, and to his shadowy family who lived somewhere beyond the village. She knew that what she felt for him she had never yet felt for any man. To Lilly it passed for love.

For a very short time she was happy in her secret way. Her love was as when a fruit is opened, and the scent flows out like a wine, never as sweet again. But soon she asked herself Well, what of it? What could she do? There was nothing in it for her, and then the sweetness was gone. If it had not been for Eleanor and for the life that Lilly had arranged for Eleanor (and so for herself) she would have set herself to seduce Paddy if she could, and perhaps she could. At least she would not have been scrupulous. She thought a little scornfully He's easy . . . a woman's only got to give a sign. She would have made talk and trouble but she would not have cared much, and she could have moved on. But about and behind her spread always her intangible and invisible Then, solid as steel, inescapable as past birth or death to come, making her Now always insecure and always scrupulous—for Eleanor. Thus, since her birth, the child Eleanor, all unknowing, had guarded her mother and had made her the blameless and silent woman that she had become, who now was crushing out her love. (But a girl's gotta right to live, hasn't she? Sure she's got a right. No, said Lilly's austerity, she has no rights at all. None.)

So Lilly banked her fires, painfully, and gave no sign, yet the fires were there. She saw Paddy daily, free with his easy little favours, but she affected not to see, and she was jealous. This was a very hard time for Lilly.

One day she saw Paddy come out of the boiler room wearing his blue overalls. He strolled into the fresh spring sunshine, and lit a cigarette. A new young laundress crossed the yard. Paddy called to her and walked towards her with his easy stride that had some grace in it. Paddy and the laundress stood and talked. Paddy was teasing her, and the girl looked up and laughed back at him. She's flip, that girl, thought Lilly scowling from the pantry window. She did not like the new laundress. The girl

flexed her arm, clenching her fist and, laughing sideways,
she straightened and bent her arm again, showing her
strength. Paddy ran his hands up and down the girl's arm
feeling its roundness for the muscle. Still with a hand on
her arm, Paddy walked with the girl as far as the laundry
door, they stood leaning against the door and talking, he
threw his cigarette away, she went in, he turned and went
back across the yard with a pleased smile on his face and
disappeared into the boiler room. He's no good, carrying
on with every woman he sees, Lilly said angrily to herself.
And so she tortured herself with nothings.

She suffered. She knew that she was ridiculous, but she
suffered. That girl, that laundress, could stand in the
yard with Paddy, and with the eyes of the hospital walls
looking on, Paddy could run his hands up and down her
arm, and he and she would meet anywhere again. But
Mrs. Hughes, mother of Eleanor Hughes, who had worked
through the gruelling weeks of winter beside him, who had
been close to him, was now as any other, and less than any
other. For the winter was over as though it had never
been, and Paddy did not stand in the spring sunshine in
the hospital yard or anywhere else and dally with Mrs.
Hughes (who was known to keep herself to herself), with
his hand on her shoulder, on the strength of a hard winter
just over. That evening, when her work was finished,
Lilly went back to her cottage and looked at herself in the
glass. She did not like her face. "You're a fool," she said
to herself. She pushed back her hair whose soft brightness
had gone, and said again to her pale image in the glass
"You're a fool, you're a fool." Yet she loved him.

Once on a Saturday afternoon the Matron took Lilly
with her and drove in her little car up the Valley towards

Harrison. On the far side of the village they passed Paddy walking with a woman and two girls. Paddy carried large paper parcels. His wife walked beside him, heavily. Lilly saw as the car passed quickly that Mrs. Wilkes, whom she had never observed before, was short and of the shape and size called comfortable. Lilly had never before seen Paddy as a family man for even one short glimpse, and the sight pierced her. She suffered at the sight of the woman who walked beside him, and slept beside him, and had borne him those two tall girls.

The Matron said "That reminds me. I must speak to Paddy. He's being silly with that new laundress, and he's spending too much time round the kitchen too. I must check him. I think he'll take it all right." And then she thought that she should not have spoken like that of one hospital employee to another, and that one Paddy. Lilly said nothing, but she thought You see, there's always somebody sees everything. There's never any freedom . . . not for me. Things don't stop, either. They go on and on and on.

That summer she became shrewish. She spoke habitually more sharply to Eleanor. The Matron took her holiday early following the exhausting winter. When she came back to the hospital she looked at Lilly and said "I'll arrange your time off. You take a good holiday this year for a change. You need it. Go up country or to one of the Gulf Islands. Take Eleanor, or if you want to leave her she can stay with the Sample girls, or I'll look after her."

But Lilly was aggravating and stubborn. "No," she said, "what would I do with a holiday? I don't care about mountains."

The Matron knew that Lilly meant that scenery had no

charms for her. But she said, "You can at least rest. You need it."

But Lilly said, "I couldn't lay around and rest. I'm not used to it. Anyway I'm saving for when Eleanor goes to the city. It won't be long now." This was true, but, above all, Lilly would not remove herself from the sight of Paddy Wilkes. She would torment herself. Her passion for him was thrown away, unrewarding, and not likely to be rewarded, but she could not help herself. As always, she lived her inner life alone, and made no sign. She could not afford that luxury.

Autumn came and the countryside was mellow and beautiful but Lilly did not notice the beauty. Eleanor was changing from a tousled school girl and was growing into neatness and beauty and perception. Lilly had reason to be proud of her daughter, and she was proud and she was hard. It was a wonder that she did not quench the girl's sparkle that year with her coldness, but youth prevailed over her. Lilly worked harder than was necessary and did any extra tasks that had to be done.

On a golden afternoon Paddy drove the little truck to Mr. Small's farm. He had in the back of the truck some old windows for the farmer to use in making a hot bed. Lilly and the gardener sat with him in the front seat. The Matron had urged Lilly to have the drive and, both willingly and unwillingly, Lilly had said "Well, I don't mind if I do." The gardener decided to stay at the farm and help Mr. Small to build the frame for the seedlings. On the way home Paddy turned off the highway and drove on a winding trail that led to a ridge overlooking the width of the Valley. Scarves of mist and smoke lay upon a landscape of golden poplars, dark conifers, broad

225

meadows, cattle grazing there, the winding river reflecting forest and sky; at the far rim of the Valley were the folded hills, and here and there were farm buildings like dolls' houses, so small they appeared that they seemed to bear no relation to bedrooms and kitchens within, or to human life.

"Pretty, isn't it," said Paddy, and idly put an arm around Lilly. She yielded herself so immediately that he was astonished. He looked at her and her eyes were closed. Her body seemed to melt and flow to him. She felt her banked fires shoot into flame. Paddy drew her close and his arms went round her and for an endless moment she lay in his arms where she had so much longed to be. A word that was not a word nor a thought but a stab of pain and mortal fear went through and through Lilly, and the word that was the pain that stabbed her was *Eleanor*. The word seemed to destroy her, and yet she could not deny it. She had to obey it. She pulled his arms roughly away, and as he tried to take her again she struck him across the face in a frenzy of fear of herself and sprang out of the truck. She stood in the long grass beside the truck, stiff and tensed but already as if in flight.

Paddy held his hand to his face and roared "Why, you . . . you . . . you hell-cat!"

"Don't you come near me! Don't you touch me!" cried Lilly in terror of herself and her desire.

"*Touch* you! *Me!*" shouted Paddy angrily, "I wouldn't touch *you*, not with a ten-foot pole!"

Lilly looked at his furious face with its reddened cheek and she began to tremble.

"I'm going," she said, and turned.

"Hey! Are you crazy? You get up here! I'm not going

226

to drive back and leave you walking. Have my wife hearing crazy talk! Like hell . . . Why," he stammered, roused and resentful, "what'd you take me for, acting like that?"

"I want to walk by myself a little ways," said Lilly piteously. "I want to walk a little ways and you come along and stop and I'll get in. Honest I will."

"O-*kay*," he growled. He lit a cigarette, collected himself a little and looked out furiously over the dreaming landscape which he no longer saw.

Lilly walked on, hurrying away. She stumbled as she hurried. Oh, Baby, Baby, it'd be the finish of you. Nothing stops right there. Everything goes on. She was still trembling and was still afraid of herself. She heard at last the truck coming up behind her and stood aside humbly, waiting. She got in with something that seemed like composure, and Paddy drove on in angry silence.

Often, now, Lilly cried out in her sleep. One night she called "Police, police!" as she had cried out so long ago. Eleanor, beside her, half awakened from deep sleep, said drowsily "Mummy, what is it . . . you said police . . ."

"Nothing, Baby," said her mother in the dark as to a little girl. She overflowed with a sad compassion both blind and dumb for Eleanor and for herself and then, as with discovery and a melancholy surprise, for anyone anywhere who might suffer or be lonely as she was lonely. "I guess it was a bad dream. Go to sleep, honey."

"All right . . . just a bad dream . . ." and Eleanor trailed off into sleep again. They were so close, yet an invisible world lay between them. Lilly, half rising and turning, put out her hand and gently felt the girl's mop of feathery curls. And my girl doesn't even know enough about the world to be scared of it, she thought, and she took comfort from this.

It was some time before the Matron noticed that her housekeeper and the handy man seemed, actually, to dislike each other. Strange I never noticed before, she thought, but she said nothing.

Lilly's poor love affair, like a sickness, passed, and was over.

XI

ELEANOR was a little thing, slim and brown. Lilly did not know that her daughter's face was enchanting. With her Martha-like care she gave Eleanor always a quick glance to see if her face were clean, if she had been putting powder on again, if the upspringing short brown curls were combed, brushed and shining, if her hands and nails were well-kept, if her dress and shoes were neat and in order.

"Other girls can paint up their nails if they like, but not you. When you're grown and earning you do what you like I guess but not now. While you're a girl all you got to do is to keep yourself neat and clean . . . no . . . not even for the party you can't."

There was a potential maturity in the girl that Lilly would never know. When that maturity would arrive, Lilly would only dimly discern it. The little girl who accepted her mother as embodied authority and love, grew into the girl who knew that her mother was limited and fallible. Lilly could not keep pace with her child, nor enter into her child's world.

"Mummy, see the smoke curling up the hillside and all those white dogwoods against the dark green fir trees! Dogwood looks prettier against forest than by itself doesn't it. O Mummy, what a heavenly heavenly day!"

"Yes. I guess I better get your winter coat on the line and put it away. There's no room for spare coats in that cupboard if they're not being used."

229

And, "Listen to this, Mummy, it's when Mr. Collins proposed to Elizabeth! *How* did Jane Austen make it so serious and so funny!"

"I haven't got time, not now. And you be careful of that book, if it's Matron's."

And, "Oh, I wish I could learn the piano! Mrs. Sample said I could practise on theirs!"

"Well, some things you can do, and some things you can't, and we can't be beholden to Samples like that. And any ways, I don't want Bobby Sample walking home with you every afternoon when you've been playing on the piano."

"Oh, Mummy, Bobby's *lovely*!"

"So you say."

Eleanor's sense of the ridiculous would send her flying into the cottage with her eyes shining, to tell her mother of some funny encounter.

"Well, I guess it was pretty impertinent all right."

"But don't you *see*, Mummy, don't you *see*, when he said Mrs. Sample was as common as an old shoe, *he* meant it for a compliment!"

"Funny kind of compliment."

Eleanor grew to reserve her fun and laughter for herself, or for the Matron or for her friends the Samples, and her love of beauty too, and her quickly spoken hopes and wishes. She was aware as time went on, without defining anything to herself, that her mother had little sense of humour and little of beauty. There is a wild disorder of nature which is beauty. Eleanor could see it and feel it and Lilly could not feel it at all. Eleanor did not often think of the time before they came to the Valley, but sometimes she was led to remember the sand spit at Comox, with the wind blowing over, and the little headstones, and the bending grasses; she remembered the boat on a blue sea as still as glass, or tossing on grey white curling water, and she wanted to see the ocean again; she remembered a great cat in the sunlight in an open glade, and its green lambent eyes; she remembered the elegance of a china horse and a china dog; she remembered vaguely stories told and books read aloud by Mrs. Butler, some she had understood, some she had not understood, but she had listened. Mrs. Butler had taught her poetry which meant nothing at all to her but she learned the succession of words and it pleased Mrs. Butler. And now, only the other day, some of these words sprang to life, and she knew with pleasure of her very own discovery what the *Psalm of Life* meant, which had been but dead words. Her mind was opening.

A time came when Eleanor began to show some increasing top-lofty young impatience with her mother. The Matron, loving the girl, noticed. I must speak to her, she thought . . . no one else will. I must.

She walked one evening slowly along the road's side with Eleanor. There was a remainder of yellow light still in the lower sky. Bats had begun to fly. Sometimes the headlights of a car approached. The car rushed past them, and lights and sound disappeared and all was still again. I must be careful, the Matron told herself, youth is easily stampeded. Eleanor thought She's going to say something to me . . . I know it . . . how tactful she can be . . . and how easy it is to see her getting tactful! . . . Her defences were up.

"Your mother's a very wonderful woman," said the Matron at last. Eleanor did not reply. Meddle meddle.

One should have the wisdom of God, the Matron thought.
I must tread delicately. She went on.

"It's struck me sometimes that now you're regarding
your mother not for the things she is, but for the things she
isn't . . . and you can't change grown-up people, Eleanor.
You know her history . . ." she paused "don't you . . . ?"

"Yes," said Eleanor, and of course she did not.

"If your father had lived," said the Matron in a very
low voice (they followed slowly the dim curve of the hedge
on the side of the road), "your mother—who was just a
country-bred girl—would have had all the advantages of
life with an educated man . . . like he was . . . and she
was deprived of it all . . . and she so young . . . not
many years older than you are . . . now . . ."

"Yes . . . yes . . . " said Eleanor. The girl's world was
dim and mysterious without and within.

The Matron had not tried to take the girl's arm and
ingratiate herself by physical contact but walked with her
arms folded. "I've thought of your mother," she continued as they went slowly along the road, "poor, yes, very
poor, Eleanor, and ignorant—yes, you know it and I know
it—fresh from the country, knowing nothing of the world,
and friendless, with herself to support, and a small baby
that was you, and no chance to think of herself and only
her own health and courage to support you both . . . I've
seen girls like that go out of the hospital, but they have
friends . . . Forgive me, darling," and here she took the
girl's arm and clasped her hand. The girl gave a sigh.
" . . . Don't mind that I said this, Eleanor, will you,
but . . . well, your mother's a puritan" (oh Yow oh
Ranny) "and you're a romantic—you don't know half
what a romantic you are, my dear . . . so you have the

232

imagination to see it all and understand more easily than she can . . . let's cross over and turn back," the night was darker now, "and I'll tell you the word I've had from Vancouver. They'll take you in the next nursing class but one." But Eleanor did not seem to hear.

"Oh, Matron, Matron, I'm a beast," she murmured.

"No, not a beast," smiled the Matron in the dark, "just a little big for the boots . . ."

Eleanor crossed the hospital yard, stood, and looked through the window at the familiar figure of her mother sitting by the fire as she so often did at the end of the day's work and turning the pages of the newspaper. It was true, her mother was a puritan. And she, Eleanor, was secretly glad and a little proud that Matron had called her a romantic although there seemed to be some kind of warning there. A faint new illumination in the girl's mind showed her mother to her not as an adult person, not wise like Matron, not light of touch like Mrs. Sample, not even as clever as Eleanor, but as a puritan girl, grown old. Eleanor felt more experienced than her mother, but not so good, nor so true, nor so strong, nor so unselfish. She went in.

"*Darling* . . . !" she said impetuously.

"Well, what?" said Lilly continuing to look at the New Westminster Sales advertisements.

"Just darling!" said Eleanor. She went down on her knees beside her mother and the firelight shone on her face.

Lilly turned from the newspaper. "Well, what is it?" she said.

Oh, *why* does she always have to be so matter of fact, thought the girl in irritation and something told her "Because she's had to be. All these years she's had to be."

"Matron's told me . . . They're taking me at the Hospital!"

Lilly laid down the paper. "You glad?" she asked.

Eleanor nodded, her eyes shining. "Give me a kiss and tell me you're glad too," she demanded. "You're awful stingy, aren't you!"

Lilly smiled and embraced her daughter.

"We'll have to see about your things," she said.

"They love each other, this woman and this girl," a wandering god would say passing near and stopping to look at these two clasped for a moment together, "and they are to part. Good. They will be much happier."

XII

IN THE second year of her hospital training in Vancouver, Eleanor wrote to tell her mother that she had become engaged to a young lawyer named Paul Lowry.

"Not finished her training!" exclaimed Lilly, at first displeased. Then she was glad. The letter telling of Eleanor's engagement was almost perfunctory. She was struck silent by her love, and could not tell her mother about it. "I can't tell you what I feel for Paul. You will know just a little by what you felt for my father. We are almost frighteningly happy."

"Well . . . " said Lilly, looking at the letter. She read further. I'm glad his folks live in Montreal, she thought, and she felt some apprehension of this Paul.

Paul Lowry heard, little by little, about Eleanor's handsome young father, who married a poor girl, broke with his family, went ranching, and was killed by a stallion before Eleanor was born. He heard of her mother's courage, and how her mother—a country girl—had withdrawn farther and farther into herself. She could have married again, but she had been too devoted to the memory of Eleanor's father. She could hardly bring herself to speak his name. "She's a very calm person. She won't kiss you or goozle at you, Paul."

"Thank God for that," said Paul looking down at Eleanor, caring nothing for her relatives and all for her, as they sat side by side in the train, travelling up the

Valley, wrapped in no ordinary magic. Nevertheless he prepared himself to see this consecrated woman and met with surprise the colourless dowdy and slender Lilly. His picture dissolved and then assembled itself again. Lilly was undecipherable. Out of her shyness and inexperience she saw him as in another place with which she was not familiar, and she stiffened in self-protection. Paul dismissed quickly his first disappointment in the mother of the incomparable Eleanor. A country girl . . . what she has done . . . what she has been through, all alone, he thought, reproaching himself. He smiled at her in his disarming way and Lilly warmed to him, but carefully.

She kissed Eleanor without demonstration, shook hands with Paul and said "I'm sure I'm pleased to meet you." Looking at him she meditated rather grimly He's got class. Eleanor'll have class married to him. Mrs. Paul Lowry! I'm certainly glad his folks don't live too handy. And she said "Come in to tea."

Lilly seemed placid, but Paul thought that this was a woman who contained herself and was in charge of her feelings. When she took them to the small hospital to introduce Paul to the Matron and to a doctor who happened to be there, he saw her manner of deference and yet of authority. Plainly she was a person in her own right. Paul corrected a little his first impression of Mrs. Walter Hughes. In any case she was Eleanor's mother and a woman to be respected, but it was clear that Eleanor must be her father's child.

Today Eleanor made a present of her happiness to everyone. She was proud of her mother to Paul and proud of Paul to her mother. She embraced the Matron and the nurses. The doctor kissed her. Everyone was happy.

Lilly heard with disapproval that Paul called her daughter Nora. This she resented as a descent from the Eleanor which (for some reason that she could not for the moment remember) had always seemed to her the highest honour that it had been in her slight power to bestow. And here was this composed young man with the grey eyes under tilted eyebrows, and the unwilling yet attractive smile, reducing the dignity of the name to an ordinary Nora. She would say nothing, but she did not like it.

"That's a good-looking young man," said the Matron after they had gone. "He's clever, too, I should say. He'll go far. You're going to have a very distinguished son-in-law some day."

"Well," said Lilly coolly, "handsome is as handsome does. As long as he's good to Eleanor . . ." and she nearly burst with pride, but not even the Matron could guess that.

XIII

THREE times following the marriage of Eleanor and Paul, Lilly spent her two weeks' annual holiday with them, and then she went no more. Paul, rather than Eleanor, divined some uneasiness in this silent woman his mother-in-law in spite of the welcome she received. During the day-time Lilly helped her daughter in the house, or went with her shopping, or went to a show. Or Lilly was taken to the houses of friends or Eleanor's friends came to tea. Lilly could find nothing to talk about. She had nothing to say. She felt that as Eleanor's mother she reflected no credit on Eleanor, and that weighed upon her. At the hospital one never made conversation for conversation's sake. But all these pleasant girls and women seemed to relate experiences which to Lilly were irrelevant. She was not at ease and she did not enjoy herself. In the evening, there they were, Paul reading or working, Eleanor reading or sewing or talking to her mother, Lilly sitting. She wished she had her rocker. She wished she had a movie magazine. Paul and Eleanor did not seem to have any movie magazines. She had looked through the magazines of which there were a great many but the names were unknown to her—hardly a picture in the lot. She did not like to buy herself a movie magazine. So she sat, and because she had nothing to do, she sucked her teeth absent-mindedly. Then, sometimes, Paul closed his books, looked up and said "Who wants some fresh air?

Anyone want to go for a drive?" and that was better,
for then they drove round the park under the trees, and
saw the lights come out on the Lions' Gate Bridge and on
the opposite shore. That was much better, for there was
no constraint. But the next evening there they were again,
sitting, and Lilly sucked her teeth in despair, or someone
came in and they sat talking, talking about goodness
knows what, and that was worse.

One afternoon Lilly came out of her bedroom door,
moving quietly as usual, just as Paul came in and ran up
the stairs. He ran up calling "Nora!" and Eleanor came
quickly out of their bedroom. They did not see Lilly, but
Lilly, standing in her doorway, saw Eleanor come up to
her husband with her face raised, and on her face a
revealed look that Lilly had never seen on Eleanor's face
nor on any face. Eleanor's face was changed and radiant.
For a moment the husband and wife looked at each
other. They did not speak. Then they kissed. Paul remained with his arms around his wife and his face to hers.
They were alone, and this moment had revealed their
felicity. What was it all about? All that had happened
was that Paul had come home to dinner. Was there some
special secret life that these two led together, of which
other people had no knowledge? There was. Of that
Lilly felt sure, as, quickly, having seen what she had seen,
she stepped back into her room and quietly closed the
door. She sat down on her bed, shaken by her daughter's
look. She had lived for nearly fifty years, and she had
never seen this thing before. So this was love, each for
each, and she had never known it. And this secret life of
love went on in this house and she had never seen it
before. She was outside it.

The third year that Lilly stayed with her children, Eleanor had a maid. Lilly had less than ever to do, and time hung very heavily. She felt that the maid thought poorly of Mrs. Lowry's mother and this disturbed her. If it were *my* home and *my* maid, she thought, it would be kinda different.

Each time she returned home to her cottage in the Valley, it was with a sense of relief. After her third visit the Matron had a severe attack of arthritis which resulted in lameness and a great deal of pain. Lilly did what she could to relieve the Matron, but it was plain that the Matron suffered a great deal. Matron looks older, thought Lilly. And then she realized that Matron *was* older, and she—Lilly—was older too, and she and Matron had worked together for nearly a quarter of a century, and something like this—arthritis, or a fall or one of those things—might happen to Lilly too. The Matron confided that she was very worried. She had been careful all these years, and had saved, but she helped to support her mother, who still lived. If she kept well and could work until she was sixty-five, and could continue to save, she would be secure—or almost secure. "That's it, for a woman," said the Matron with unusual bitterness, "work, work, work, save and scrimp, and then arthritis and then old age and what do you get out of life?" Lilly, who had begun to have a nice little savings account in the bank in the village, now saved to the point of meanness. Her only luxury was her visit to town; a visit, it was true, but it had begun to cost money.

"Darling," Eleanor had said, "do you know you're letting yourself go a bit? And you're really so pretty! You should have your hair styled while you're in town."

"Styled? What's styled?" asked Lilly. And she had not gone to have her hair styled. But she had bought a new hat to do Eleanor and Paul credit, and she had bought a long unnecessary dress for the same reason and somehow it looked wrong. Eleanor had wanted to pay for it but that Lilly would not allow. And she had given the maid a preposterous tip out of pride, and she had paid visits to the dentist. The last trip had cost her over two hundred dollars. She was horrified. She would not go again.

Over and above all reasons was another. While living in the Valley she never thought of Lilly Waller. But in Vancouver, fear was with her (like a taste, or a smell) that some day, in the town, someone who had known young Lilly Waller in her vagrant years would look at her, and look again, and would come up and say to her "Say, aren't you Lilly Waller? I remember you!" It was not likely, but it was possible. In the night she would wake and smell this fear, and the sweat would break out upon her as she thought, not of herself, but of Eleanor, and Paul, and their secret life, and the children that they would some day have. She would not come again.

It was easy enough. Safe in the Valley she could write, or she could telephone. She could explain "I'm going to stay home this year and take time and cover my chesterfield and chair. You come along up and see me." Or she might say "Matron's arthritis is not so good. I guess I'll take my holiday later this year," and then she would not take a holiday at all. And her small bank account grew. When Eleanor had one boy, and then another, and then another, Lilly had, after all, to go to town to see each new baby, but she could not be induced to stay unless she was needed for a few days in the house. The oldest boy was christened Walter Hughes Lowry which was a nice tribute to Walter Hughes. Lilly loved the boys in a way, but she was not a grandmother by nature.

One evening in the last brilliance before twilight Lilly was standing at the sink in her cottage kitchen. She gave the sink a final wipe. It was pearly clean. She wrung the dishcloth quickly and neatly, looking out of the window at the late sunshine as she did so. A man was crossing the yard that divided her cottage from the hospital. He walked with a swaggering gait, a swaggering roll. He had a cigar in his mouth. He removed it. He spat. He put the cigar back into his mouth. Walking slowly with his swaggering gait, he looked as would a stranger from side to side of the hospital yard, from the hospital building to Lilly's cottage and back to the hospital. Although he wore western clothes, Lilly saw that he was Chinese. His hat, tilted sideways and backwards, revealed a drooping eyelid. Through his wide nostrils he blew cigar smoke. He was formidable. His face was insolent. Lilly, drawing back and back into the shade of her kitchen curtains like a silent animal withdrawing into the cover of the forest, saw, beyond any possibility of doubt, that this man was Yow.

XIV

When poor Lilly recognized the Chinaman, the import of what she saw caused her such terror that the blood rushed from her head and she fell like a stone. She began to gain consciousness, but the horror of what she had seen overwhelmed her and she sank back again. When at last she was able to raise herself she crawled towards the cottage door, reached up and bolted it. She at last rose dizzily to her feet. She drew herself into the bedroom, where she half fell upon the bed.

Year after year now she had lived in an obscurity that was so planned and safe that there were times when it seemed that the years of vagrancy had never been. They had become a dream and hardly a dream, yet a recurring dream. Her faked past had almost become her reality. She had forgotten the associates of her vagrant years, and here was Yow, the most dangerous, the most violent of them all. There was a bicycle, wasn't there, and there were some underclothes. There was Yow in her room on Cordova Street. There was Yow at Lam Sing's and the bicycle. There were other men. There was Lilly working at Lam Sing's. There was the murky half-lit night of Chinatown. There was the bicycle again. There were the police; the police! and Yow's cries in the night, and Lilly hiding in the bushes, and Lilly running, running in the dark from the police, and the same Lilly now a desperate elderly woman.

Oh God, said Lilly aloud for the first time in her life, crouching on her bed, what shall I do? I done the best I could didn't I and what'll happen to me now? There's Eleanor . . . and Paul . . . and Walter and little Paul and the baby and their swell home and their swell friends. If it wasn't for them I'd just go and drown myself . . . but there's Matron and all the folks . . . I done the best I could. Pain shot through her head. Did I hurt myself when I fell down, I guess I did. Lilly drew herself up on the bed (she could not think lying down) and the same support of boldness and hard sense that had saved her before began to be felt through the waves of sick terror and fear and pain.

I needn't fool myself, she knew. I've changed some but he'd remember me sure. I guess he's come after Wong's job . . . I'd see him every day . . . I could wear black glasses but he'd know me—I knew him—and he's the kind that wouldn't have no mercy. She remembered more and more clearly the terrifying fondness on Yow's violent face, and she remembered his words "I killem you", and, she thought, I guess he went to jail and had time to learn to hate me plenty. She could see his derisive face, she could hear his contemptuous voice saying "This woman! I know she! She alla same my woman, she stealem bicycle, I go jail she stealem lady pant, stocking, dress, bicycle everything . . ." She could not face it out. He was too strong for her. Oh, she cried aloud again, God God *what* shall I do? It's like I was in a trap. There's not one person I can turn around to, not Matron and not Eleanor and not Paul and those little kids, I gotta go on protecting them and I gotta go on by myself. I gotta get away . . . right away. And at the thought of what she had to find to do, at once, and at the thought of leaving those who were her life and all because of that vicious man whom she would destroy if she knew how, Lilly, who had never indulged herself in weeping, wept painfully, and wept hopelessly, and wept alone, in the dark of her room.

She felt weak, but she was determined, and, by the time that morning came, her plans were made and she had done with crying.

XV

IT WAS nearly ten o'clock the next morning when Lilly heard the tap that she knew would come on her door.

"Yes?" she called.

"It's Ruthie, Mrs. Hughes," said the voice of the young nurse-in-training. "Matron sent me over to see if you're all right."

"Wait," said Lilly, and got slowly off the bed.

"Oh, Mrs. Hughes, what is it? You're ill! Come back to bed," said the girl, shocked at Lilly's ravaged face.

Lilly gave herself a careless passing glance in the mirror and saw her face, pale, puffed, streaked with weeping and sleeplessness, and bruised on the forehead.

"No," she said with a short laugh, "I'm not sick, Ruthie. I fell, I fainted I guess, and I had bad news from back East and I didn't get much sleep. Ask Matron can she step over when she's got a minute, and oh, Ruthie, get me a pair of dark glasses, the bigger the better, my head hurts and my eyes don't seem to stand the light."

In the evening Lilly caught the eastbound train at Mission. Before boarding the train she telephoned Eleanor from the station telephone. She had not gone to the hospital all day. She would not run that risk.

"Eleanor," she said, "that you? I've only got a minute. Now listen. Your Aunty Mabel's sick, she's living in Toronto now . . . I know . . . neither did I . . . I'd forgotten too . . . but she's all alone and I got a letter from her yesterday that just broke me up. The doctor says she hasn't got long, she might go right away or . . . and she says she's gotta see me . . . no, now listen . . . she's plenty of money it's just she wants me *with* her . . . it was awful pathetic. Matron ran me down to the bank to see Mr. Walker and I drew money for my fare and he'll wire some to the bank when I let him know . . . sure, I'll be at Aunty Mabel's place . . . I'll wire you . . . I gotta go . . . the train's coming in . . . give Paul my love and the boys . . . now don't you worry . . . what's that?" and Lilly hung up the telephone because she had to. For once she had made a long and hurried speech. She had said all she had to say and she could say no more. She had not telephoned earlier because she dared not risk Eleanor's intervention. She said goodbye to Matron and took her seat in the train and smelt the unfamiliar train smell. She felt very tired. Had she covered up all her tracks? Yes, she thought she had. In the small change of daily living, Lilly gave and expected truth. But at the crises that misfortune had brought into her humble life ever since her childhood she had not scrupled to lie for expediency. And now as she dodged again, she lied again, and felt no guilt, only involvedness—a girl's gotta live, hasn't she? Sure, a girl's gotta live.

Lilly resolutely turned to the new experience of travelling on the train. She would not look forward—yet. She could not plan her future—yet. She had got safely away, and that was enough. She dared not look backwards. Perhaps her own cottage would stand there without her and she might never see it again; and Matron, bewildered as time went on, would be without her help; and Eleanor, whom she had moulded with infinite work and care, would continue her happy and sufficient life without her mother, anxious, of course, yet deceived and unaware . . . and for how long? She discovered bitterly how much she loved. She felt the strange taste of sorrow in her throat, and in her stomach the cold core of lead that only the desolate know.

When, two days later, the stubbled prairies spread around her far to the horizons, Lilly, sitting with folded hands, looked intently at the tiny buildings of lonely farms as the train sped on and left the farms behind, disclosing more. Afar off, remote from village or train, she saw small isolated dwellings. Was it there I lived? she thought with a slight sardonic smile, or there, with Walter Hughes? She took the train guide and memorized the names of stations through which the railroad passed. At least, she knew now where she had lived, and the unfamiliar and endless prairie was her nearest familiar friend.

XVI

When Lilly arrived in Toronto she wasted no time in renting a small room and securing employment as a chambermaid in one of the lesser hotels. She did her work well and easily.

Eleanor wrote anxiously. "Are you all right, or shall I come? Tell me, dearest dearest M." Lilly's flat reassurance to Eleanor as to her aunt's health and her mother's easy circumstances, . . . "She's doing pretty good now . . . it's a bit of a change for me, but I'll be coming back pretty soon," satisfied her. The Matron was busy and wrote seldom. "We're getting on," she wrote, "but I never realized how much I rely on you. Mrs. Wilkes is filling in fairly well. The new Chinaman is an excellent cook but very bad-tempered. Poor Ruthie, he terrified her. You know Wong's big kitchen knife? He twiddled it at her and said I killem you. I spoke sharply to him about it and he went black as thunder and said he was only fooling. I don't want to lose him, he's so clean and quick, but if that happens again, away he goes. Now don't hurry, take a rest if you can, but how glad I shall be . . ."

Lilly's mouth pulled down in a wry grimace. She contemplated the Matron's letter. How clearly she saw it all. Matron, unknowing, had warned her away and she could not return. Lilly lay awake, night after night, looking into the darkness, seeking a way.

After her working hours she had nothing to do. Shows cost money, and she would not spend money, so she found in the shop windows her cheapest occupation. She wandered along Yonge Street and Bloor Street without any fear of recognition, and as she looked in the great shop windows a new world was disclosed to her in which all women were beautiful. All the models, standing sleek-haired and frozen in elegant attitude, seemed to be young. But as Lilly watched with interested eyes the women in the hotel, in the streets, in the cafés, she saw many older women also whose well-groomed heads seemed to be the key to an appearance which she admired. She's been styled, I suppose, she thought, as she saw some white or grey neatly modelled head. As the days went on, a plan matured in her mind. Why wouldn't I be styled so's it would change me a bit? And it would please Eleanor; she wanted me to be styled. Lilly was desperately lonely. If she could see a time coming when she could go to her own home and people and not spend her life cleaning hotel bedrooms in a foreign city, walking the streets, and going back to a rooming house, then she could endure, for a time.

Late one afternoon Lilly walked into the most expensive looking Beauty Shop that she could find. She went up to the girl sitting at the desk and said "I want to be styled, and I'd like my hair dyed white. It's kinda mousey now."

The girl at the desk looked at her and said "You'd better see Miss Larue. I doubt whether she'll dye your hair white, but if you'll take a seat I'll call her, and then she'll tell you."

Lilly was soon seated in a chair in a small and elegant booth whose appearance surprised her. She looked at herself in a large gilt-framed mirror and did not like what she saw. A small untidy woman in a crumpled white uniform entered the booth. "Good afternoon," said the woman. "Good afternoon," said Lilly, and thought Why don't you style your own self? She did not know that this woman was a power, privileged, and an artist who modelled in human clay.

The woman surveyed Lilly's dowdy figure in the mirror. She ran her fingers through Lilly's sparse and faded hair, lifting it, dropping it. "Well?" she said, and surveyed her again.

"I want my hair dyed white, and styled," said Lilly.

"I couldn't dye your hair white. I could dye your hair platinum but I wouldn't. It would look terrible. You wouldn't suit it. It'd be a terror to the nations," said Miss Larue, looking dispassionately up and down the figure in the glass. Lilly felt her every weakness magnified and revealed in the fine mirror as she, too, looked at herself.

"Well, what were you *really* wanting?" asked Miss Larue who had dyed innocents and thieves in her time, and had no illusions.

Guess I'd better tell her if I'm going to get anything out of this, thought Lilly. She said "I want to be styled. I come from out West. I live in the country and my daughter lives in the city. She's married and she's well fixed, and she's got three fine boys and I figure their grandmother could do them a whole lot more credit. She's been at me and at me to get styled so I thought while I was in Toronto I'd get something done about it. But I can see," continued Lilly humbly, "that it wouldn't be any good me having my hair fixed and everything else looking wrong."

"You're dead right it wouldn't," said Miss Larue. She leaned her elbow on a cupboard and nonchalantly regarded Lilly. "I can tell you what to do, and I can do something for you, but it's going to change you quite a bit if you do what I say."

"My daughter won't mind, and she's the only one I care about," said Lilly, and hope leapt within her.

"All right. I'll tell you. Maybe you won't like it, but you just listen to me." Lilly nodded. "First, we make you a wig." Lilly started, and began to say "A wig . . .!" But Miss Larue silenced her. "You listen to me. First we make you a wig, grey, a bit iron grey, not white, very neat, modelled waves, not curls—every woman starts bleating when I say 'wig'—well, call it what you like, call it an 'adaptation' if you like, but it's a wig, and that's the first thing we'd do. Then I'll touch your eyebrows and lashes just a little, and you'll have to wear a bit of lipstick . . ."

"I never use . . ." began Lilly.

"No, I know you don't," said Miss Larue with asperity, "but you should. Now am I telling you or are you telling me?" Lilly's lips moved silently. "Okay. Then you've got to throw out that print you're wearing. You go to one of the big stores and get you a plain black suit, no trimmings, no fancy sleeves, just plain classic tailored. You've got a good figure, slim in the hips but you might need a coupla cheaters." ("Cheaters?" wondered Lilly.) "Then you get you a small—smaller the better—black hat, head-fitting cap effect, no trimming, no nothing. You can get 'em for seventy-five dollars or you can get 'em for four ninety-five—no veil, no nothing, you get a feather or a veil later when you've got more assurance.

252

You get you black gloves, a plain black handbag, and plain black pumps, *not* fancy. You can wreck the whole outfit if you get fancy pumps. Do you know what court pumps are?" Lilly shook her head. "Well, you ask 'em for court pumps. Cold weather's coming on. You get you a plain black coat, warm, not fancy. I *think*, for you, better get form-fitting." Lilly nodded. "If you could run to a short Persian lamb, loose back, as well, it . . ."

Lilly spoke. "No Persian lamb coat. What do you think . . .?" She could speak frankly with this woman.

"Okay, okay," said Miss Larue soothingly, "you don't *haf* to. I'm just telling you. You've got to get all black for a start. I wouldn't trust you with colours. Your suit won't cost you an awful lot. I can't say about the coat, it all depends, your hat'll come cheap, your bag and your shoes—don't you try to scrimp on them. Your wig'll come most expensive. But I'm telling you, when you've done those simple things, your own daughter'll have to take three looks at you before she knows you, and then she'll be crazy about you. And what'll you have done? Nothing but make the best of yourself and it's high time. You can't do a thing with *that* hair, not to look like anything," and she ran disparaging fingers again through Lilly's wispy hair. "You've got to change the whole works and it's easy if you can pay for it. There you are—take it or leave it, but don't ask me to style your hair and then go round looking the way you do."

"What'd the . . . what did you call it, well, the . . . wig . . . cost?" asked Lilly, bracing herself.

"Oh, anywheres from a hundred and fifty to about two hundred dollars, according," said Miss Larue. Hundreds were nothing to her.

Lilly considered the wig. She would have to spend too much of her savings which were so precious to her. But with this money she could open a gate wide through which she could go safely home. What release, to walk Vancouver streets with Eleanor without fear! She must do it all, or not at all. She saw the justice of what Miss Larue had told her. With an effort she said "Okay."

Miss Larue patted her shoulder. "Good for you, honey," she said. "I like to see a woman who can make up her mind and not fuss."

"I don't fuss," said Lilly.

"There's one more thing I've got to tell you," said Miss Larue, "if you can take it."

"I can take it," said Lilly.

"When you get your new outfit, pitch out that dress and that maroon coat . . . and that hat too. Give 'em away. Sell 'em. Don't own 'em." She saw Lilly's lips move. " No," she said, "don't keep that dress nor any other, to wear working round the house. Forget 'em. Pitch 'em out even if you've only a coupla cotton uniforms to wear round the house. If you keep those clothes you keep some of your old-fashion self. And when you get kinda caught up, buy you a thin grey wool dress, plain, not fancy. That'll do you for anything in the house except formal, and you can wait for that. You don't mind me telling you, all this, do you, dearie? . . . Oh and . . ." she continued rather apologetically, for she had begun to like this slim silent practical woman who had, probably, little money to spare, "*if* you can run to it, when you've got the other things—but they're the essentials— get you a pair of plain pearl or silver earrings, large buttons, or clips, nothing that dangles, silver with your hair not gold, and some pearls . . . no no no, imitation . . . or a silver link necklace . . . cost you one ninety-eight or a bit less or more. Oh, and you'd better stay home nights awhile and cream your skin. We'll start you off with a coupla facials if you like but you don't *haf* to. Your skin's pretty good." Miss Larue, on a fine creative spree, was assisting at the rebirth of a free woman, Mrs. Walter Hughes. She fell silent, looking Lilly over with her artist's eyes. Lilly looked mistily past the woman in the glass to the new Mrs. Walter Hughes, hardly recognizable even to Eleanor, yet justifiable to Eleanor. ("Why, Mother . . .!" "Yes, I know, but I thought I might as well get styled while I had the chance.") She was sure that Eleanor, after the first quick intake of surprise, would be pleased; she was not so sure of Matron, yet she thought Matron would be pleased. But, whether or not they were pleased, Lilly knew that she was committed, that she was glad, and that there would be no turning back. But will it change me? Shall I be safe? I think so.

XVII

Mr. J. B. Sprockett was one of the passengers who boarded the east-bound train at Winnipeg on a Monday evening. He was overcast, and in spite of the fact that he wished very much at this moment to leave his home in Winnipeg, his feeling was rather one of reprieve than relief. He found his car, shouldered himself on to the train, made his way to his seat, disposed of his bag, brief-case, coat and hat, sat down, looked through the dark and rather opaque window at nothing in particular, and said to himself What the hell.

I never knew before, he said to himself again, that you could go through your life, and be real happy, and then get to be sixty-four and have the most awful thing happen to you. It's not fair, when you're—he dismissed "elderly" and tried "getting older". It's not fair to have trouble when you're getting older and can't stand it the way maybe when you were young and had your way to make. And then he thought again that after all he was only one of the millions upon millions of people who are getting older for whom are reserved the most crushing indiscriminate and callous blows of life and fate. That don't make it any easier, he said to himself. And so he brooded. The train jerked, and after trying again, it started. He felt a faint sensation of release as the train drew out of the station. He took his evening paper and found that he didn't care for it. Headlines, talk, advertisements, all

were the same, yet all different because Bessy was dead,
and Mr. Sprockett while suffering the almost irremediable
homesickness of bereavement had now become tram-
melled in events to which he would never have thought it
possible to be exposed. No more would Bessy, he thought.
What had happened? Nothing out of the ordinary, yet
he was now what is called a widower. Mr. Sprockett was
shaken from time to time by such discoveries as that he was
lost, that he was irrelevant, that he was no longer the self
into which he had grown after thirty-nine years of living—
not in rapture but in the perfect satisfaction which is one
equation of love—round the days, the weeks, the years
with Bessy Sprockett, and he knew now in an obscure way
how taut yet tenuous are the filaments that bind our
beings, and how death changes the aspect of a street, of
a house, particularly of a room—yes, of everything in life.
Bessy had been ripped away from him without warning
(thirty-nine years of shared mortality had not served to
warn him), and those filaments had been torn and only a
vestigial Mr. Sprockett remained. And yet he appeared
very much the same. He could see that in his mirror when
he looked.

"Good evening," said the man who took the seat
opposite him.

"Good evening," said Mr. Sprockett and chose to look
at the blind dumb window. Gosh, those sure were two
awful parties, Saturday night at Ed's place when they had
Bertha's sister, and last night at Al's place when they had
that second Aldridge girl. Brrrr, went Mr. Sprockett,
blowing through his lips and shaking his head rapidly,
forgetting the man across the way. He thought with
distaste of Bertha's sister, with her fat cheeks painted too

bright (no brighter, if he had known it, than Bessy's used
to be), with her constant treble cry "Oh say!" (no more
shrill than Bessy's treble cry), and her air that was cosy,
as if he and she understood. And the second Aldridge girl,
I guess she'd be about fifty, or more'n that now, well, that's
okay, but . . . well, those Aldridge girls they all look the
same to me, marry one, marry all three. Why can't they
leave me *alone!* he thought in a rage. Yet Mr. Sprockett
could not bear to be alone, and he knew it. He almost felt
that Bessy, taken away in surprise, had failed him and
had not been faithful in this, but he checked the thought.

"Make up your berth, sir," said the porter in his rich
husky voice. "Observation car's three cars back."

Mr. Sprockett, followed by his companion, walked
lurching down the aisle of the train, steadying himself as
he walked. It was surprising how much alike the two men
were, and, as they entered the end car, an interested
observer might notice two or three more Mr. Sprocketts
already leaning back on the comfortable chairs, reading
the magazines, looking through the dark windows at the
Canadian landscape which they could not see but which
fell backwards and backwards behind the moving cars,
and contributing to the cloud of tobacco smoke that
blended richly yet acridly with the smell of train.

It is all very well to say that Mr. Sprockett was a type,
but that settles nothing for *him.* He was the only Mr.
J. B. Sprockett on that train who had irrevocably lost his
wife Bessy, and who could not live alone, and who was
heading east through the night (this time alone) on a
business trip which (his friends said to each other) would
serve to take his mind off of things and would jolt him
out of himself and would help him come to some decision

about himself when he got back, so let's give him a send-off and a coupla little parties. Because (they said) it's just terrible to see the way he's going, I mean poor old J.B., he's got to go through with it the way other people do. Everybody has to go through *something some* time. He's no different.

So that's what Mr. Sprockett was doing; he was going through with it. Sitting down in the observation car he continued to go through with it, and then when he thought the porter had had enough time he went back to the sleeper and climbed up into the upper berth and undressed in the discomfort that he could no longer make a good joke of because who cared, and he continued to go through with it until he slept.

When he arrived in Toronto he went to the hotel where he usually stayed. He covered a good deal of business in the first two days. He spoke to all the porters and waitresses and clerks and bell boys that he possibly could, and it cheered him a bit because to them he was just another travelling man and not someone who was going through with it and must be treated differently from other people. This disguise, or anonymity, was, unknown to Mr. Sprockett, of some service to him, and gave him back an entity, spurious perhaps and still vulnerable, but restoring.

He forgot, sometimes, that he had to return to Winnipeg and the grey unpalatable dish of life. But three or four days soon pass, and the inescapable moment was drawing near.

XVIII

MR. SPROCKETT looked gloomily out of his bedroom window. The day was fair, clouds raced, the wind blew the chimney smokes and the smoke of a far-off ship on the lake in flat streaming banners. Business was good. Two days more would finish it. Mr. Sprockett's digestion was good, but he had no appetite, or perhaps food had no taste. Last year when he had made his annual trip east he had been alone but he had not been lonely. The year before that he had brought Bessy with him and her loud and cheerful presence had filled his space. Perhaps he had taken her for granted . . . well, perhaps he had. But he wouldn't have done anything different, he had nothing to reproach himself with and neither had Bessy. I mean if it had been me that passed away and not Bessy she wouldn't have had a thing to reproach herself with neither. It was like that.

In two days' time Mr. Sprockett would board the train and go west to Winnipeg and open up the house whose air was lifeless and depleted. Once a week there were the signs that the cleaning woman had been there. But when he went home at nights never a thing was stirring in that house, empty from wall to wall. Never a sound from the kitchen, never the long telephone conversation with "the girls" about Lodge, never the shrieks of laughter. Bessy had been a great laugher, like a great big girl, buxom, a bright dresser. Somehow he had never thought that life would not go on in the same way forever. He shrank from the harsh truth and finality of the words "Bessy died"; she had passed away, a refinement of speech which tempered the fact. And now because it was six months since Bessy had passed away the boys and their wives had begun to ask him out with their sisters or unmarried friends and the meaning was plain. And one of these days he would find himself marrying Bertha's sister or Herb's cousin or one of the Aldridge girls because he couldn't help it. And the boys were beginning to joke him a bit about a nice young lady. He was not moping exactly but his empty house was desolate. Yet it was still a refuge, and sometimes he sat there and never even answered the telephone. It was no good. Maybe one of these days he'd come around to one of the Aldridge girls.

As he continued to gaze gloomily out of his bedroom window, revolving his unprofitable thoughts and tasting the ashes in his mouth, he heard someone enter the room. He looked round indifferently and saw that the chambermaid had come in, bringing fresh linen and cleaning utensils.

"Good morning," said Mr. Sprockett.

"Good morning," said the chambermaid.

Mr. Sprockett resumed his staring out of the window.

In his domestic, social, and business dealings, Mr. Sprockett had always been a jokey man. But now the springs of his jokiness had dried up within him. The habits of communication remained, and so he turned again to the chambermaid and said "It's a fine day."

"Yes," said the chambermaid, neatly unfolding and spreading a sheet. Mr. Sprockett watched her moodily instead of watching the smoke blowing across the skies of Toronto.

"Tronno your home?" asked Mr. Sprockett, more from force of habit than anything else.

"No," said the chambermaid, moving quickly round the end of the bed and causing Mr. Sprockett to step smartly backwards. It did not occur to him that he was in the way.

The chambermaid moved well and neatly. It seemed as if order flowed from her fingertips, and sheets, pillow-slips, blankets, bedcover fell obediently into place instead of standing up to her and wrestling with her and intentionally crumpling themselves and falling out of line as they do in less gifted hands. She was a good-looking woman with too much reserve. A little friendliness wouldn't hurt, thought Mr. Sprockett, what does she think I am! Her figure was young and slim but her neat head was grey. He caught glimpses, as she turned and turned about, of a face worn but pleasing. Fifty-four? fifty-six? thought Mr. Sprockett who made a hobby of ages.

I wish he'd get out of my way, thought Lilly. If he stands there any longer I'm going on to three hundred and seven.

"And what's your name, if I may ask?" said Mr. Sprockett who liked to call people by their names.

"Mrs. Walter Hughes," said the chambermaid.

"Is that right!" said Mr. Sprockett who was for one moment surprised and taken out of himself. "Your husband . . . er . . . in business here?" He said that naturally, because while Mr. *Hughes* might be absent through death or divorce Mr. *Walter* Hughes sounded present and active.

"I'm a widow," said the chambermaid, deftly adjusting the bedcover. She had not turned toward Mr. Sprockett.

Mr. Sprockett, who until this moment had looked at everything—including Lilly—that came within his vision with the lack of interest shown by fishes, came to life, looked at Lilly, and really saw her. He had always regarded widows as a social or business classification (fill out Form A Section 3, state whether unmarried, married, widowed or divorced) without emotional overtones or connotations, but now he knew what the word meant. I guess, he thought, married women know things that spinsters don't know, and widows know a whole lot that married women don't know. So *that's* what it is.

"Is *that* right!" he said with some feeling.

Lilly straightened herself and looked at him. She really was very . . . well, unusual.

"I'll go on to my next room and come back when you're through," she said, and did so.

That night Mr. Sprockett had nothing in particular to do so he went to a show. He did not like it. Before Bessy passed away they used to like going to a show, they went to lots of shows. They had their favourites. And if he was in—say—Toronto alone, he'd go alone, or ask someone he met to go with him, and that was fine, because everything was all right and when you went out again into the street everything used to seem natural. But now, he had to force himself to go to a show, because the minute you emerged into the street, into real life, it wasn't real life, it was the same kind of nightmare again, you knew again that you were irrelevant, you belonged nowhere, things had no meaning and were indifferent to you, and you were in a devastated country. But returning home to

Winnipeg was much worse than going to a show. He did not want to stay in Toronto, but he did not want to go home. Maybe all this feeling would get better some day. Lots of people had to go through with it. In this frame of mind Mr. Sprockett went back to the hotel and went to bed. He slept a bit but did not rest.

Next morning Mr. Sprockett telephoned the man whom he was meeting at nine o'clock and told him that he could not make it at nine o'clock and would eleven do. If he could not make it by eleven he'd let him know. The man said that would be okay, as a matter of fact it suited him better. Mr. Sprockett then took papers out of his brief-case and scattered them upon a round table. He pulled the armchair over beside the table, selected a folder, sat back in the armchair with his fountain pen in his hand, as if lost in thought. The door was slightly open.

Mr. Sprockett was becoming tired of going through the same folder when the door opened wide and the chambermaid came in. She stopped. "Oh," she said, "I didn't know."

Mr. Sprockett waved a slightly lordly hand that said "Come in and don't mind me," gave a perfunctory smile and became again immersed in the folder in which he made notations from time to time. The chambermaid made the bed.

Mr. Sprockett at last gave the sigh of one who has finished his work, closed the folder, and looked up at the chambermaid. He said almost austerely "May I have a few words with you," and his tone was rather that of polite command than of question.

"Well, I'm busy," said the chambermaid, hesitating a

little, but her words had an upward inflection which did
not denote finality.

"Mrs. Hughes," said Mr. Sprockett, and a huskiness
crept into his voice, "you are a widow and you will
understand what I am going to say to you."

Lilly said nothing, but looked at him with her soft
brown eyes that were made finer by the delicate new
darkness of her brows and lashes.

"I ... er ... come from Winnapeg," said Mr. Sprockett.
"That is, my home is in Winnapeg and I am returning
there day after tomorrow. I . . . er . . . lost Mrs.
Sprockett recently. She passed away last May. And I
must say . . ." But Mr. Sprockett could not say it. Lilly
did not help him; she stood there silent, her look not
quite as impersonal as before.

Mr. Sprockett continued. "You may be a family
woman yourself, Mrs. Hughes?"

"I gotta married daughter," said Lilly.

"Is that right!" said Mr. Sprockett.

He was, for some obscure reason, pleased.

"Her husband in business?" asked Mr. Sprockett who
always liked to know these things.

"He's a lawyer," said Lilly shortly. Then "Not here.
In Vancouver."

"Is *that* right!" said Mr. Sprockett. He was both
pleased and amazed. The fact that Mrs. Walter Hughes
had a daughter married to a lawyer seemed to make
the suggestion that he was about to offer both right and
reasonable.

"Mrs. Sprockett and I . . . we had no family, and so it
makes it all the worse . . ." Lilly nodded, and he was
grateful to her for the nod and for no more.

265

"Well, I was going to suggest to you, Mrs. Hughes, seeing I don't know any ladies in Tronno, at least I do know two ladies but I have no wish to invite these ladies, no wish at all, if you would be kind enough to have a bite of dinner with me tonight and go to a show . . . I'm going back to Winnapeg almost right away you understand so it isn't as if . . ." his voice tailed away, "what I meantersay I wouldn't be in any way . . ."

Lilly looked, hesitated, and said "I don't mind if I do." The acceptance was not warm, but Mr. Sprockett appreciated her almost guarded manner. A woman can't be too careful, not a nice woman.

XIX

At half-past six that evening at the time of transition in the sky, when the streets were growing dark and bright and the feeling of night came down on the city, McCloskey's was loud with chatter and clatter, and Mr. Sprockett who was waiting there for Mrs. Walter Hughes was feeling nervous. Now that he sat there, expecting his chambermaid to dinner, he began to think that he had been a bit silly. What was she going to look like anyway? I don't know what Bessy would think of me, but I guess Bessy would understand. You *gotta* have some female diversion like and I'm scared pink of Bessy's friends with marriage in their eye and a person like this who doesn't expect anything is kind of a relief. I never did just such a thing as this in all my life before but then I never was so unhappy in all my life before. What's the odds! Lilly, slim, scared, smart, stepped inside the swing door and stood.

A man sitting alone at a table looked at her under deeply furrowed brows. Clasping her bag she stood, her small grey head held straight and well, and her brown eyes widened, looking to right and left. A deer in the city, thought the man, a deer dressed in black, and see the sabled delicate deer startled on the edge of the multitude startle darkle crash and clash the voices of the multitude startle the delicate elegant deer, and so he went on. But Mr. Sprockett did not think that Lilly was a deer dressed in black. He breathed relief as he saw that she was a

darn good-looking woman and knew how to dress,
different, of course, from Bessy who had been plump
and liked a bit of colour, but very stylish.

"This is very kind of you, Mrs. Hughes," said Mr.
Sprockett as they sat down.

"Oh no," said Lilly with her small seldom smile.

Mr. Sprockett read from a menu that bewildered
Lilly. "You choose," she said, so he chose. Mr. Sprockett,
although chiefly engrossed in his own solitariness, had
become interested as to why Mrs. Walter Hughes, a
good-looking woman and stylish in appearance, with a
daughter married to a lawyer in Vancouver should be
working as a chambermaid in a Toronto hotel. He
considered. How should he set about a little delicate
questioning? He did not know how, so he said, straight
out, "Mrs. Hughes, I don't want to seem inquisitive, but
does your dotter *know* that you're working as a chambermaid in a hotel?"

Lilly flushed ever so little all over her pale face and
shook her head.

"Ah, I thought not," said Mr. Sprockett, feeling
pleased with himself. "Or your son-in-law? Is he a
nice fella?"

"Paul's lovely," said Lilly with something near
enthusiasm.

"Well, then," said Mr. Sprockett, speaking rather like
an uncle, "wouldn't they want to help you, if it's money,
I mean?"

"Oh yes," said Lilly, "that's it. I don't want them
to." ("I thought as much," nodded Mr. Sprockett.)
Lilly felt that she had better explain, although she was
not much good at explaining.

"I came east in a hurry. My sister was sick and I
nursed her and she died." (Lilly was familiar with life
and death, and in her experience people used no euphe-
misms about death; they did not pass on, over, or away,
they simply died.) "And after my sister died I was sick.
I guess I was tired out, and when I got everything fixed
up there wasn't much money," (How clear it all became
to Mr. Sprockett, listening as he watched Lilly, with her
worn and pretty face with its agreeable snub nose, sitting
there and telling her simple lies) "and I knew I could
get a job like that tempory, so I thought I'd save a bit
before I went home. Eleanor doesn't know. I didn't
even tell her her aunty died after all or I was sick. She
just thinks I'm staying at her aunty's place. There's no
reason why they should worry now. I'll tell them some
day. They'd send me the money to go home sure, but
they got three little kids. I'll soon have enough to go
home on my own. Paul's doing fine but it costs money
to get on, and I got my health," and she stopped.

Mr. Sprockett was touched. "You're a very very fine
woman, Mrs. Hughes, if you don't mind me saying
so."

"Oh no," said Lilly simply, without argument.

"And do you live with your dotter, Mrs. Hughes?"

"No, I work. Up the Valley."

"Work?"

"I help Matron in the hospital there."

"You a nurse?" respectfully.

"No. But I guess I can do anything round a hospital.
I worked with Matron there for getting on twenty-five
years or more." There was no boasting in Lilly's talk,
simply a statement of fact while she ate her dinner, and

269

a statement of fact that happened to be also a statement of character.

"Is *that* right!" said Mr. Sprockett, feeling more respectful every minute.

Lilly was not expert in communication, and did not try to draw Mr. Sprockett out although it would have been easy. But as soon as Mr. Sprockett's curiosity about Lilly was satisfied he began, naturally, to talk about himself.

He talked about Bessy, her illness, death and burial. He told Mrs. Hughes where he first met Bessy, what she wore, liked, cooked, ate, about his Order and her Lodge, about the boys (most of whom were now bald boys), and the girls (most of whom were now grey girls). Lilly did not respond very much; she ate with care; listened; and became a well into which Mr. Sprockett poured himself.

"And now," he said, "I can see perfectly well, the boys are kind of ganging up on me. I guess the girls are behind it. And I know they mean well. I might under sim'lar circumstances do the same myself. But it just goes to show they don't understand, not till they've been through it like me—and like you, Mrs. Hughes." Lilly nodded. "You can take a horse to the water I always say, but you can't make it drink. Mrs. Sprockett was always one for being lively and the house feels just terrible. I can't hardly stand the thought of going back home. There's the Aldridge girls that Mrs. Sprockett went to school with, and sometimes I get thinking I'd better settle for one of the Aldridge girls though I must say I wouldn't for choice. I guess, Mrs. Hughes, you being an attractive woman, there's more than once you been approached on the subject of matrimony since your husband passed on?"

"Yes," said Lilly.

"And might I ask," said Mr. Sprockett, leaning across the steaming plates, "what it was stopped you marrying some nice fella? I bet I could tell you."

"I always felt that Mr. Hughes . . ." began Lilly, and stopped. There was no reason why she should not be frank, because, come to think of it, Eleanor was the reason why she had not married, Eleanor and the desire that Lilly had to possess herself.

"It was my daughter," she said. "I wanted her brought up like so, and if I married they mightn't have liked each other. So I worked and gave her an edjcation. Mr. Hughes' family was edjcated and a bit high steppers and I hadn't what you'd call an edjcation myself and I wanted Eleanor should have everything in the way of an edjcation. And she did."

"I knew! I knew!" said Mr. Sprockett. "You sacrificed yourself on the altar of . . . You're a very very lovely woman, Mrs. Hughes. You've had a hard life and come through!"

"Oh, I don't know," said Lilly. "It's been kinda happy too."

XX

MR. SPROCKETT arose the next morning in a state of exhilaration such as he had not known for years and years and years. It was quite different from his normal arisings of several decades, except perhaps when he and Bessy were going on a holiday. His normal awakening was into optimism, flecked sometimes by business cares, and was followed at once by dressing and shaving noisily and cheerfully while Bessy made kitchen clatter, calling or, rather, shrieking to him sometimes from kitchen to bathroom. And since then there had been this interminable interval of horrible awakenings into emptiness and silence, alone in the bed, the room, the house, the void. And today a feeling of hope, some kind of hope, any kind of hope.

He made his plans for the day, and arranged that he should encounter Mrs. Hughes in the hotel corridor, which he did. Lilly was moving between bedrooms and carried a bundle of crumpled sheets. She looked at him over the bundle of sheets. She was as trim and neat this morning in her white cotton working dress as she had been last night in her elegant black. A warm and pleased feeling came over Lilly when Mr. Sprockett accosted her genially in the hall.

"Well, and how are we this morning," he enquired heartily.

Lilly's lips moved in a smile. "Fine," she said.

"I'm off in a hurry," said Mr. Sprockett looking down

at his watch. "I gotta lot to catch up today before I leave tomorrow. I thought if you are free to have dinner with me again tonight it would certny make a nice little wind-up for me before leaving Tronno—that is to say if convenient to *you*."

Lilly and Mr. Sprockett had progressed last night into that pleasant stream-fed meadow-land in which men and women find themselves, where no names are used, a place of more or less magical anonymity which words do not describe. Sometimes you return to the street names and shop names of daily living. Less frequently, but sometimes in nearly every life, progress is made further into personally owned and fenced-in territory. They had not arrived there yet.

Lilly said "I'd be glad to."

"Fine . . . fine . . ." said Mr. Sprockett, "same place, same time." He said this beaming and with emphasis, and went hurriedly on his way down the hall. Lilly disposed of the laundry and entered the next bedroom, feeling different.

Mr. Sprockett was not quite honest with Lilly. He had now no intention of leaving Toronto the next day. It would all depend on his own finesse, on Lilly's disposition, and on luck. He was excited.

When Lilly entered McCloskey's that night, no poet would have called her a startled deer—a deer perhaps, but a self-possessed deer that Mr. Sprockett did not wish to frighten. They sat down.

"Well well well, feels kind of nice, doesn't it?" said Mr. Sprockett snugly.

Lilly thought He *is* a nice man, and smiled. The smile softened and lit her face.

273

"My my, I hope you don't mind me saying," said Mr. Sprockett, leaning forward with oh so happy and shining a look upon him as if he had been polished, "but you do have pretty teeth!"

Words from the days when Mrs. Butler read and taught old tales to Eleanor floated up in Lilly's mind.

"All the better to eat you with," she said unexpectedly and was astounded at herself.

At this they both laughed and laughed, and the feeling that had pervaded Mr. Sprockett for the last twenty-four hours pulsed more strongly up from his feet, to his stomach, and flowed out to the end of his fingers but particularly into his head and face.

"Would you mind if I ast you your name, your Christian name?" he said.

"Lilly," said Lilly.

"Lily, Lily!" he repeated, seeing lilies. This woman was perfect! The voice of a spirit in his brain said Lily Sprockett Lilian Sprockett Lily Sprockett Lilian Sprockett. "Would you mind me calling you Lilian? I always thought it was a very handsome name."

"No," said Lilly, "I wouldn't mind."

The waiter stood over them. Mr. Sprockett ordered shrewdly. When the waiter had left, Mr. Sprockett knew that he had a good long time to talk without interruption.

"When I told you this morning that I was going to Winnapeg tomorrow that wasn't strictly true. I been very busy today finding out certain things and I find that . . . I find that . . . Well, I'll tell you." He looked earnestly at his fingers and Lilly looked at them too. Then he looked up and spoke in a serious voice. He had mastered the excitement that possessed him because you have to do these things properly. "If you and I were to get married right here in Tronno—and go back home and settle right in at the house it would be wonderful, wonderful! Now just a minute just a minute . . . all Mrs. Sprockett's and my friends would be crazy about you and . . ." his voice was tender, "I'll say this now and I'll not say it again . . . I have a feel that Bessy would be kind of pleased it was you and not one of the girls. *Now* . . ." he said in his ordinary voice.

"But what about the Aldridge girls?"

"I don't *haf*ta marry the Aldridge girls," he said vehemently. "That's just one of the things I don't want to do!" and he looked urgently at Lilly.

Her lips moved.

"What did you say?"

"I don't know what to say," said Lilly.

Mr. Sprockett's happy look faded. Lilly knew that he thought that she did not know what to answer, but she meant that she did not know how to answer him. He looked very anxious.

"I don't mean what you mean," she said, "I just don't know what to say." She looked at her lap.

Truly it seemed a long time to Mr. Sprockett that he sat there suffused by wavering emotions as he waited for Lilly's answer to him. Between the putting of a proposal of marriage and the Yes or the No, the interval is forever and intolerable. Lilly took a long time to answer him, long by the clock, and immeasurable to Mr. Sprockett.

She wished to marry him. She had never hoped so high. But her almost fatal caution made her pause to examine. Could there be any flaw, or any possibility of discovery that still might wreck her—and him? She thought

275

not. She felt that this man was kinder, perhaps, than any man that she had ever known, and he was hers for a look or the speaking of a word. She recognized, of course, that not only herself had charmed him, but that he had turned to her in his extremity. She knew now that when he had first addressed her, only yesterday, he was desperately trying to dodge the future towards which he was compelled to turn again. The taste had gone out of his life. He was cornered. And then he met her. He'd never have turned to me so quick if he hadn't been unhappy, she thought. . . and I can make him happy, and comfortable too . . . him happy, and me . . . why, I've never been to say happy like that, have I, in my life. While these thoughts threaded light and quick through Lilly's mind and she still sat silent, looking downwards, the man opposite to her grew more gloomy. But she had not finished yet. Every moment brought her nearer to her answer, for herself yes, and yes again and again. But the old habits of mind and heart that rushed first to the care of her daughter, and then to Matron, still delayed her. Yet she knew before she asked herself the question that this marriage would not divide her from her children. She would be proud of it, and they would be glad for her. And as she thought Perhaps by and by he'd let Matron come and stay with us for a bit and I could look after her, the soft look that came on her face caused the fog of Mr. Sprockett's gloom to lift a little. Before ever she said a word to the man who was waiting on the other side of the table, she wanted to call to Eleanor, and to Paul, and to Matron at once, and again and again, joyfully, "I am going to marry Mr. Sprockett!" She looked up at him with a look that seemed to be, that was, for him only.

"Will you tell me this, then? Could you love me, d'you think?" asked Mr. Sprockett, speaking very low.

Lilly examined this question. If loving Mr. Sprockett meant looking after him and thinking for him and caring for him and guarding him from harm and keeping things nice like she'd always done for Eleanor and for Matron, then she could love him, and she was his, and he was hers.

"Yes, I could," she said. Then she said with a faint and apologetic smile "I could make you very comfortable too."

This simple statement caused Mr. Sprockett so much rapture that he cursed himself that he had not deferred the whole of this conversation until after dinner, because he wanted to kiss Lilly for saying that, and here came the waiter. He felt that, failing putting his arms round her which was not very easy at the table at McCloskey's, he must make some kind of declaration, so after an interval he said solemnly "You have made me a very happy man."

Lilly was happy too, happier than she had ever been and with a different variety of happiness. Perhaps what she chiefly felt was gratitude but she did not enquire of herself. She had the same kind of confidence in Mr. Sprockett that she had in Matron with the added pleasure that he was a man. She would be without fear; nothing, surely, could touch her now. There would be security and a life of her very own in the house of Mr. and Mrs. Sprockett. She would be content that she should share a ménage à trois with Bessy Sprockett and her husband. But still two shadows fell upon her, one small, one great.

Mr. Sprockett saw that Lilly was about to speak, and he held back the stream of information that was bubbling for release.

She spoke slowly.

"There's one thing that sorta scares me . . . and it's kinda hard to say . . . I don't always talk very good, and if I try to talk good I talk worse. I don't know why I talk like I do," she said plaintively, "but when I'm with folks that are edjcated, I get nervous and I just *know* I don't talk right and so I stay quiet. I guess it's because I was just a country girl and never had advantages. I wouldn't like to make you ashamed ever. I don't know about Paul and Eleanor, but they never . . ."

"Think nothing of it," almost shouted Mr. Sprockett. "I'm not so hot myself. My my my, how I remember Bessy calling me down for something I'd say—kind of in joke! She was a great reader, all the magazines; movie magazines and everything," (Lilly breathed a freer air) "there was nothing she didn't know, but she'd just jolly me along. You talk fine! . . . Now let me tell you something. The law here says we can't get married for three days after I get the licence. You fire the hotel tomorrow and get yourself fixed up." Into Lilly's vision swam Miss Larue's grey woollen dress, followed by a pair of white gloves, in at the left side, out at the right. Into Mr. Sprockett's vision swam the fur coat that he would soon get for Lilian Sprockett. How good he was! Yes, he was good.

"I don't need anything but one thing and maybe a pair of white gloves to get married," said Lilly. "I dress plain."

(This woman is a wonder!) "Now you must let *me* . . ." said Mr. Sprockett, making feeling motions on his hip.

"No, I won't, I certny won't," she said stubbornly. "I got plenty."

"Lilian, you're a great kid! And just taking me on trust!" (Trust! thought Lilly.) "You got a right to know

278

if I can support you. Well, I can, same way Bessy and I lived and a bit for when we get old."

What blessed words—yet over all still hung the second shadow. I gotta tell him, she thought, I can't marry him not telling him and keep him in the dark . . . it wouldn't be fair and him so good to me . . . and maybe he won't want me then and and . . .

Tears rose to her eyes at the thought of what she was going to disclose and what she might be about to lose and Mr. Sprockett not wanting her. The tears formed into round drops and hung trembling at her eyelids. Mr. Sprockett was dismayed.

"Lilian, what's the trouble?" stretching out a hand to hers.

She took her hand away and said as firmly as she could "I gotta tell you something else . . . I wouldn't feel right if I didn't tell you right now before you start getting the licence and everything. It wouldn't be fair."

As he looked at her, all his joy flowed down, away, and out, and where the joy had been was a nausea of cold fear. Is there another husband somewhere? thinks Mr. Sprockett in cold fear (what a fool I've been!). Is there a brother an alcoholic or in jail or is there madness in the family (what a fool I've been!)? He grew dizzy with the dimensions of his folly. In cold soberness he saw that he was proposing and planning to marry immediately and put into Bessy's place a woman whom three days ago he had never seen. He was mad, mad! If anyone had told him that he would do this thing he'd have said they were crazy. If Herb or Al or Eddy did a thing like this, he'd say they were crazy, too. Well, he hadn't done it yet but . . .

279

The waiter took away the plates, brought the coffee, and stayed too near the table. Mr. Sprockett was nearly sick with this cold fear. What had he done? He waited. It was insupportable. Lilly's two tears stopped trembling, and rolled down her cheeks. She did not wipe them away. She looked piteous and quite childish.

When the waiter had gone, Lilly began in a low tone. She could not bear it if her joy were taken away from her, but she must tell him now, not later.

"I told you," she said in her low tone, "that my sister was sick." Mr. Sprockett assented. "And I told you she died and then I was sick."

"Yes."

"Well, when I began to get better my hair started to fall out something awful, and they said there was nothing would save it but to cut it all off and make me an Adaptation."

"A what?"

"An Adaptation. It's when they take and cut your hair and fix it so's you can put it on again."

"Is *that* right!"

"It's your own hair. I said no at first because I thought they meant a wig and I couldn't ever wear a wig, but they said no, they just take your own hair and make up an Adaptation. So they did."

Mr. Sprockett stared and stared at her.

"And is that what you had to tell me and upset you like that?" He was so much relieved that he could have cheered.

Lilly nodded, still uncertain. "I wouldn't have liked to deceive you," she said, "ever. I wouldn't want to have anything to hide." Then she felt that her cheeks were still damp so she rummaged for her handkerchief and wiped each side of her little nose.

Oh, this perfect perfect woman! She's like a little girl! Mr. Sprockett got up from his side of the table and came over and put his arms round Lilly and kissed her in McCloskey's (old guy must be tight, said someone).

When he sat down again (oh no, he's not tight) he said fondly "We can have the ceremony at a minister's house or in a church   Which would *you* like?"

"I think the house would be nice and private."

"Would you like a corsage or a *bo*kay?"

"Oh . . ." said Lilly and her reassurance and joy made her eyes to shine, "I *would* like a *bo*kay. I never had one ever."

"What of?"

"You choose," said Lilly who did not know the names of florists' flowers.

"And now," said Mr. Sprockett at the end of the meal, tucking Lilly's arm in his, "we'll go and have a little glass of something."

"I don't take licker," said Lilly, hesitating.

"Just what Bessy used to say," said Mr. Sprockett triumphantly, "but we'd have a glass of something just the same . . . Oh, say! I never ast you what church!"

Lilly thought quickly back to the days when she used to take Eleanor to the little church in Comox, and then to a different kind of little church in the Valley.

She was just going to say "Whichever's handy" but she checked herself.

"United," she said almost inaudibly, faint with her happiness.

THE END